POTUS DOWN

Global Espionage, Assassination, AI, and Resilience:
The Unforgettable Stand-Only Sequel to
First Spouse of the United States

JR STRAYVE JR

ADZ Press

San Diego, CA

ADZ Press
3650 Third Ave., Suite #3
San Diego, CA 92103

Printed in the United States of America
First Printing March 2023 Jerome R. Strayve, Jr.
All rights reserved.
Cover and Internal Design: Tamara Merrill
Content editor: Tamara Merrill
Line Editor: Sandra Yeaman

ISBN: 978-1-7371243-5-1 (paperback)
ISBN: 978-1-7371243-6-8 (eBook)
First printing edition 2023
ADZ Press
3650 Third Ave., Suite #3
San Diego, CA 92103

If you enjoyed this book, please add a review on Amazon for JR STRAYVE JR:

DEDICATION

It is with deep humility and immeasurable gratitude that I dedicate this book to my dear friend and fellow author,

TAMARA MERRILL

She has been my constant cheerleader and mistress of accountability throughout the writing of POTUS DOWN.
She makes me a better writer.

Thank you, Tamara!

Contents

CHAPTER 1

Newly elected President Nicholas Chambers-Jeffries, his spouse Rocky, and their children left the inaugural viewing stand and crossed the lawn headed toward the White House.

The president positioned himself between Rick and Brooke and placed his arms around their shoulders.

Rocky walked alongside Brooke, holding her hand as they stepped on to the White House drive.

A shot rang out.

The president slumped forward, his arms falling from the shoulders of his children. He crumpled, his knees hitting the driveway, careened forward, falling face down on the lawn.

Rick and Brooke screamed, "DAD! DAD!"

Rocky stumbled forward. "Nicky, no! Nicky!"

They collapsed to the ground and surrounded the president. Rocky pressed his hand against the wound trying to stop the flow of blood pouring from Nick's head.

People shouted.

Secret Service agents raced forward, engulfing them in a protective circle. They swept up Brooke and Rick and carried them toward the safety of the White House.

Rocky, an athletic fifty-two-year-old man, fought to stay with his husband, but to no avail. Three agents forcibly overpowered him and hauled him toward the White House portico.

Resisting the agents, Rocky screamed, "Nicky, Nicky!"

"Stop fighting us! It's for your own good, your protection, sir," an agent said. "Please stop fighting us."

Physically overwhelmed by the agents, he craned his head back toward the driveway. His heart ached; his head felt like it would explode. He saw Nick, face down on the lawn of the White House, surrounded by a phalanx of Secret Service and medical personnel.

Secret Service agents could be heard on their radios shouting,

"POTUS DOWN!"

The unconscious president's body was placed on a stretcher, his head turned to the side, his white shirt and black suit saturated with blood. His limp arm fell to the side as the Secret Service members carrying the stretcher ran toward the White House.

Four medical types removed the president from the stretcher and placed him on a hospital gurney. The White House doctor and paramedics swarmed the president, providing life support as he was wheeled to the White House infirmary.

The grounds of the Executive Mansion teemed with Secret Service and military personnel. Sirens filled the air, muffling the sound of helicopters flying overhead. Machine gun-toting civilian and military personnel lined the cast iron fence, cordoning off the 18-acre perimeter. Anti-aircraft guns positioned on the mansion's roof were flanked by a dozen snipers.

"Get back! Get away from the fence!" could be heard being shouted by armed guards as thousands of onlookers pressed against the ten-foot-high cast-iron fence surrounding the White House.

The crisp, sunny January day faded as an east wind ushered in low gray clouds, and the temperature plummeted. Personnel not directly assisting with the president's care huddled in groups, the chill-infected conversations framing a dirge-like mood. *Who had shot the president? Were they still out there? Were they watching us now? Here?*

The packed mass of onlookers strained to understand what was happening. Some cried, others prayed, and a cacophony of angry voices could be heard. "Is the president alive?" "Did the haters finally get 'em?" "Who shot him, right wingers?" "Who's the fuckin' murderer?" "That sodomite had it coming!" "He was a good man, dear God, save him!" "He's going to hell for sure!" "Pray for our president!"

∞

Rocky, Brooke, and Rick were ushered by Secret Service agents to the White House's second story residence. Agents closed all the drapes and window coverings on the second floor. Armed men stood guard at the doors leading into the residence.

Rocky slumped on one of the sofas in the West Sitting Hall with his children on either side. The sound of wailing sirens in the distance cast an eerie pall throughout the residence.

With his arms wrapped around shell-shocked Brooke and Rick, Rocky cringed and experienced an eerie déjà vu moment. *It seems so very long ago, twenty-five plus years ago that I sat here with my parents, brother, sister, and Josephine Tanner. She's dead. President Tanner's dead, both assassinated, now Nicky's close to death. A Greek tragedy?* He closed his eyes, leaned back against the sofa, and released a deep guttural groan.

The quiet of the room was broken only by Brooke's muffled sobbing.

Rick and Brooke rested their heads on their father's shoulder. Rocky's chest—his coat, shirt, and tie—absorbed the three adults' tears.

Rick shifted his weight and then sat upright slipping his hands into those of his father and sister. "Let's pray for him."

"Please, let's." Brooke sat up and used the back of her hand to wipe her tears, regaining her composure.

"I have," Rocky said softly.

A moment later, Rocky's voice quivered; tears cascaded, his head now cradled in his hands. "Dear God, help Nicky, help our children's father. Please save uh, um, him."

"Please make him well, God. Please," Brooke said looking at her father's tear-washed, tormented face.

Brooke reached up and used her fingers to gently wipe away tears pooling on her father's face.

"Excuse me," someone said.

Rocky sat up and turned toward an unfamiliar voice. "Yes?"

The tall, fit, African American, thirty-five-year-old man, with an earpiece in his right ear, wearing a black suit, white shirt, addressed Rocky. "General, we have not met. We were to be introduced following the Inaugural Parade." He cleared his throat. "I'm Special Agent Hunter, head of the White House security detail."

Rocky felt as if he had been lifted out of the moment, divorced from the reality he and his family were experiencing. He thought, General, *interesting. Ever since Nick was elected, that's what I'm called. Not, Mr. Chambers-Jeffries. Why haven't I thought about that before now? Must be everyone feels the need to* butch-up *the First Spouse thing. Beats the hell out of Mrs. Chambers-Jeffries. I guess focusing on my career in the Marine Reserves works for everyone. When will this gay shit go away?*

Rocky's focus returned to the moment. The three huddled on the sofa focused on Special Agent Hunter.

"Yes?" Rocky said again.

"Sir, the president has been moved to the White House infirmary. As you are most certainly aware, his condition is very serious, critical. He's on life support. I've been told he has been placed in a medically induced coma."

Rick shot to his feet. "Is my dad going to make it?"

"The doctors don't know. It's too early to tell. But he's alive."

Brooke, holding one her father's hands with both of hers, said, "I suppose it is useless to try and see him now." She rose from the sofa, flattened her palms, and straightened her dress. She made a futile attempt to arrange her hair, then wiped her eyes, leaving broad mascara lines across her face.

"Yes, no one, not even my agents are allowed in the medical area. Things are very intense. A lot's happening. The medical team is considering bringing the necessary equipment to keep him in the White House to avoid moving him. The security team is not confident it can guarantee his safety if he is moved. They don't know if they can protect the president if he is transported to Bethesda or any hospital. The situation is too fluid. We have no idea who shot him or why. However, the vice president has recommended moving him to a better-equipped facility, Georgetown Hospital."

Startling everyone, Rocky stood. "They will bring the necessary equipment here! They will not move him! Have I made myself clear?"

"Sir, that is not my decision to make. But I will make your wishes known to the appropriate people."

"He's my husband." Rocky glared at Hunter. "I have the final say on this and EVERYTHING else that pertains to the well-being concerning him and our family. Understood?"

Straightening to attention, Special Agent Hunter said, "Sir! Yes, sir!"

"Now, get the lead doctor on the phone and let me speak with him."

Special Agent Hunter stood frozen in place.

"Get on with it!" Rocky said, immediately regretting the way in which he had spoken to Hunter.

Hunter raised his hand to his right ear. "The president's spouse, er husband, demands to speak to the physician in charge." He paused. "Just do it. That's an order. Now!" The agent rocked back and forth on his heels. He looked at Rocky. "It'll be a moment, sir."

Rocky moved to the large Venetian window, facing the Executive Office Building, the only window in the residence not covered. He stared out, oblivious to the building's extravagant French Second Empire architecture, often referred to by onlookers as the *wedding cake* building. Brooke and Rick joined their father on either side. Rocky wrapped his arms around them.

"Good call, Dad," Rick said.

The agent, removing his earpiece, walked over to Rocky. He extended his hand holding the earpiece. "I know it's not protocol, but why don't you take this, sir, so you'll be on the line when the doctor gets on?"

"Thanks," said Rocky as he took the device from the agent. "In the meantime, please get me an update on the president's parents and siblings and their whereabouts. Mine, my family, too. I haven't seen any of them since leaving the viewing stands. Have them brought to the residence."

"Sir, the White House is locked down."

"Damn it! I don't care!" Rocky paused and sighed. "I'm sorry. Forgive me, my outbursts. Please just do as I say."

"Yes, sir."

The agent picked up the receiver from a nearby phone. He pressed a button on the console and issued Rocky's order. Hunter paused, listening, then said, "Just do as you're ordered and bring them to the residence as soon as they arrive."

Rocky used one hand to support the small device now in his ear. "Yes, Doctor. I'm here . . . How is he?" Rocky listened intently, pacing the room. "Yeah, uh huh, okay. That is good to know, encouraging . . . Yes, yes and the . . .?" Moments passed. "Okay. I understand. Maybe tomorrow. Doctor, thank you for what you and your team are doing. My family and I truly appreciate everyone's efforts . . . Yes . . . Right. I agree, moving him could be problematic. So, yeah, it's the equipment. Okay, keep him here. That's my direction on behalf of the family. Take whatever steps you need to get the necessary supplies and equipment. Thank you, Doctor."

Rocky handed the earpiece to the agent. "Thank you, Special Agent Hunter." Rocky folded his arms. "Where is the vice president?"

"As acting president, he has called a meeting in the situation room with Joint Chiefs, Speakers of House and Senate, and other officials."

"Interesting, hmm." Rocky's mind raced, *perhaps I am reading too much into this. It's been six hours since Nick was shot. Why hasn't someone from Vice President Goulet's office or Goulet himself reached out? I told Nick I didn't think the man was to be trusted. I need to calm down.* "When he has a moment, I would appreciate it if he would meet with me in the president's private office. Just have someone let me know when it's convenient for him."

"Yes, sir."

Rocky turned to join Brooke and Rick and noticed the agent, face tilted a bit downward, his hands to his side.

"Is there anything else, Agent Hunter?"

Special Agent Hunter cleared his throat. "Sir, er, um, I want you to know that we are doing our best to protect the president and your family. It is horrific what has happened. We all feel responsible and are heartsick. Please know that our prayers and thoughts are with all of you." He was visibly holding back a dam that was sure to burst. He swallowed and turned to leave the room.

Rocky walked over and placed a hand on his shoulder. "I know, it's awful. You and your team have been put through a lot. I also believe it is not your fault or your team's fault. This president is not the first president to have been shot. Sadly, he may not be the last." Rocky paused, and with a shallow smile, said, "Hopefully, he'll recover soon, and we will all be spending a lot of time together."

"Thank you, sir." The agent turned to leave as the families rushed down the Center Hallway toward them, their anxious voices echoing throughout the residence.

Rocky's mother, Consuelo, ran to her grandchildren and wrapped her arms around them. She had been the first person to reject Rocky when, as a high school senior, he had come to her admitting being gay. Falling back on her staunch Catholicism, she had failed him. Her rejection launched his life in another direction, one that defined his life today. Only when he had been shot while defending his future husband did she come around. She had swallowed her pride and surrendered to love of family.

In a thick Spanish accent, she said, *"Hay Dios mio, mis nietos! Estas bien?* This is so horrible! Come close, I will protect you."

Rick and Brooke surrendered to their step-grandmother's cries and embrace.

Rocky took a few moments to comfort, as best he could, Nick's parents and siblings before taking his father aside.

Rocky's father said, "Rocky, I am so sorry. I am so sorry." He inhaled and placed his right palm aside Rocky's face. "How are you and the kids doing?"

"Okay, I guess, Dad." He sighed and took solace in his father's touch. "Listen, Dad, I have some business to attend to. I need to excuse myself to meet with the vice president. Could you keep an eye on things here?"

Placing a hand on one of Rocky's arms, his father said, "Sure son, I am more than happy to." And with a twinkle in his eye, he continued, "It looks like Brooke and Rick will have plenty of support here."

"Thanks, Dad."

The White House butler, an Asian man named Simon, approached. "Excuse me, General, the vice president is available to meet with you as soon as he gets out of his meeting with the cabinet and the Joint Chiefs."

"Thank you. Please tell him I'll be right down, and in the meantime, arrange for our families to be able to remain in the Blair House and Executive Guest Houses. There's no need for them to have to relocate for the foreseeable future."

"Yes, sir."

"One more thing, if you don't mind, please contact and ask the president's chief of staff to attend my meeting with the vice president."

"Yes, sir."

Rocky thought, *I guess it's not really the butler's place to make requests of the chief of staff. I'll apologize later.* He looked about the room and breathed a sigh of relief. The family was safely huddled together in conversation, comforting one another.

Rocky stepped over to speak with his mother-in-law again. She had been a mountain of strength and a font of wisdom over the years. She had been there for the kids when they were very young and when their mother was dying. She had provided unsolicited but wise counsel when Nicky had run for the House, the Senate, and the presidency. "Mom, I know they're adults, but all the same, would you keep an eye on the kids? My folks are on it too. If all this attention gets a bit overwhelming, perhaps you can make sure everyone gets some space. I have arranged accommodations for the families. Simon will let you know when the rooms are available."

She hugged him and in her rich modulated southern drawl, whispered in his ear, "Sure, Rocky, I'll handle it. Now, go about your meetings. I know that my Nicholas would want you to be tending to the business at hand." She squeezed his hand. "Please forgive me for saying this, but remember, not everyone has my son's or your best interests at heart."

A chill ran down Rocky's spine. He stepped back and with a look of surprise, then apprehension, said, "I had thought about that. But thought perhaps I'm overreacting."

She patted his cheek. "You have a good head on your shoulders. Trust your instincts."

"I'm glad you're here." Rocky hugged her. "Thank you."

She offered a warm smile and kissed him on both cheeks.

Brooke pulled her brother aside, "I suppose you have noticed Dad raising his voice."

"Yeah. Not used to it. Haven't heard him that angry, that loud, ever."

"He's always been in control, cool, calm, collected."

"Yeah. He loves Dad, must be totally afraid of losing him."

Rocky walked over to Brooke and Rick. "You'll be in good hands. Whenever you feel like it, you're free to excuse yourselves. You're adults now, please help your grandmothers. I've got to go meet with the VP."

Rick stepped up beside them. The three hugged.

In unison, Brooke and Rick said, "Love you, Dad."

"Love you back." Rocky stepped away, blew them each a kiss. He turned and walked down the broad Center Hall. Passing through the door to the stair landing, he turned to the right into the private, very private Treaty Room. Closing the door, Rocky paused, then turned the elegant brass knob below the door handle. The door was now locked.

He made a few calls, took a few more minutes and scanned news feeds and social media and prepared himself for the meeting with the vice president.

Exiting the Treaty Room ten minutes later, he crossed the stair landing and bounded down the Grand Staircase to the ground floor. Next stop, the Oval Office.

Rocky stepped out of the mansion onto the outdoor Colonnade bordering the Rose Garden. He stopped. A distant memory flooded his mind. A memory, decades old, when as a young Marine Corps fighter pilot having been awarded the Medal of Honor by President Turner. Following the presentation, he had been escorted along this same walkway into the Oval Office, which led to his assignation with the most powerful man in the world. An interlude that changed the course of Rocky's life and perhaps that of the nation.

As he pulled his mind out of the past, he noticed daylight waning on the dreary gray winter Rose Garden. He braced himself against the cold January wind's onslaught, wrapped his arms about his coatless body, bent his head forward, and jogged toward the Oval Office.

Shivering, he said, "What a dumb-ass idea, why didn't I just use the entrance from inside the West Wing? Is there one?" He knew why he hadn't—he needed to clear his head. Fresh air was supposed to do that.

Entering the Oval Office, he straightened up and faced forward. Furtively trying to fend off the cold, he used his hands to rub his shoulders and arms. This time, the experience in the Oval would be different. He was, once again, entering the most important room in the world. This time, he wasn't the proverbial lamb headed to the slaughter. But perhaps the only person capable of heading off a coup. *A coup?* Why had such a thought entered his mind. *I must really be losing it.* Then he remembered Nicky's mother saying, "Trust your instincts."

A fire roared in the fireplace, the flickering flames dappling the dimly lit room's walls. Adjusting his eyes to the low light, he noted the pristine elegance was somewhat obscured by collapsed cardboard boxes littering the center of the carpeted floor. He thought, *what a shame, the presidential seal covered by boxes and crumpled packing paper . . .*

At one end of the room stood four partially opened boxes. They were labeled "President Chambers-Jeffries/Oval." Another set of cartons lay empty and flattened, piled by the door leading to the outer offices. They were marked VP Goulet/WH Office.

His eyebrows raised. *Why weren't these boxes in either the VP's West Wing office or in his Executive Building office? This is bizarre. Whose idea was this? Naw, couldn't be. Stupid! Blatant! Dangerous!*

Rocky, still confused, looked around the room. None of Nick's personal items were there. Unfamiliar objects sat on shelves, on the president's desk and behind it. Rocky's insides cratered as he recognized people in the pictures and memorabilia on which another's name stood prominent. *This is the VP's stuff.* "What the fuck?" *Nick's not even dead and the son-of-a-bitch's movin' in!* Rocky felt the color leave his face; his stomach turned. *I knew Goulet wasn't to be trusted. Asshole! Nick's mother was right. Snake in the grass. We'll see about that!*

Holding his cell phone to his ear, he said "Please get the president's chief of staff and ask her to meet me in the Oval. Be discreet; only her, no one else. I'll be waiting." Rocky placed the phone in his pocket and began unpacking Nick's things and placing them where he assumed they belonged.

Ninety minutes later Vice President Christopher Goulet emerged from his meeting with the cabinet, Joint Chiefs and various intelligence agency heads. He was informed General Ricardo Chamber-Jeffries USMC(R) was waiting for him in the president's private office.

The vice president left the situation room and made his way to the president's private office.

Rocky rose from his chair and stood silent as the vice president entered the room.

Goulet walked over to Rocky. Sticking out one hand, he clapped Rocky on the shoulder with his other hand.

The vice president looked around the room, his eyebrows squished. He released Rocky's hand and tugged at his own ear, as if something was amiss. A smirk in his tone, he said, "Hello, General. How are you doing? Such a horrible time. So tragic. Mrs. Goulet and I, I mean, Margaret and I are praying for the president."

"Thank you, Chris. We and the nation can use all the prayers we can get. You, particularly, sir. I don't envy your task at hand. I asked the chief of staff to join us, but she is otherwise detained."

"Well, you know, General," he paused, and in a condescending voice asked, "may I call you Rocky?"

Rocky considered what he had just heard. *This guy is just what I thought, a simpleton masked behind bravado, wrapped in unbridled ambition.*

"Of course. Nothing changes along that line. It is my husband who is president. Let me offer you something to drink."

Rocky, daring not to betray his feelings, gestured toward the wet bar encased in a bookshelf flanked by several of Nick and Rocky's family photos.

Rocky's lips formed a level line. "As you can see, many of my husband's things are already unpacked and in place. Let's ferret out the scotch, shall we?" He knew precisely where it was. He had put it in its place ten minutes earlier.

"Sure, Rocky. I'm surprised everything has been already unpacked and put in place, under the circumstances."

Rocky, his back to the vice president, inwardly raged at the viper's statement and poured the contents of a decanter into two glasses.

"Yes, it has all come together," Rocky said, his back still facing away. "We need to have everything perfect for Nick when he recovers and assumes his duties as president."

"Ahem," escaped Goulet's throat.

Rocky seethed. He turned and handed Goulet the two fingers of scotch.

Brandishing a half smile, the glass's recipient said, "To the president and his quick return to excellent health."

As Goulet took a large gulp, Rocky said, "I had your shit moved out of the Oval Office too."

Goulet, caught off-guard mid-gulp, choked and spewed out the amber drink.

Wiping his mouth with his sleeve, the VP coughed. "What, what are you talking about?"

"Oh, I beg your pardon, Chris. Didn't you know? Someone had packed up Nick's things in both offices and had commenced arranging your personal items in their stead. Odd, isn't it? As far as I know, the president is still the president, at least under these uh, as you said, circumstances. Strange, isn't it?"

Rocky stood sipping his scotch, his eyes boring into Goulet.

The overzealous politician placed his glass on a nearby table. He stood with both hands clasped in front of him. "I'm sorry. That was very insensitive of my staff."

"I hope you have better control of the country than you do your staff, sir," Rocky said, his tone syrupy with sarcasm.

"That's not fair!" Goulet said.

"What isn't fair is the callousness and unchecked ambition you have displayed." Rocky girded himself for what he knew would be an eruption. "It has already compromised you as a leader. While your tenure as acting president may be temporary, it remains the most important and sacred position of trust in the world. I refuse to let you squander it. Your actions reflect poorly on both your staff and my husband's. After your inappropriate move into an office that does not belong to you, the staffs will be unable to think of anything else. Can you blame them? It's a friggin' shit show! Nick's staff and your staff are talking, positioning themselves and jousting and yes, joking about nothing else. Including your antics during the meeting in the situation room."

"My antics in the situa–?"

Rocky held up his hand and moved in on the befuddled acting president.

Goulet tried to step back and bumped up against a built in bookcase, trapped.

Rocky got within inches of Goulet's face. In a low even tone, he said, "Yes, Trish Smart and I discussed your actions, your duplicity."

"General, was it you who called her out of my very important meeting?"

Rocky ignored the question. "You have embarrassed the administration with your actions. The very thought of occupying a man's offices while he is fighting for his life is unconscionable. It smacks of a desperate grab for power. You have the power. You don't have to seize it. Your actions are dividing the house. And we all know, divided houses fall. Wait until the press gets ahold of this! If they haven't already."

Rocky paused, turned, and walked halfway across the room, stopped, then turned back toward the frozen figure. "You lack gravitas and bearing. I pray to God you have some semblance of integrity somewhere inside you. God protect us."

"You may be a general, but I am the acting president of the United States!"

"Yes, Mr. Vice President, and you are acting badly."

"Your lack of respect may force my hand," Goulet said.

"To do what, sir? Form a coup to unseat the president? Ram through evoking the 25th Amendment?"

"How dare you suggest such a thing! That would be just short of treason!"

"Yes, it would, Mr. Vice President. And my sources indicate you have taken adroit ambitious steps to solidify your position. Rather prematurely, I might add. Should the president survive, you will have a great deal of explaining to do. Either way, you will have lost any confidence he may have had in you."

Rocky, armed with his renowned command presence, pointed to a chair. "Now, sit down, Mr. Vice President. We have a lot to discuss."

∞

Two hours later Rocky sat in the East Wing dressed in a muted wool sports jacket and open-collared plaid shirt. He faced the assembled national media's White House television cameras.

The East Wing historically functioned as the offices for the First Lady. Now Rocky, the First Spouse of the United States, and his staff would soon occupy the offices. He sat on a large maroon leather wingback chair. Behind him stood a bookshelf which held quickly assembled photos of the Chambers-Jeffries family.

The lights blared bright enough to intimidate those unfamiliar with the intense heat and glare. However, accustomed to speaking to people and cameras, Rocky was nonplussed. There was no prepared speech and no teleprompter.

The White House Communications Director raised his hand as he spoke from behind the camera, "General, we're on in 3-2-1 . . ." He pointed. "You're live!"

"My fellow Americans, Vice President Goulet has graciously allowed me to speak to you on behalf of my family. He has asked that I share with you some of what has happened. The president's physicians feel the president's health is a personal matter, a family matter. The vice president has agreed and feels that it would be best that I personally keep the nation informed of the president's health during his anticipated recovery." Rocky paused. "Thank you, Mr. Vice President.

Rocky continued, "Your president, my husband, our children's father, has been shot. He lies in a medically induced coma. Assassinations and attempted assassinations have happened before. They are something one fears. Something we had feared. The very thing we had hoped would never happen again, has happened".

Rocky paused for effect. "As a nation, what do we do now?"

Rocky looked down for a moment, then raised his head slightly up and to the right. He took a breath and looked back into the camera. "I'll tell you what's next. First, please accept our family's sincerest gratitude for your thoughts and prayers. Rick, Brooke, our extended family, and I ask you to keep the faith and keep Nick, us, and the country in your prayers. Reach out to one another and comfort those in need of your love and compassion. The president is still alive and fighting bravely for his life. You, the American people, must continue to go about your lives steadfastly and compassionately. Be there for one another."

Vice President Goulet stood behind the cameras glaring at Rocky.

"As a nation, we are blessed to have elected a time-tested representative of the people, Vice President Christopher Goulet, to serve alongside my husband. Now, the duties of acting president have fallen on his shoulders." Rocky inhaled and then said slowly, "To temporarily," he paused again and continued, "take up the mantle as acting president to protect and defend our nation."

Rocky sat back in his chair. He folded his hands in his lap. "Vice President Goulet and I have just spent an hour in the president's private office. Yes, it is still the president's office, as is the Oval Office. My husband's personal items are awaiting his arrival." Rocky sat up straighter. "The vice president feels, as do all of us, that the administration needs to move forward as if President Chambers-Jeffries was at the helm. The promises made to you, the nation's people, must be kept. Now, I know many of you are concerned that things could change during the president's recovery. That will not happen. Vice President Goulet is committed to fulfilling every promise and every facet of President Chambers-Jeffries' and the vice president's platform. The vice president is honoring this commitment by submitting the mutually agreed upon Cabinet and judicial nominations tomorrow, as planned."

Rocky glanced down at his hands and then back to the camera. "As you know, all the nominees were selected and vetted during the presidential transition period following the election. They make up a balance of qualified men and women representative of our nation's interests and priorities. Thank you in advance, Mr. Vice President, for bravely fulfilling the will of the people."

Leaning toward the camera, he smiled softly as a bit of a sparkle danced in his eyes. "Thank you again for your prayers. Please know that I will be in regular contact with you, the American people, personally, keeping you up to date on our president's recovery. Again, the president's family thanks each and every one of you. God bless America. Goodnight."

The following morning headlines on social media and in newspapers blared:

**VICE PRESIDENT DEFIES PRESIDENT
AND CONTRADICTS HUSBAND.**

VP TRASHES PRESIDENT'S TRANSITION TEAM

**GOULET SUBMITS ONLY PARTIAL LIST OF NOMINEES
TO SENATE**

WHITE HOUSE IN DISARRAY!

CHAPTER 2

At 6:00 a.m. that same morning, Rocky, Brooke, and Rick, holding hands, stood beside Nick's bed. The frigid, over-air-conditioned room was shrouded in low light. Beeping monitors punctuated the silence. The president lay quiet, head elevated by several pillows. Tubes and wires were draped over and around his body, his head heavily bandaged.

Brooke shivered.

The three stood silent, looking down at the comatose president, father, and husband. Brooke released her brother's hand and took Nick's in hers. Rick placed his arm around his sister's shoulder and gave her a gentle squeeze.

She spoke to her father. "Dad, we love you. We're praying for you." She stroked Nick's arm with her free hand. "I know you'll recover. You're strong, you're a fighter. We're here for you." She sniffled. "One of us will be here for you 'round the clock." Brooke squeezed her stricken father's hand. "Remember when Mom was in her hospital bed? She let us know she could hear us by squeezing our hands. You can do that too."

Rocky thought back to the days Nick and the twins, Rick and Brooke, and he had stood vigil by Sheila's bedside as she lay dying, struck down by a stroke at age 42. Sheila had been a wonderful and loving mother and a strong supportive wife to Nick and had always accepted Nick and Rocky's love for one another.

Twenty five years ago, when Rocky met with Sheila in a café in Brussels. he had been impressed with her sophistication, charm, and ambition. She had surprised him by confessing that she suspected he and her fiancé, Nick, were romantically involved. He was stunned when she offered to share Nick with him. She had said, "Continue together as you always have. I want Nick. He wants you. He wants to run for Congress, and I'm part of what will make that possible. He can't really run and remain a single man forever. Sooner or later, he'd be outed." Her acceptance and a ménage à trois assignation weeks before Sheila and Nick's marriage had led to her being impregnated by both men. A DNA test attested to Nick having fathered Brooke and Rocky being Rick's father vis à vis heteropaternal superfecundation. After discussing the DNA results, Sheila, Rick, and Nick decided to never tell the twins their respective parentage until they were older, adults. A decision they had yet to regret.

Rick placed his hand on top of his sister's and leaned over his father. Placing his lips close to Nick's ear he whispered, "Brooke's right, Dad. One of us will be here with you. We love you, Dad."

Rick gave a forced chuckle. "We thought getting you elected was a rough journey. Well, it looks like we're on another one." He kissed Nick on the bandages covering his forehead. A tear escaped, landing just below the president's bandages. "We're in this together."

Rocky stood behind Brooke and Rick and gently rubbed their shoulders. "Okay, I think we need to let him rest now."

They drew together in a warm embrace.

Rocky's voice shook as he said, "I ordered breakfast. It should be waiting for you upstairs. I'll be here if you need me."

Brooke and Rick smiled at Rocky, turned, and looked down at their father. They held hands as they left the room.

The door closed, leaving the husband and husband alone for the first time since Inauguration morning. *What a difference a day makes*, Rocky thought to himself.

Years earlier, when Sheila passed, Nick had been a US congressman running for the Senate. The media attention had riveted the nation on Sheila, Nick, Rick, and Brooke during their ordeal. The election polls had been too close to call prior to her death. The sympathy vote cast after her passing was said to have clinched the election for Nick.

Sheila had been confronted with concerns for her health just as she and Nick had decided he would run for the US Senate. Alarmed by headaches and what she assumed were petit mal seizures, she consulted her physician. The prognosis had been devastating. Her seizures would increase in frequency and intensity. To spare the family the suffering that would accompany her health issues, she never shared her health condition with anyone but her parents. Nick and Rocky were surprised to find that, during this time, Sheila had left a letter for them and one for each of her children.

In the letter addressed to Nick and Rocky, she encouraged them to move on with their lives, together. She had written, "I think it's time for you two to lead a proper life together. I am blessed to have a child from each of you. You are, and always have been, a family. It's time you lived openly like one. This is my challenge to both of you: Get married. Rocky, I hope you will adopt the children when the two of you are married."

Nick and Rocky had decided to keep the letters Sheila had written to Rick and Brooke for another seven years, until they had reached their twenty-first birthdays. Nick and Rocky felt the truth of their parentage was too much for teenagers to absorb. Rocky had wondered when or if there would ever be a good time to reveal the truth.

Rocky studied the monitors for a moment. He pulled a chair up beside the bed and sat holding Nick's hand.

The whispering whirling monitor created a soothing white noise accented by endless irritating beeps. Beep, beep, beep . . .

"So, old man. Here we are."

Rocky thought back to years ago when they celebrated their engagement. And when he had taken the bullet that a crazed man had meant for Nick.

"This time you're the one that caught the bullet, and I'm here looking after you. So sorry. I wish it were the other way around, again." Rocky squeezed Nick's hand and waited for a moment. There was no response. His heart aching, he swallowed hard.

In a halting voice, Rocky continued, "I remember regaining consciousness when you sat at my side at Georgetown Hospital. Seeing you at my bedside made my heart skip a beat. Having you there revitalized me. I hope one of us will be here for you when you, you, uh, wake up." He wiped a tear from his eye.

Rocky looked around the room. "You know the twins, well, they're holding up pretty okay. You have to recover fast. As you know, Brooke put her job at the law firm on hold to help with the campaign. She was supposed to start back today. Rick is not where he needs to be, running Chambers Enterprises." He swallowed. "They are good kids, um, uh, adults. What would Sheila have said about all this? My guess she would—"

"Good morning, General," Dr. Samson said entering the room. The round, preppy, bespeckled physician transferred the thick folder he was carrying to his left hand in order to shake Rocky's hand.

Rocky looked him up and down and smiled. "You look like a politician."

"Yes, sir," he said, "I want the patient to feel at home."

Amused and hopeful, Rocky said, "You've got that right! I'm sure it will help. So, what's my husband's status? Prognosis?"

Samson, still holding the folder, crossed both hands in front of himself. "We're not exactly sure. With the medically induced coma, we're waiting for the body, the brain, to take over and heal itself. The bullet is lodged just inside his skull, a precarious spot. Swelling is an issue. You'll note the thick cold packs on his head. Operating before the swelling diminishes is not an option."

This is the first time Rocky had thought about the heavy bandages and what appeared to be tubes weaving through the bandages and most certainly into Nick's head. He thought, *I*

guess there must be shunts in there draining fluid from his brain, Jesus
Christ . . . and who knows what else.

Rocky sat motionless. He smiled down at Nick and reached
out to squeeze his husband's shoulder. "Looks like it's up to you,
babe." Turning to Samson, he said, "Doctor, how long will it take
to get the swelling down? What are the chances of brain dam—"
Rocky choked on his words.

Brooke and Rick sat in the residence's kitchen. Shoulders
stooped and faces drawn, they contemplated the meal in front of
them. Despite not having eaten since lunch the previous day,
they poked at their food. A steward arrived with a stack of newspapers, placed them on the kitchen counter, and left the room.

Rick looked over at the stack. "What's this? Do people still read
newspapers?" He paused, staring at the pile. "I don't think I want
to see what they have to say."

They both turned their attention back to their breakfast and
began to eat.

Rick, with his mouth full, said, "Isn't that a bit outdated? Who
reads newspapers these days, anyway?"

"You're repeating yourself. And yes, some do. I do, sometimes," Brooke said, mid-bite.

She jumped up, grabbed the pile from off the counter, and
dropped it in the middle of the breakfast table. "Finish eating
and let's get through these. Maybe there is something in them
we didn't get on our feeds."

She picked one off the top of the pile and thumbing through
the *New York Times*, she continued, "Let's see what's happening in

the outside world. Grandma said someone has to look out for Dad's interests!"

"Dad's interests? Really? What're you talking about? Ever since you got that law degree you've, well ... forget it."

She ignored him and picked up another paper and placed it in front of her. Moments later she drew the paper to one side and looked at her brother. "There're people out there that want to take advantage of Dad's being injured ... the assassination ... attempt."

Annoyed, Rick said, "So what? What can we do about it? Besides, I'm a businessman, not a politician. I've got Chambers Enterprises to keep me busy, especially since Dad is First Spouse of The United States, um, FSOTUS, now."

"FSOTUS, POTUS, President of the United States. Weird." She picked up her phone and scrolled. "Two thirds of the country may be sad and prayerful; the other third's conniving to take advantage of the attempted assassination. Remember, it's all about power!" Brooke looked up at her brother, steely-eyed. "Now either get online or read these papers. Let's at least try to do something!"

Rick exhaled. "I'm sorry, sis. I'm just a bit overcome with all this. I don't really know what to do."

"I don't believe you. You run a multinational corporation. Most of the time you're a hard ass. If it wasn't our dad who was shot, you'd be all over this."

He picked up a linen napkin and blew his nose. Sighing, he removed a paper from the stack and tossed it on top of his breakfast, splattering the fried eggs and home-fries. "Fuck! Sorry."

He then ignored the mess he'd made and stared at the blank TV screen on the wall behind Brooke. "Brooke, grab that remote from behind you and turn on the TV . . . the news."

Brooke, having put down the paper and was now scrolling, pulled her phone closer. "I don't believe this! What's going on? It says that the Senate received only a partial list of Cabinet nominations Dad and the governor, I mean vice president, agreed to put forward." She shook her head and kept reading.

Incredulous, Rick said, "Didn't Dad work that out with Goulet like over a month ago? The Cabinet and judicial nominations are the foundation of the platform. They had to put something together to get the right wing to go along with the platform and all that stuff, right?"

"Yep, that's what they said and that's what they did. Let's see who the veep left off the list of nominees."

Reading further, she said while looking at her phone, "So, it seems you did get your head out of the corporate offices now and then and pay a little attention."

"You know what, Brooke?"

"What?"

"Never mind."

She put the phone down, stood up, and left the kitchen. Moments later she returned with two legal pads and pens. "Let's take notes on everything and anything we find. Maybe there's something we can discover that will help. Anything at all."

Rick looked at his sister and grinned. "Okay, counselor, let's sleuth. Then we can pass what we find to the *General*. I mean the FSOTUS." They both let out subdued laughs.

Rick and Brooke looked at one another. Simultaneously they said, "I am so glad we're here together."

They reflexively high-fived one another.

"Always happens!" They said.

Rick stood and stretched. "I'll record NBC, CBS, ABC, MSNBC, the BBC, NEWSMAX and FOX." He grabbed the remote and started clicking.

"We can check Twitter and RSS feeds too. Then there is Google News Reader, News Laundry—you know them better than me."

"I know, I'm on it, jeez."

Fifteen minutes later, after having flipped through the various cable news networks, Rick put the TV on mute.

"Why did you do that?" Brooke said, fixated on her phone.

"They are repeating old news. We can watch the banner running across the bottom, that's where we'll see anything new, not from the talking heads."

"Yeah, I never understood why the dads always kept the TV on. I was always way ahead of them with my feeds." She paused and looked up from her phone. "Wait a minute, why don't we put some feelers out?"

"What d'ya mean, sis?"

"We both have Facebook, Instagram, and Twitter. Let's send a little message of thanks for support and prayers, and that kinda thing, and ask our followers to feed us anything that might help figure out who, why, and how Dad was shot?"

"You've got to be shitting me!" Rick said.

"Why not?"

"That'll piss a lot of people off, you know, like the Secret Service, the FBI, and for Christ's sake, Dad!"

"Listen Rick, I'm a lawyer, you're a corporate guy. You know everyone has an agenda. It is all about power. What if the people that are trying to figure this out, like someone in the FBI, CIA, NSA, are the bad guys? Remember those dudes that got canned from the Department of Justice and the FBI and the National Security Agency for the crap they pulled and then pretended to investigate it? No way am I gonna trust anyone to get to the bottom of this! If we catch a lot of crap, we just say sorry. Besides, we have the sympathy angle working for us if we really screw up."

Rick sat back and stared blankly at the TV for several minutes. He picked up his phone and started tapping away. "Let's do it."

"This is unbelievable!" said the president's chief of staff Trish Smart, into her speaker phone. "The VP's done an end run. What does he think he is going to accomplish? Leaving Labor, Education, and Housing and Urban Development off the slate of nominees is not only confusing and dangerous. The entire world will begin to second-guess the administration; he'll split the party wide open! What the hell?"

Rocky sat in Trish Smart's office opposite her desk. His once magnificently golden hair had mellowed, as had he, entering his sixth decade. He'd maintained an athletic build by alternating his days either running or hitting the gym five out of seven days a week. Today, he felt tired, no, exhausted. Certainly not athletic, but every bit his age and older. He stared out the window and listened to the conversation.

The Senate Majority Leader Debbie Tatsu's voice echoed from the speaker phone. "You're right, this has caught us all off-guard. I never liked the slate and don't agree with some of the picks, but it was a deal. Shit, I just don't . . . hell, we gotta figure this out. We have to come up with a story for the press and both sides of the aisle." She paused. "Can you say the other nominees weren't finalized, like the vetting hadn't been finalized or something like that?" She paused again. "That does sound a bit week, damn."

Trish, observing Rocky's blank stare, said, "That's not the point, Senator. The point is the veep has done something under-handed. He's cutting the legs out from under a man who could be dying at this very moment! You know as well as I do that the president and vice president had agreed to the list. Even the Senate Republicans, your party, you, the leadership, signaled you would accept it in total. The vice president elect literally signed off on the list alongside the president elect's signature when I sent the draft up to the Hill weeks ago."

The Leader continued, "It's already a crisis. You're right, it just might turn into something bigger, dare say, a constitutional crisis. It's vital we head it off at the pass. Think about what I said and get back to me with something. Something we can live with whether or not the president survives and assumes his duties."

"Well, Senator, I don't know what it'll be."

Stress lines appeared on Trish's forehead as she pondered the senator's request. "Maybe you could put out a statement from the Hill. Something to the effect that the White House will be sending up more nominees over the next week or so. If they ask why they were not sent up with the other nominees, just say that it's only the second day of an administration and that it has been dealt a severe blow. You know the drill. Senator, appeal to people's sympathies. Oh, and may I suggest you direct them to the prayer vigils being held all over the country. Let's work together to see what we can do to keep the focus on the president's recovery, not speculating about a rogue veep. This is as the general said, a house divided. I'll get back to you."

Trish hung up the phone. "Rocky, you heard that. I hope . . . Are you, are you okay with it?"

Rocky turned his gaze from the window and folded his hands in his lap. "Sure, you did a good job. Who ever thought we would be working side-by-side with the Democrat Leader trying to keep a Republican vice president from compromising an administration to which he had been elected?" He shook his head.

"The Senate leader's politics are left of Mao, but she's an honorable woman. Unlike that character Goulet across the street."

"Do we have anyone in the veep's office we can trust?"

"Not really, but I've been thinking about who in his inner circle we might be able to turn. I think I may have someone."

"What are you talking about? Turn?" The mere use of the word "turn" caused him to adjust his position. *What would Nick want me, want us to do?* He thought back to when Nick had been serving in Congress and Rocky had had to insist that Nick man up. Man up by throwing caution to the wind and supporting LGBT rights. Nick, then though not out as a gay, bi-sexual man, and representing a conservative electorate, in the end, exhibited great courage and followed his heart. Another reason, one of many, Rocky loved Nick.

Trish stood and paced behind her desk. "We need to know what is going on in the veep's office. Obviously, he's got his own agenda. We need to know what it is. Officially, my office is still running things in the White House, for the time being, anyway. We've got to avoid the Cabinet triggering the 25th Amendment and sending it to Congress."

"Doesn't that usually come from the Cabinet," Rocky said.

"Yes, but it can originate in Congress too. Fortunately, or not, the president's Cabinet has not been seated. I don't doubt the holdovers from the previous administration are scrambling to find some way or another to end up on a winning side. Most of them are, for sure, jostling for positions elsewhere, knowing full well they are not on the list of nominees."

Her pained frustration vibrated in her voice. "I'm supposed to be coordinating things between the White House and Capitol Hill. So, why didn't I know about the vice president's changes until five minutes before it happened? Why? I should have known. Had I known, I could have and would have stopped it dead in its tracks, at least stalled it."

"No doubt," Rocky said, "He knows you would have pushed back, had you been aware of what was going on. The man is feckless. He and I had agreed before I addressed the nation last night that he would implement the president's agenda, including sending the agreed upon nominees to the Hill. Goulet is a lying, manipulative, deceitful son-of-a bitch!"

The chief of staff used both hands to pull her long red hair away from her face, flicked it behind her shoulders, folded her arms across her chest, and nodded in agreement. "I am afraid you are right."

They sat silent for several moments.

She slapped her desk in frustration and rose to pace behind her desk. "Things like this take time and must follow time-tested White House protocols. Names placed in nomination don't magically appear on the Hill. Goulet had to have his people working overtime soon after the president was shot. They must have been working all night in the Executive Office Building to have the scheme in place this morning. Still there just wasn't enough time to get it done in less than ten or twelve hours, overnight!"

"As Will Shakespeare said, 'Something is rotten in Denmark.'" Rocky said.

"I wasn't sure this was important, but I had the Secret Service check his schedule. He didn't get back to the vice president's residence at the National Observatory until 6:00 a.m this morning. The revamped nominee list story went viral shortly thereafter. I didn't see it at the time. Again, the president's staff, my staff, knew nothing about it."

Rocky ran his index finger's knuckle atop his upper lip. He then steepled his fingers under his chin and slowly repeated what he had said earlier. "Something just isn't right."

He stood. "By 'turning someone,' I suppose you mean we need to find someone loyal to the Constitution, more so than ideology, right?"

"Right, sorta."

"The person you have in mind needs to have integrity. We can't have 'fair weather' friends in our camp. It never works."

The chief of staff returned to her seat behind the desk and folded her arms. "I agree. We need someone in the veep's office. Someone that can be our eyes and ears."

Rocky looked askance at Trish.

"The person I have in mind," she said, "is a constitutionalist. She's kind of a right winger, a hold-over from the last administration. She's a real academic. Gorgeous, a bit aloof. I think she's some sort of Ayn Rand devotee, if you know what I mean. She knows her stuff and has kept a lot of people out of trouble. She's a straight shooter."

Rocky's jaw dropped. "Oh, do you mean Merrill Spaulding? There is a rumor that Goulet asked her to submit her resignation."

"Where did you hear that?"

"One of Nick's transition people overheard something about someone refusing to resign . . . in the White House mess earlier this morning."

Trish looked directly at Rocky. "She was waiting for me in my office when I arrived this morning . . . and handed me her resignation. I was surprised she had offered it to me. She does not work for the president. I asked her why she hadn't given it to Goulet's chief of staff. She said, 'Wait till you see what's broken on the wires.'"

"Then what did you do?"

"I handed it back to her."

Rocky leaned forward in his chair. "That's it? Nothing more?"

A knowing smirk crossed Trish's face. "Now, Rocky, we have known each other a long time. You know me better than that."

He inhaled deeply and sat back in his chair and slowly exhaled. He crossed his arms across his chest and shook his head side to side; a narrow smile and a twinkle in his eye confirmed his hope that Trish had made an arrangement with Merrill.

Trish said, "As she was walking out of my office, she turned and said, 'Ms. Smart, you know I can be very helpful to the president and the country.' I replied, I know that. Isn't that why you are here, here in my office? Perhaps we can follow up on this conversation and how you can help later today? She then appeared to bite her lower lip, offered a slight nod, and left my office. And that was that."

"That puts her in a tough position," Rocky said.

"She's tough and a real professional. I suspect she was covering her backside and playing it safe by tendering her resignation to me and not Goulet. No doubt, she is delighted to still be in the thick of things."

"What're you going to do?" Rocky asked. "I believe the president will survive this. But if Goulet is left unchecked for very long . . . The way things are going, this will not be the last letter of resignation. People will start balking at coming aboard or remaining with this circus. We could have a flood of resignations. Resignations from people we need, people of character and good reputation. People we've nominated will start bailing."

Trish sat back in her chair. A Cheshire-cat grin formed on her face. "I sent a memo over to Goulet's office twenty minutes ago informing them of a new White House policy. It says, in part, 'due to extraordinary circumstances associated with the president's health, the White House is not accepting any resignations for the foreseeable future.'"

Rocky sat up straight in his chair.

She continued in a whimsical voice, "I told them it would remain in effect until the president had recovered or had been removed by Congress from office vis à vis the 25th amendment."

"I bet that pissed off Goulet! Are you sure you have the authority to do that? After all, he is the acting president."

"I am the president's Chief of Staff."

"And again, for now, anyway."

"Oh, and by the way, he doesn't know about the memo yet." Trish laughed. "His staff replied saying that the VP was in meetings behind closed doors most of the day and has ordered that he not be disturbed. They said they would bring it to his attention at the earliest opportunity."

"So, I guess maybe that means Nick keeps all his people, perhaps even you and your staff in place for the time being."

She sat up in her chair. "It was leaked to the media about ten minutes ago."

Rocky chuckled. "Goulet will have to live with it! It will be almost impossible to reel that back in now that it's out there. But be ready, you'll probably be the first to go, if and when Congress votes."

"If Goulet gets the nod from Congress, I am outa here before the bastard can turn around."

"With any luck, Nick will be back on his feet and the administration will get back on track."

Trish nodded a caring smile, sat back, and folded her hands in her lap. "General, we're going to need your help as this heats up."

"You have it. Let me know what you need." With a conspiratorial smile, he said, "Oh, and I've got some ideas of my own."

∞

Vice President Goulet and the Director of the Secret Service, Craig Hamilcar, sat at a worktable in the veep's office in the Executive Office Building.

The men rose as Rocky entered the room.

Interesting, Rocky thought, *they both outrank me.* He stifled a smile. *That's right, like a first lady, wife to the president. Will I ever get used to this?*

"Good afternoon, General," Goulet said, motioning him to join them at the table. "May I introduce Craig Hamilcar, Director of the Secret Service?"

Hamilcar extended his hand.

"It's a pleasure to meet you, Director." Rocky shook the proffered hand and took a seat across from the others.

"The pleasure is mine, sir," Director Hamilcar said.

The vice president opened the meeting. "As I've said before, my prayers and those of the nation are with you and your family. We are all praying for the president's quick recovery."

Rocky forced a smile. "Thank you, Chris." *This guy is full of shit.* "Our children and I appreciate your thoughts and prayers."

In a sincere tone, Hamilcar said, "The men and women of the Service regret not being able to protect the president. We are determined to find the perpetrator or perpetrators of this heinous act."

Rocky said, "As I expressed to Special Agent Hunter yesterday afternoon, my family and I do not fault the Service."

The director twisted a ring on his right hand.

"Director, would you please bring us up to date on what you have?" the vice president asked.

"Yes, sir. We are in a quandary. Simply put, there is nothing definitive as to how or who attempted to carry out the assassination. Of course, it's early in the investigation."

The vice president sat back in his chair and let his head fall back.

Rocky inhaled and crossed his arms. "Nothing? It's been over twenty-four hours, and nothing? I don't understand. The act was carried out in broad daylight and in the most secure and highly controlled environment in the country. Why is there nothing?"

"Yes, sir. I understand. The Service is as perplexed as everyone else. We locked down the entire city within minutes. Every bridge and thoroughfare were secured and remain so. We're searching every vehicle leaving the city, every boat on the river, everything and everyone leaving the District of Columbia. We've photographed vehicles and documented all occupants. Flights in and out of Reagan have been cancelled. Only essential personnel are allowed to come into the city. The mayor of DC declared martial law. It'll remain in place for the foreseeable future." The director paused and shifted his weight, and continued, "I would have thought, you, Mr. Vice President, would have beat the mayor to the punch." The director stopped speaking when he realized what he had said and to whom he was speaking. "I, uh, beg your pardon, Mr. Vice President."

Rocky quickly interjected, "Neither the president nor the vice president can declare martial law, Only states, territories, and the District of Columbia can do that."

Vice President Goulet opened his mouth to speak.

"The Supreme Court ruled on that years ago," Rocky said. "I remember my husband and I discussing it when President Tanner was in office. It was a wise move then and remains a good one now."

"But Lincoln, Pearl Harbor, and in any number of instances throughout our history, the president has declared martial law," the vice president said.

Rocky repeated, "The Supreme Court ruled on that years ago, sir."

Rocky placed his elbows on the table, rubbing the palms of his hands together. "Satellites. I'd like to see the satellite pictures."

Goulet did a double take, looking first at the director, then Rocky, and back to the director.

Rocky continued, "As you know, gentlemen, I am assigned as a reserve flag officer to the Directorate for intelligence, J-2, which supports the Joint Staff and Unified Commands."

The director sat up in his chair and cocked his head. Speaking to Rocky, "Have you been talking to NSA, CIA? I know you have the security clearances, but I need to know who's been talking."

The vice president's phone buzzed.

He picked up the phone. "Yes, what is it? Who? I'm in a meeting. She'll have to make an appointment. Yes, I know who she is." He hung up and turned his attention to Rocky. "General?"

"I've spoken to no one," Rocky said.

The office door opened. A short, round woman entered, assisted by a cane. Her blond, streaked hair was pulled into a messy chignon. Her trifocals covered half her pasty puffy expressionless face. "Gentlemen give me a moment while I waddle over. This is the slowest damn cane on the planet!"

Goulet snorted. "Dr. Parsons, I told my secretary to tell you I was busy."

"I heard you. We are all busy, Mr. Vice President. You will want to hear what I have to say."

"General Chambers-Jeffries, you probably haven't met our best and brightest, Dr. Parsons." The vice president paused. "NSA and a host of other intelligence folks rely on her expertise."

The three men rose from their seats, saying nothing until she placed herself in a chair beside Rocky.

"Mr. Vice President, Director, General." She looked directly at Rocky. "General, it grieves me to make your acquaintance under such trying circumstances."

Rocky nodded. "Thank you. I as well, Doctor."

As the vice president was about to speak, Dr. Parsons interrupted, "Sit down, the three of you. Let's get to it. My guess is," she said, looking over at Rocky, "you've figured something out or may have a wild ass guess why I have insisted on joining this powwow."

The VP and Director Hamilcar appeared to be competing as to who could don the most sheepish look.

"Yes, Doctor, it seems so. I was just inquiring about satellite surveillance."

"Well, I think you may be on to something." She placed her cane on top of the table next to an oversized folder she had carried into the room. "My duties at NSA involve just that, satellites. I am also tasked with interfacing drone technology and surveillance as they relate to the Space Force. We are currently marrying the two for purposes of this investigation."

Dr. Parsons sat for a moment allowing the three men to digest what she had said. "By chance, we may have something. I'm not sure. I've designated this operation investigating our suspicions as they relate to the assassination attempt, the *Maltese Falcon*, or MF."

The vice president chuckled. "MF!"

Rocky and the director glared at Goulet.

The doctor ignored the vice president's remark and continued. "When we surveil areas, we are continually distracted by events and activities that occur naturally. We find ourselves watching small animals, movement in trees caused by gusts of wind, drunks relieving themselves on the sidewalk, children chasing one another around, and other such natural phenomena. We use Artificial Intelligence, AI, to ferret out the normal from the abnormal."

'AI' caught the men's attention. They sat up and inched closer to the table.

"Do you mean Artificial Superintelligence, ASI, Dr. Parsons?" Rocky asked.

She smiled and nodded. "Yes, General, I do."

Goulet's and the director's looks competed once again, this time for being the most perplexed.

"Even ASI is limited by the tedious process of tabulating millions upon millions of pieces of information being collected and reviewed. It's a matter of mathematics and algorithms. It takes time. Twenty hours after the shot was fired, we hit on something. An outlier."

Director Hamilcar asked a poignant question, one attesting to his rapid assimilation of what the doctor was saying. "What is the difference between an anomaly and an outlier?"

Parsons said, "An outlier, a statistical—"

Giving a quick shake of his head, visibly alarmed, Goulet interrupted, "What are you talking about?"

Irritated by his interruption, the three looked at Goulet.

Dr. Parsons sat for a moment, silent.

Annoyed, Rocky shook his head. "Please continue, Doctor."

"As I was saying, this outlier, well, it's remarkably peculiar, but fascinating," she said, baiting the vice president. "Anomalies usually represent abnormal behavior. In this instance, it is an outlier, because we cannot classify it as abnormal behavior. Because we do not know what is *normal* for this situation. It may be perfectly normal in this instance. It is therefore an outlier because we do not know how to measure the behavior, yet."

Rocky suppressed a chuckle, and the director ran his tongue around the inside of his cheeks holding back an urge to laugh.

"Maltese Falcon," Dr. Parsons said, "because the ASI noticed an anomalous flight pattern executed by a bird. A bird that had remained stationary until well after the shot that struck the president rang out. Rang out being the operative word here."

"So, what's so odd about a bird flying a strange pattern?" Goulet asked, lips pursed.

"Thank you, Mr. Vice President. That's what we wanted to know. Why would a bird not fly normally? And then why did it not move an inch for hours?" She paused and made every attempt to suppress a sarcastic tone. "You have made my job here so much easier, sir. Thank you."

Director Hamilcar and Rocky both folded their hands and placed them in their laps tightening their jaws in a not so successful attempt to suppress their irritation and disdain for the vice president.

Dr. Parsons went on to say, "Remember gentlemen, the shot that rang out. The same sound that had emptied the trees of all fowl within a quarter mile. However, this bird didn't move. It didn't move so much as an inch until hours later. Hours after things had calmed down considerably."

Dr. Parsons reached for the folder and drew it to her. She eyed her audience and then placed it in front of the three men, opened it, and withdrew three photographs, positioning them in front of them.

The director's and Rocky's jaws dropped.

The vice president's countenance took on that of a stunned wax Madame Tussaud's figure.

"Mr. Vice President. Are you all right?" the doctor asked.

Goulet, ashen faced, stared nowhere and remained frozen in place.

Rocky alarmed, wondered, *is he having a heart attack, a stroke? Bad time for the SOB to croak. The vice president's successor, the Speaker of the House, is a Dem. Nicky will hate that.*

The director turned toward the V.P., and asked, "Mr. Vice President?"

Rocky reached over to a tray holding several bottles of water. He unscrewed the cap on one of the bottles, handing it across the table. "Mr. Vice President, drink this."

Goulet turned his gaze toward Rocky and reached for the water.

"Thank you." He drank half its contents, his hands shaking, he returned the bottle to the table.

The four sat for another moment as Goulet collected himself.

"Please, go on," Goulet said.

"We have rerun video and satellite images over and over. These images document the subject, which I will refer to as the MF." Parsons let out a quiet cough framed in a smirk. "It shows the flight to the 'roosting' place forty minutes prior to the time the shot was fired and its eventual flight from the tree, four hours later."

"Is this some sort of trained bird?" the director asked.

"No, not exactly," Parsons said. "MF swooped in and landed on a tree on the White House grounds near the VIP viewing stand during one of the loudest points of the parade. ASI alerted us to the fact that the flight of this large fowl seemed less natural and somewhat contrived or mechanical. It's landing was more like a VTOL, a vertical, take-off, and landing aircraft, like a Harrier or Osprey."

Director Hamilcar said, "Certainly an outlier!"

Rocky nodded.

The vice president listened intently, first crossing and uncrossing his legs, then his arms. Tiny beads of sweat formed on his brow.

Parsons continued. "Our ASI had compared the flight of falcons and hawks in the wild to the flight of this one. Though subtle, MF's maneuvering is more contrived, robotic. Most importantly, the bird remained perfectly still for over four hours."

The three men focused on Dr. Parsons as she removed a tissue from her pocket and silently blew her nose. She returned the tissue to her pocket and began again. "The MF did not move once it landed on the tree branch. At least that's what we perceived from a temporary video camera focused on the rear of the viewing stand. It appears that it was a last minute decision to place the camera there." Looking at Director Hamilcar, she said, "I believe your people made that happen."

Hamilcar nodded.

Parsons said, "Without that having been done, we would not have this information."

"That is our good fortune," Hamilcar said. "I believe the area was thought to be a blind spot. Just a coincidence, I suppose. Though, perhaps, and it remains to be seen, a fortuitous one."

Parsons continued. "The camera was put in place just before the inauguration. Since the bird sat on the periphery, it went undetected by computers running algorithms and by personnel manning video monitors. MF was positioned quite a distance from the camera. The image was pixilated and too unresolved to attract attention. The MF remained stationary."

Dr. Parsons placed another folder, an unopened folder in front of the three men. "MF didn't move until just before the shot was fired. Even then, it was barely noticeable. Except from some sort of bracing action taken before the shot was fired. We simply don't have a sufficiently clear picture, even after doing our best to get one. However, we do have this. You might want to stand on my side of the table to look over my shoulder for best effect."

Dr. Parsons opened the folder exposing its contents, a large photograph.

CHAPTER 3

The three men stood dumbstruck, viewing the photograph. Each sensed the air being sucked out of the room. A chill enveloped them. Rocky's gaze hardened in anger.

Goulet swallowed hard. Fear wrapped its icy fingers around his throat.

The Director of the United States Secret Service, absorbed in extrapolating what he saw, leaned against the table for support.

Dr. Parsons observed the various reactions. She grinned inwardly, knowing she had been validated. There was more to come, but just not yet.

She whispered to herself, "Let them squirm and cower a bit more. Then hit them with the hard truth!"

The paralyzing silence was interrupted by a beeping tone from the veep's office phone.

Only Dr. Parsons seemed to take note of the singular sound as it continued to squawk. None of the men acknowledged it.

Parsons said in a condescending voice, "Mr. Vice President, aren't you going to answer your phone?"

Goulet glared at Dr. Parsons, walked to his desk to reach for the phone, lifted the receiver several inches, and dropped it back into the cradle. The beeping ceased.

The vice president sat and motioned to the others. "Gentlemen, er, and lady, I mean, uh, everyone, sit down."

The ornate latch on the office's paneled door clicked. All heads turned.

Special Agent Hunter entered the room. "Mr. Vice President, I apologize for the interruption, but when you didn't answer the—"

Goulet tapped a pen on his desk. "What's so important that you're interrupting this meeting?"

"Sir, the president has regained consciousness."

Goulet's face paled. He slumped down into his chair.

Noting Goulet's reaction, Parsons and Hamilcar exchanged glances. They turned and focused immediately on Rocky, watching a smile expand across his face.

"Thank you, Special Agent Hunter," Rocky said. "I, for one, appreciate the interruption. Let's go see the president." Rocky made a mental note of the veep's defeated posture. "Let's pick this up at the Residence in a couple of hours." Reaching for the folder, he closed it and handed it to Dr. Parsons. "Doctor, please bring this and any additional data you have to the meeting."

He turned to the VP. "Chris, don't you think it a good idea to include the FBI and Homeland Security in that meeting?"

Goulet, sitting with his hands folded in his lap, sighed. "Sure, why not?"

"And Chris," Rocky said, walking to the door with his back to the vice president. He twisted the door handle and turned to face the VP. "I would appreciate your immediately releasing an official announcement pertaining to Nick's improved condition."

Rocky, giddy with hope, did not wait for an answer.

∞

Special Agent Hunter and Rocky made use of the underground tunnel between the Executive Office Building and the White House on their way to the infirmary. The last thing Rocky wanted was for a vigilant press corps to draw conclusions, usually incorrect conclusions, about his or anyone else's movements. *It's their job to create news. Why make it easier?*

As they ran down the stairs from the second floor office to the tunnel in the subbasement, Rocky anxiously spoke, almost shouting, "What else can you tell me? What happened? When did he wake up? How is he?"

Hunter, doing his best to keep up with the now sprinting Rocky, said, "I, uh, I don't really know, sir. All I know is that he's, he's awake."

Hunter ran his fingers around the back of his sweat-soaked collar as they came to the end of the tunnel. Refusing to wait for the elevator, Rocky and Hunter shot up the stairs, then down the hall. Rocky was not going to let another second pass before he was back at Nick's bedside.

Brooke and Rick stood on either side of their father as he lay in the bed, eyes closed.

Rocky paused before entering the room. He wanted to indelibly capture this moment in his mind. Succumbing to the urgent need to be close to his husband, to touch him, he stepped into the room.

Brooke and Rick turned toward Rocky. Both faces bathed in tears and celebratory grins; eyes radiating love, warmth, and hope. Brooke motioned her father to join them. He wanted to move forward, to join them. He was afraid it was a dream, and he would wake up to find Nicky wasn't conscious. Maybe worse, worse, much worse.

Rick went over and pulled his hesitant father toward the hospital bed. "Dad, come over here."

Rick moved to the side of the bed.

Rocky took Nick's hand in his. He struggled to hold back his surging emotions, emotions of every stripe. He strengthened his will not to break down by focusing not on Nick, but on Brooke and Rick as they gazed at their father. He concentrated, biting his lower lip, and paced each breath.

"What are you looking at them for? Aren't you here to see me?" Nick said softly.

Rocky used his hand to steady himself, startled, not daring to believe it was the voice of the man he loved, who had nearly been assassinated. The man he wanted to rise up and live, like Lazarus. *Was it true? Is he speaking to me? Or is this a fanciful dream? A dream that will end with a horrible reality.*

He looked down at Nick and saw dopey eyes peering from beneath half open lids, atop a lazy smile. Rocky bent over in joyful disbelief. "Hey, you."

Nick smiled.

"I've missed you," Rocky said.

"I must have missed you," Nick said, sporting a drowsy grin.

"I love you; I love you so much." Rocky teared and sniffled.

The momentary brightness in Nick's face began to slide away.

"I love you too," Nick said. He smiled and squeezed Rocky's hand. "Think I'll rest a bit."

"Good idea, hon."

Nick's eyes closed.

Dr. Samson entered the room and stood beside Rocky. "Surprised, huh?" He smiled at Rocky, then Brooke and Rick. The doctor studied the monitors. "Let's allow the president to rest. We can go to my office and bring everyone up to date."

Rocky leaned down and planted a kiss on his husband's cheek. "We'll be back to see you after your rest."

Moments later, in the doctor's office, "This is amazing Doctor. How did this happen, so quickly? Expert care?" Rocky asked, smiling.

"We get the credit for this one," Brooke said.

"Yep, we worked miracles!" Rick agreed.

The doctor was amused and decided to play along. "Yep, that's right. It's called the 'Miracle of the Twins!' All they had to do is show up and be there with him and voila! He opened his eyes, and here we are!"

Everyone laughed and exchanged victory grins.

"Very funny everybody," Rocky said, amused and eager to learn more about Nick's recovery.

"Actually Dad, it's true. It was my turn to sit with him. I came in to chill with Brooke for a few minutes before I was supposed to go on 'dad duty.' So, while he was asleep, we were letting him know what was going on in the world, especially as it pertains to him. We were telling him how we were doing our own investigation on the assassination attempt. He now knows everything about us and you, too."

The doctor coughed, uncomfortable with the direction the conversation was taking, not sure he should be part of the non-medical private family discussion.

Rocky said, "Doc, so share with us what you believe is going on."

Brooke, eager to continue, said, "We didn't bother him with details. Well, not all the details, just a detail here and there. We were trying to entertain him. Maybe help him out of his coma, even though it's medically induced. Just that kind of stupid stuff. We also said you were keeping an eye on—"

"Ok, that's good," Rocky said. "What, when, er, how did he wake up?"

"That's just it," Brooke said. "When we told him that you were keeping tabs on 'he who shall not be mentioned,' and how'd you'd made him move his stuff out of the office, that's when he opened his eyes and said, 'What are you talking about?' I couldn't believe it! Wow, were we shocked? Surprised and happy!"

"Amazing!" Rocky said.

"It sure is," Rick agreed. "Then we started talking a little bit, back and forth. That's when I stuck my head out the door and asked the nurse to get in touch with you. It seemed to take a long time for you to get here."

"I wasn't in the building."

"Oh."

Rocky looked at the doctor, "You realize this conversation is confidential, right?"

"Yes, sir."

Rocky nodded. "So, Doc, what do think this is all about? Medically, I mean."

"I think a rapid reduction in cranial swelling played a big part. Reducing the intracranial pressure improved the flow of blood and oxygen and decreased the chances of permanent damage.

"When do you think you can remove the bullet?" Rick asked.

"Sooner than you think. As you probably noticed," the doctor said with a knowing grin, "The president is getting closer and closer to being off life support. As soon as he regains some of his strength, we'll go in and get it. The last thing we want is a piece of metal running around his brain."

"Are we talking days?"

"More like a week."

"Oh, another thing, I thought his coma was medically induced," Rocky said. "How did he get out of it?"

"It wasn't until his swelling started to suddenly decrease, rapidly. At that point, we started backing off the medication. He surprised us. It's unusual for someone to respond as fast as he did. He seemed to really want out of the coma."

"I guess that's good news?" Rocky said quizzically.

"It means he is in excellent physical condition. As far as I can tell, he'll likely make a full recovery. It'll be a while, but he'll recover."

"Great, thank you. How about giving me some notes on his condition. You know, throw in some medical jargon, so I can keep my promise to the American people and update them?"

"Yes, sir. I'll send that up in the next thirty minutes."

∞

An hour later Rocky and Rick sat with Brooke in her bedroom in the White House Residence looking at her computer. "How did you get this information?" Rocky asked looking at Brooke. "Conspiracy? Sounds like a coup attempt. This is taking on a sinister dimension. Okay, what else?"

Brooke hesitated and went on to explain. "That's what we're saying. We, I mean I, went online, and don't get pissed, we, er, me, not Rick, got into the server. It looks like a DOD server. Firewalls and all, but I found something you need to take a look at. We can't figure it out. I think Dad could still be in danger."

The unfamiliar laptop caught Rocky's attention. "Where are the stickers? Don't you still have those 'Chainsmokers' and 'Chili Peppers' stickers?" Rocky reached for the computer.

Brooke pulled it toward her and out of her father's reach. "I borrowed it, sort of. What I mean is, well . . . " She paused and closed the laptop and folded her hands on the cover. "I couldn't find my computer. The people that unpacked our stuff must have put it somewhere. I simply couldn't find it. So, I went looking for it. I thought it might be in Dad's office in the West Wing. Remember when he told us we could go to the West Wing whenever we wanted?"

"Okay, Brooke, quit stalling. Where did you get it?" Rocky folded his arms and tightened his jaw.

"Um. I was just about ready to enter, you know, the—"

Rick interrupted, his tone positive and supportive. "You mean the Oval Office? Right, Brooke?"

"Yeah, Oval for short," Brooke said.

"And?" their father asked.

"I was just about to enter the Oval, like earlier this afternoon, when I overheard the vice president talking to some guy. He was really irritated and sounded like he was nervous and in a hurry. He was sitting at Dad's desk, the president's desk, trying to get into his computer. He was really ticked off.

"I heard him tell some guy to just fix the computer, so he didn't have to remember a password. The vice president doesn't seem to be very tech savvy. Besides, I've never liked him much. But you know that. Gives me the creeps."

"But every computer needs a password." Rocky said.

"Yeah, and after a few minutes whoever was helping the vice president asked him what it was. I heard him tell the other guy it was 'G-O-U-L-E-T.'"

"Shit! What a dumbass," Rick said.

Brooke looked at Rick. Her eyes pleading for support.

Rocky leaned forward in his chair and placed his folded arms on the table. "Brooke, you're stalling. That's the vice president's laptop. You absconded with it? You, you stole it, didn't you?"

"There are mitigating circumstances, tell him how, why," Rick said.

Enunciating each word, she slowly nodded her head while looking at the floor. "He then said something really cruel."

Rocky cocked his head. "What? What did he say? I thought we were talking about the laptop."

"I heard the vice president say." She paused. "'That queer won't last long, and I want my stuff in here and his stuff out, now!'" She swiped at falling tears.

Rick said, "Dad's recovering, Brooke. He'll be okay."

"I know." Brooke sniffled. "It's just hearing those awful words cut so deep."

Rocky knelt beside Brooke and drew her into his arms. Her head rested on his shoulder. "I am so sorry Brooke." A moment later, he said, "Did you hear anything else?"

She managed a nod. "He said, I've got some things I need done as soon as I'm sworn in, maybe sooner. Then I heard glass clinking, and something pouring, must've been alcohol. He belched, it must have been Goulet, 'cause then he said, 'Christ, I sure as hell hope he doesn't last long.'" Tearing, Brooke sniffled. "I didn't know if I was going to throw up or curl up and die."

Rick said, "What a horrible thing for you to have to hear."

"I'll be okay, but I'm worried about Dad." She pulled away, wiping her tears with her hands and in a strong voice said, "Let's get on with it! He'll pay!"

Rocky stood and, in an anxious whisper, said, "Did anyone see you there?"

"No and thank goodness he and whoever he was talking to walked out the opposite door."

Rick said, "And listen to this, the next part is unbelievable, I swear, I don't have any idea how she does it. I sure can't do what she does."

"Gawd!" Brooke said.

Brooke and Rick exchanged fist bumps. She thanked him with her eyes and then turned toward her father.

Rocky felt lightheaded for a moment, suddenly transported to thinking about the secrecy surrounding their parentage. For the first time, not telling them seemed wrong. He shook his head to rid himself of the thought.

"I couldn't believe what I heard," Brooke said. "The offices were eerily quiet. I don't know how long I stood there. But the longer I did the more friggin' pissed off I got."

Rocky raised an eyebrow.

Rick smirked and grinned at his sister.

Her face flushed, she continued. "It was so weird. I stuck my head in the Oval, no one was there. This sounds stupid, but I felt like I was being pushed or something, like someone had their hand on the small of my back. I just marched right into the office, to the desk, grabbed the laptop and walked right out the door and back here."

"You know there's video cameras everywhere," Rick said. "And eventually White House security is going to tell Goulet about it. He's the acting president."

A pregnant silence filled the room.

"Yeah, there are, but we can make some sort of excuse..." Rocky said. "Maybe I can get to Hamilcar and defuse it before Goulet hears about it."

"Like, I needed a computer and thought it was Dad's," Brooke said.

Rocky, internalizing the difficulties Brooke taking the computer might have created, said, "You know, this whole thing is getting out of hand. What you did is probably illegal. You're an attorney; you both are adults. You're on camera. There could be some long term legal ramifications here."

The twins exchanged their familiar 'Dad's-overreacting-but-don't-say-a-word look.' A look they often shared growing up.

Brooke turned back to Goulet's computer.

"Okay, I'll deal with that later," Rocky said. "It's obvious you found something on the computer. And how do you know so much about computers, anyway? I sent you to law school, right?"

"Messing with computers is something I picked up while at law school. A nice guy, kinda nerdy, got me really interested in IT. It helped to get my head out of studying. It's almost meditative/therapeutic." Her hands flew over the keyboard as she spoke. "We had a small group of us that would meet up, blow off steam, and show off new stuff we'd picked up. We would swap routines, talk hacks, rip apart code. It was fun and we learned a lot. I'm pretty good at it."

"You better believe it," Rick said, beaming at his twin sister. "I could use her at Chambers Enterprises."

Rocky shook his head. "I am very concerned. Theft of government property, and now hacking into government sites. Your Dad could be really damaged politically should this get out. His own adult children, felons."

Brooke stopped typing for a moment, looked up at her father, inhaled, and returned to her keyboard.

"Dad," Rick said, "It wasn't our plan to do anything illegal. We won't do anything illegal anymore, if we can avoid it, but we have to find out who and why someone tried to kill Dad.

Rick walked over to the bedroom door, closed it, and continued, "C'mon Dad, relax, give us a chance to tell you what we know so far."

Light from the dimly lit chandelier bounced off the pearl painted fourteen-foot-high bedroom walls. The ceiling to floor ivory Damask curtains and matching upholstered furniture provided a cool sophisticated ambience. The contrasting blue glare from the computer screen lit up Brooke's furrowed brow.

Father and son stood behind Brooke's chair looking at the screen.

"I have no idea what we are looking at," Rocky said and folded his arms.

As she typed, Brooke couldn't help from commenting, "Not to get off-topic, but Goulet sounded scared or agitated or something. Like I said, he creeps me out."

Keeping the conversation on track, Rick said, "Okay Brooke, show Dad what you have so far."

"Well, what I think I've found is that someone has gone to a great deal of effort to conceal something. Normally, this stuff would be impossible to access, given we're probably on the most secure network on the planet. But, luckily for us, Goulet is a walking, talking security breach. Can you believe it? He saved all his passwords on his desktop!"

"What Brooke is trying to say, Dad, is that she has located a server that isn't part of the White House equipment."

"You have got to be kidding me!" Rocky said. "How did you figure this out? Why were you even looking?"

Rick said, "After Dad was shot, we were sitting in the kitchen, trying to figure out how to help. Brooke came up with this idea. I think she's really on to something."

"What idea, Brooke?"

Focusing on her screen, her fingers flying across the keyboard, she said, "We started getting a lot of feedback, conspiracy theories from our social media followers, most of them crackpot ideas. Nothing that we thought credible, but it did get us think-ing. It really got us thinking. Things are really weird." She paused for a moment. "We need to wipe Goulet's computer of any sign of my trolling. Need to get it back to him." She shrugged. "We'll figure that out later."

"Anyway," Rick said, "with the laptop, we now have access to the internet. It's so much easier than trying to do all this on our phones."

Brooke said matter-of-factly, "So, I'm sitting on this 'hot' com-puter, and I find a link to an off-site server. That's not weird in itself, but what I found on the server was crazy."

"What was crazy?" Rocky asked.

"Well, the server, it's insanely powerful, more powerful than anything used for data storage or day to day stuff. But it's sitting idle most of the time monitoring all kinds of activity. Traffic, video, and surveillance stuff. There are cameras pointed to vari-ous parts of the White House grounds and it's also linked to other cameras in other parts of the city. Data is streaming, but I don't know why. But if I were to guess it seems that it has served its purpose and should have been shut down."

Rick said, "There wasn't much going on until just before, dur-ing, and after the inauguration. Lots of logging action. And then nothing since a few hours after Dad was shot."

Brooke leaned back in her chair, hands clasped behind her head, and stared at the screen, "If it's the White House's server, they made a big mistake. They left it on, and apparently, it's run-ning, and from the logs, it doesn't look like it's being monitored. I'm totally inside it, thanks to VP dumbass. I can see everything. It's got amazing analytics. They're showing all traffic in and out of the White House and surrounding buildings. There's a camera network showing tons of angles but many of the cameras are focused on trees and bushes and...Why anyone would need cameras there I don't know. I think the server is monitoring cell phone towers along with GPS coordinates of specific phones or something. Can't tell yet. So far, this is way beyond anything I can imagine."

Rocky's hair stood up on his neck. It felt like every inch of his skin tingled. He shifted his feet and clasped his hands behind his back, trying to steady his nerves. *This parallels the intel from Dr. Parsons. It's Top Secret. Crap! Brooke's on to it and I can't share what I know. I can't pull them any deeper into this. What the fuck!*

Rocky returned to the conversation. "I still don't understand what that has to do with anything?"

Brooke looked away from the screen and back at her father. "Let's check something. The cameras might have caught an image, the shooter. Like I said, what I can tell from looking at the logs for when this server was powered on, there are only three times the server was actively running: during the parade, the shooting, and several hours after the shooting." She paused taking a deep breath. "During the same time that Dad was shot."

Brooke stopped speaking, allowing time for what she had said a second time, to sink in.

Rocky and Rick exchanged *oh shit* glances.

"Other than that, it's been quiet, just eavesdropping, watching, not processing data. It makes no sense for sophisticated equipment that can collate massive amounts of data to be so inactive most of the time, yet so active at just the right time. There's *no doubt* it's somehow related to Dad being shot!"

"I was wondering, video, is there any video?" Rick asked.

Brooke answered, "Hm, has to be, somewhere."

Rocky's mind leapt back to the conversation held in the VP's office earlier in the day. *Parson's photograph!* Slightly swaying, he steadied himself with a hand on the back of Brooke's chair.

Rick picked up where Brooke had left off. "Then, looking at the logs, it tried to shut down. We aren't sure if it shut down or not, but something happened. It came back up and is running now."

"You know this, how?" Rocky asked.

"It's just, you know, in the logs," Brooke said. "When the server didn't go down, it remained online, and we found it. My guess is that it was supposed to shut down and disappear, like virtually, not really shut down. You know what I mean." Brooke leaned forward and steepled her hands under her chin.

"I can't say for sure about the distance, I mean where the server is physically located. It's a hunch, I have a hunch, based on signal strength, power levels, and GPS coordinates. I need to see what I can pull together, then triangulate. Not sure that is the right word. It also must be in a secure location. What's safer than the White House?" She snorted, startling herself. "Supposedly, supposed to be safe, anyway."

She sat back in her chair, reaching across and took her father's hand in hers. "It doesn't appear to be doing anything. Like it is waiting for an interrupt or a command. I'm not sure why." Moments later she said, "Hm, wait a minute." She let go of his hand and leaned forward toward the computer and let her fingers fly again across the keyboard. "Look at this, Dad. This map has tons of data. It shows the cell towers, cameras, and stuff around DC. I need to spend some time trying to understand it. There's gotta be something here."

"Is that Google Maps?" Rick asked.

"Nope, some program called Prism," Brooke said focusing on the screen. "It is much more complex than Google. The data is much more specific, GIS database, I think."

"When did you start 'hacking,' Brooke?" Rocky asked.

Brooke and Rick looked at each other, eyes wide, in disbelief and then at their father with concern.

Rick placed his hand on his father's shoulder. "Research, Dad. Research."

"Yeah, right." Rocky chuckled. "Well, keep researching. But keep it between the three of us. Better yet." Rocky chuckled again. "I didn't hear this and I didn't see anything."

Brooke and Rick shook their heads, amused.

Rocky opened his mouth to speak, paused to collect his thoughts, then said, "Brooke, Rick, get the word out to everyone, I mean everyone. Make sure it goes viral, that your father has regained consciousness!"

"Good idea, Dad!" Brooke said.

"Yeah, good thinking," Rick added.

Rocky asked, "Brooke, so you think you can accomplish those tasks you and Rick have been talking about, right?"

"Sure, I think so."

"Okay then," Rocky said. "In the meantime, clone that computer and take it back to the Oval after you have inserted malware to monitor it. Rick, go back to the townhouse and see if Brooke's computer is still there. If it's not there, get the laptop I put in the safe and bring it here and give it to your sister. Then keep an eye on that server and see if anything changes."

The twin's jaws dropped.

"What's this Tom Clancy espionage thing your strutting?" Rick asked.

Rocky chuckled. "Remember? My reserve duty? What I do with the Joint Chiefs of Staff at the Pentagon?"

Nick was partially elevated; some color having returned to his face. *He looks so much thinner, smaller, frail, diminutive. How could this be? How could just a couple of days diminish a man, such a vibrant man?* Rocky swallowed hard and did his best to project strength, holding one of Nick's hands in both of his as he sat on the side of the bed.

Nick's eyes slowly emerged from behind his lids. As if on cue, a grin erupted catching sight of Rocky smiling back at him. Nick, his voice somewhat resilient, said, "Hey old man, how're ya handling this?"

"Me?"

"Yeah, you. Seems to me I'd be pretty bummed out if it were you lying here and not me," Nick said. "Been there, done that."

Rocky grinned. "You'd certainly know, it hasn't been that long ago . . . that . . . well, you know."

"Yep, I do. Now, come here and give me a kiss, ya' big lug!"

Rocky leaned over in childish anticipation framed in caution, not wanting to hurt his man, but oh so desperately wanting to grab ahold and hug him tight.

A gentle kiss on salve-moistened lips would have to do, for now.

Rocky brought his cheek alongside Nick's. "I love you so much."

"I love you too," Nick said and turned toward Rocky just quick enough to snag another kiss.

Rocky beamed and found his place in the chair next to Nick.

"Okay, so what's happening in the world? I gotta know. I'm still the president, right?"

Nick's feigned chuckle didn't fool either of them.

"You are for the moment. The 25th Amendment has been bantered about. As you know, Goulet is the acting president. No action by the Cabinet yet, thank God."

"What? You're kidding me? They should have done that right away."

Rocky inhaled, forced to acknowledge the inevitable. Nick's recovery would have to share the spotlight with the reality of politics and the outside world. "Well, they were seriously considering it, until Goulet stepped on his crank, unforced error on his part, moving his stuff into the Oval. Cabinet got nervous him moving so fast when they found out."

"Huh?" Nick raised up a few inches, grimaced, and fell back. "Fuck, that hurt."

"Sweetie, c'mon, don't do that, be careful!"

"Yow! I get it . . . ow . . . okay, keep going, explain, I'll stay still. Ooh." He took a deep breath and moved around a bit searching for a comfortable position.

"I caught him packing your stuff in the Oval and moving his crap in the night you got shot."

"What the fuck? Jesus!"

"I cornered him in the private office and read him the riot act. Then the next day—"

Nick's face blanched as he placed a hand alongside his bandaged head.

"Are you all right, Nick? Should I get the doctor?"

The president shook his head. "I am okay, and please, you're gonna tell me. What about the next day?"

Rocky shifted his weight in the chair and was about to protest that Nick needed to rest but thought better of it.

Reaching for Rocky's hand, Nick said, "Make yourself comfortable, hon, then spit it out. Tell be everything. I can handle it."

Rocky moved closer to the bed. "Do you remember when Gene and I told you we didn't totally trust Goulet? Remember when we said we thought he was the epitome, the personification of the 'Peter Principle,' you know, likely to be surpassing his potential?"

"Yeah," Nick said, "but we agreed we needed him to round out the ticket, we had to secure the 'fly-over' states."

"Well," Rocky said, "we may have underestimated him. His ambition."

"We won the election, what else could he want?" Nick asked.

"I really can't say," Rocky said, raking a hand through his hair. "It seems as if something just isn't right."

"Right? Like what? He paused and then exclaimed, "Rocky!"

"That's the problem, I can't. So much shit is whirling around my head. Stuff that makes no sense. If I am half right, you getting shot is much deeper than someone wanting you dead, you know, the hate thing. More complex." Rocky sat for a minute, his hands clasped behind his head, tilting back, staring at the ceiling."

"Tell me everything you know."

"You need your rest. Maybe tomorrow."

"My ass is stuck in this bed. Nothing to do but lie here feeling like shit. Useless! Resting!"

"How about healing? Recovering?" Rocky reached over and patted Nick's hand resting on his abdomen. "I love you and want you to get better fast. We need you, alive and well." Rocky stood up and caressed the patient's face and placed a kiss on his forehead. "I need you to get well. The kids need you well. The country needs you out of this bed and in the Oval Office."

Nick grunted and offered a wilting look. "Please tell me what you know, babe. Then leave me to rest. Let me have something to think on. Something to take my mind off of my misery. I promise, I'll rest after you fill me in."

Rocky sat back in his chair and flexed his neck, rotating his head side to side. He began with one word, "Treason." And spent the next thirty minutes bringing Nick up to date on the nominees the vice president had not sent to the Hill and then on Brooke's, Rick's, and Dr. Parson's findings.

Merrill Spaulding stood 5' 10" tall, her height was accentuated by an athletic build and a tailored black vicuña wool Moshita business skirt suit. The no-nonsense, mid-length, full-bodied platinum blond hair crowned the head of one of the most respected minds in Washington.

"Merrill, please, come in and have a seat," Trish Smart said, rising from behind her desk. The late afternoon sun filled her large office with an eerie light.

"Thank you," Merrill said.

Ms. Smart motioned to one of the chairs in front of the desk.

Both women sat and Smart said, "Please, call me Trish."

"Thank you," Merrill said.

"I appreciate your coming. I know it is late, but my schedule was such that I was unavailable earlier."

"I understand, Chief. These are busy times. Perhaps it is for the best, as there were developments in the vice president's office, including a visit to my office from Vice President Goulet."

"Really? Interesting."

"Yes, he came by my office in the Executive Building this afternoon."

"Do tell, his mood? I am sure that by then he had been apprised of the memo my office sent out regarding resignations."

"Yes, indeed. He appeared a little flustered. He mentioned that he had heard from his people that I had tendered my resignation to the president, directly. He inferred that my action was probably responsible for the memo and that all-in-all it might have been for the best."

Trish sat up. "Remarkable. What do think he meant by that?"

"He actually told me himself. He opened up. His comments indicated he valued my political acumen. I was taken aback, as you can imagine. He requested I provide him with a memo

outlining the specifics of the 25th amendment, including specifically how Congress is to implement it if the Cabinet does not
take action."

Trish's eyes opened wide. "I am a little surprised he had not
ascertained exactly what was involved in triggering the amendment by now."

Merrill, eyes wide, incredulous, said, "You don't, you can't
mean this was premeditated?"

"I can't say. It does, however, beg the question." Trish placed
her hands on her hips. She looked down at her lap and then
looked back up. "His actions, in the long run, could be inter-
preted as a premeditated attempt to seize power!"

Merrill swallowed hard. "No doubt, Ms. . . . er, Trish.

Trish wondered out loud, "Okay, enough of that." She sighed.
"Where does that leave us? I mean, what is your interpretation?"
She paused. "The 25th Amendment. What can Congress do?
Where do we stand?"

Merrill flattened her skirt and folded her hands in her lap.
"There are a couple of scenarios that exist. The first one, is if the
president is injured, unconscious, paralyzed or unable to communicate his decision to give powers to the vice president to
assume the duties of acting president. The vice president automatically becomes acting president. That is the situation we
currently find ourselves in."

"Yes, I understand, Merrill. But he has not been removed as
president. At least not permanently. This is all so nebulous, confusing. Goulet is acting president. I believe that all the president
needs to do is notify the Senate he is ready to resume his office

when he feels he is healthy enough to do so. But now, with Goulet and his machinations . . . My fear is that the vice president wants to permanently remove President Chambers-Jeffries from office."

"Your concern is well founded. But that won't be so easy. If the Cabinet majority votes to remove the president, they can do so, but not right away. The Cabinet must send a letter to the Hill and both houses have to act, vote, within 21 days."

"And if the Cabinet does not act?" Trish asked.

Merrill continued, "Congress can appoint a panel to take up the question. If the panel or the Cabinet vote to designate the vice president acting president, the president can object."

"What do you mean, Merrill?"

"If Congress is not in session, it is required to convene within 48 hours of the 25th Amendment being invoked. Then they have the 21 days to vote to remove the president."

"Does the president have any recourse?"

"Yes, as I mentioned, he can object. He must notify Congress that no cognitive or debilitating physical disability exists that would limit his ability to perform his duties as president. This is all while the vice president is functioning as the acting president. Like Goulet is now. The president has four days to challenge or file an objection to the Cabinet's or Congress's challenge. It requires a two-thirds majority of both the Senate and the House to designate the vice president as acting president until the president can resume his duties."

"That sounds quite precarious, almost arbitrary," Trish said."

"Not really. Perhaps for an unconscious president, for there is no opportunity for an unconscious president to contest. But in our case, the president is conscious."

"Thank God,' Trish remarked. "One would hope that would give Goulet reason to rethink his position. The people are instinctively not inclined to have an elected president removed from office. It might seem to appear as somewhat like a coup."

"Well," Merrill said, "perceptions are everything. If Congress feels the president may be able to function or soon be able to assume the duties of his office, they are less likely to remove him. Interestingly, the president can refile his petition should a vote to remove him be successful."

"My concern is the long run. Does the acting president remain the acting president for the remainder of the president's term in office?"

Merrill said, "That is not clear. I have yet to find anything on that. Also, it appears the president can continue to appeal the vote ad infinitum. There has never been a lot written of consequence by legal experts on this. If there has, it doesn't have much validity, as nothing has been tested in the courts. We have never found ourselves in this situation before."

"For God's sake, what a mess. Where is James Madison when we need him?" Trish said.

"I suppose we will just have to cross that bridge when and if we come to it. It might not be a bad idea to start educating the public on exactly how the 25th Amendment works. If it can be shown that it could be seen as going down a rabbit hole, especially since the president seems to be recovering, perhaps Goulet will be forced to back off just by the sheer force of public opinion and not wanting to be seen as grabbing for power."

"I think you may be right about that. Polling strongly indicates the president has the heartfelt support, even across party lines, that he recovers."

Merrill slowly scratched her neck. "You are aware of course of the sensation the president's children have created on social media."

"Not really, I have been totally absorbed and have not spoken with—"

"Well," Merrill said, let me tell you, the president's health and the increasingly suspicious nature of the attempted assassination have gone viral."

"Really? What's that all about? I can understand such things going viral, but how are Rick and Brooke involved? That is a bit out of the ordinary."

"It appears that prior to the president regaining consciousness, they put out an appeal to their massive following for help in ascertaining what might have happened. #solvetheassasinationattemptmystery and #whodoneit and #coupattempt."

Trish ran her fingers through her hair and sat back. "That is truly remarkable. What a boon for the president. This will certainly make Goulet think twice about the 25th."

"Oh, he's thinking about it, hard. I understand he may be making a move as early as tomorrow to meet with the Cabinet. All he needs is eight of them to agree and Congress will be notified to act. As Congress is currently in session, things could move fast. Worst case, the president has four days to act should the Cabinet send the 25th to the Hill."

CHAPTER 4

Rick and Rocky sat in the Treaty Room at a large oval inlaid table littered with notepads, maps, and files.

Brooke entered and joined them at the table, pushed everything aside, and placed herself across from her father and brother. A glint in her eyes, her lips painting a conspiratorial smile.

Rick grinned. "Yo, Brooke, what's up? I know that look!"

Brooke's index finger pushed a tiny diamond across the table.

The two men sat up and leaned forward.

Rocky looked at Brooke. "Okay, what's this all about?"

"It was stuck between the F2 and the F3 keys on Goulet's laptop. I would never have noticed, but it caught my eye when I tilted the laptop as I was getting ready to return it to the Oval very early this morning." She smiled her full-toothed Cheshire-cat grin and pushed a larger diamond across the table. "I found this under the desk in the Oval. And these." Brooke placed a folded tissue on the table. She opened the tissue, revealing six diamonds of varying sizes.

Rocky and Rick exchanged wide-eyed glances and returned their attention to the diamonds.

"This makes no sense," Rocky said. "How could anyone be so careless?"

"Maybe they were in a hurry?" Rick said.

"It must have been that snake, the vice president, he is the only one that could have had access to the Oval," Brooke said. "Well, there are of course others with access to the room, but not many."

"The diamonds, where did you find them?" Rocky asked.

"Like I said, under the desk."

"Which desk?" Rocky asked.

"Remember, the Oval, the one in the Oval, the ceremonial desk? What's with you two? I've already told you."

Incredulous, Rick said, "What were you doing under the desk?"

"I thought it would be a good idea to put the laptop next to where the chair slides in under the desk. So it might look like Goulet'd misplaced it."

"You mean the kneehole?" Rocky asked.

She waived her hand across the diamonds. "That, what you call the kneehole, is where I found these. It was as if they had fallen out of a pocket, or perhaps a bag, randomly scattered up against the right panel where the chair would have slid in if the arms were not so large. You know, I heard it is an armored chair. It sure's heavy enough."

Reaching for one of the larger stones, Rick said, "Too bad the facet surfaces are too small to capture a finger print."

"Stop!" Brooke snapped, blocking his hand with hers. "Maybe there is some DNA residue or something like that on one of them."

"Maybe, but not likely, Rocky said.

"Probably not, but perhaps some markings or identifiers on the stones," Rick said.

"What do you mean, identifiers?" Brooke said.

"Lasered on identifiers," Rocky said. "Diamond graders have all manner of ways to keep track of different stones."

"Really?" Brooke asked. "I thought any kind of mark on any stone would compromise its quality."

"How do you know about diamonds, Dad?" Rick asked.

"When your parents and I were in Brussels before they were married, the three of us went engagement ring shopping."

Brooke toyed with a three-carat square cut diamond suspended on a platinum chain around her neck. "You mean this diamond?"

"Yes."

Brooke swallowed and Rick exhaled.

"If you had a magnifying glass, you could look at the stone's girdle, the outer edge between the crown and where the bottom meets, the widest point. I remember your father having to have that number to give to the insurance company when he bought it."

Caught up in their own thoughts, the three sat silent for several moments.

"Dad?" Rick's voice snapped Rocky out of his reverie.

"Time to get back on track here," Rocky said, recouping his place. "I am going to reach out to a jeweler friend of mine. Rick, you may know him, Sam Roth."

"Yes, I do," Rick said nodding his head. "He's the guy at Chambers Industries in the Boston research facility. Very smart, seems to know a little and sometimes a lot about everything."

"He does indeed," Rocky said.

Brooke said, "How do you think he can help? Does he have some sort of background in gemology?"

"Yes, he runs the geology division," Rick said. "The one involved with our mining and exploration projects."

"Sounds perfect to me," Brooke said. "Can we trust him to keep quiet?"

"We can. Definitely," Rocky said. "Everything that takes place in the labs he runs remains confidential."

"Do we have anyone that could help me analyze the data I'm running across on the servers?"

Rick cocked his head and looked at his father.

Rocky slowly nodded approval.

Rick folded his arms. "We have the best IT minds in the country, maybe the world. The company has been recruiting IT engineers for years. There must be someone there that can help."

"You know who I am thinking about?" Rocky asked, looking at his son.

"Not sure, Dad," Rick said. "Maybe Buck Gerard?"

"That's the one, good guess, son," Rocky said pointing his finger at Rick.

"And why would he be the one, the right one to assist me? There are a lot of good ones out there, why him?" Brooke asked.

"Well, ever since Dad began spending more time helping in the campaign, I have become more involved in managing many of the more sensitive corporate projects. Buck is the guy I go to when I need detailed information on just about any of our technical programs, such as AI and evolving technology."

"Tell me more," she said sitting back in her chair.

"He graduated top in his class at MIT, excelled in graduate work at Oxford and the Technical University of Berlin. He was awarded a doctorate in Information Science from Cornell University." Rick grinned, and continued, lightheartedly, "Qualified? I'd say so. And he's our age and a good soccer player."

Nick sat propped up on the hospital bed. The large head bandage had been replaced with a much smaller one. One tube led into the back of his head. Clean shaven, focused on his phone, he looked up as his husband entered the infirmary room.

"Hey babe!" Rocky beamed taking note of Nick sitting upright and focused on his phone. "How'd you get ahold of that? I thought you were supposed to be resting."

"You forget, I'm the President of the United States." He smiled mischievously. "I've got lots of pull. They say I am the most powerful man in the world. Not feel'n it yet, though."

"That you are, my dear."

"Rocky, what's the status on the 25th? Is it official, has Congress declared Goulet acting president? I don't see anything here in the newsfeeds. I thought for sure, by now, something would have happened."

"Nope, not yet, but he's up on the Hill and has a Cabinet meeting planned for later today. The Cabinet is probably over their initial shock at Goulet rushing to occupy the Oval. I suspect it will happen then. You know, the Cabinet voting and then sending it up to the Hill."

Nick adjusted his position and placed the phone on the tray in front of him. "So, in four days, in four days, well—"

"Well, you have four days to object. Congress just needs to re-convene within a couple of days of the 25th being sent up to the Hill. "Since Congress is already in session, that does not apply here. Assuming you are going to object, well, they then need to conference and meet, talk about it. Perhaps take it to committee. They have twenty-one days to act. Naw, it'll take longer than one might think."

The president slowly exhaled. "Even without the vote he is act-ing president. It's just that having the powers officially transferred would seem so final."

"Actually, as you know, you can get them back, but yeah, pos-session is nine-tenths. Who knows what could happen when Goulet feels emboldened? His right wing cronies will play him like a drum. I can't imagine the flurry of executive orders that would rain down from on high as soon as he knows he's got the vote."

"And reining the executive orders back in could prove very difficult and would certainly result in a political quagmire. Talk about a political party and administration being ripped apart!"

Rocky stood at the bedside. "We need to determine which av-enue we want to take. I am, of course, assuming you want to remain president."

Head cocked to one side, mouth ajar, his chin resting between his thumb and index finger, Nick said, "No shit, Sherlock!"

Both men laughed. "Just ask'n," Rocky said.

The mood lightened.

Rocky took a seat on the bed next to Nick and grabbed hold of his hand. "How are you feeling, Mr. President?"

"Better all the time. They are going to let me get up and use the bathroom unattended the next time I need to go. Sounds silly, but I can't wait to do that, get out of this bed."

"Nervous?"

"Sorta. Not sure how I'll do walking. I just want to heal fast."

"We all want you to heal, honey. And we know you'll be smart about it. Think long term."

Nick squeezed Rocky's hand. "Please don't be angry, hon'. But I have instructed Trish Smart to arrange to have a crew film me in a wheelchair. Not too close and just for a second, but me looking like I am wheeling myself into a room or something like that."

"You mean get out of the bed and get in a chair?"

"Yeah."

"And the doctor, what does he say?"

"He's not crazy about it."

"Does Vice President Goulet know about any of this?"

"No. It's part of my plan to keep him off balance."

"Maybe if you are up for a short while. It sure will add a whole new perspective to your state of health. It might give us some time on the Hill for them not to officially strip you of your office so fast." Rocky folded his arms. "Are you sure you want to chance it?"

"Why not? I have to do something to impede Goulet. In the meantime, there is something else I want to talk to you about. Something you and I should have done a long time ago."

Rocky perked up. "What is it?"

"You remember how we agreed to tell the kids about who their biological parents are?"

"Of course, I do." Rocky took hold of Nick's hands.

A moment of silence followed, and they looked into the other's eyes.

Nick said, "Kids are caught in the middle of everything and then this. It's too much for everyone. We brought them up to be strong and independent, Rocky. They can handle this. We've been unfair and now it's time to rectify the situation. You and I will have to pay the price for not letting them know years ago. It's only fair."

Rocky said, "It doesn't have to be that way. We could hold off, wait until things are more in order."

Nick lifted Rocky's chin so that they looked at each other.

"What if the operation doesn't go well? Then what?"

Rocky slowly whispered, "Then, well, I don't know. Tell them someday or maybe never. Just how important is it that they know?" He averted Nick's gaze. "Maybe important, but not now."

"Is there any way you can see my side of it, my wanting to do this?"

"Sure, Nick. I can see your side. But I can also see my position. Their current situation. Your current situation. Like I said, this just does not seem like the time to do it."

"And if I die before we tell them?" Nick lay back in the bed and maintained a vacuous stare focused on the ceiling.

Gently, Rocky said, "I don't think you are going to die and neither do you."

"You never know," Nick said, staring at the ceiling.

Rocky thought to himself, *what if he is right and he does die. I will have stood in the way of what could very well be a last wish, perversely, a dying wish. Would it make a difference one way or another to Brooke and Rick? I don't know. I guess so, maybe. It's his decision, not mine. Ultimately, it truly has nothing to do with me, but between him and the kids. Yeah, but I'll be affected and not so well. Why can't he leave well enough alone? Fuck! God damn it!*

Rocky stood and placed his hands in his pockets. "Have it your way. I don't like it but have it your way."

Still staring at the ceiling, Nick said, "Thank you, Rocky. It means so much to be able to take care of this one thing . . . just in case.

Rocky nodded.

"There is something else."

With an exhausted groan, Rocky said, "What?"

"The operation to relieve the pressure on my brain and remove the bullet is scheduled just after my wheelchair debut."

Startled, Rocky shouted, "You have got to be kidding! What the fuck?"

Rocky stared past Nick at the medical equipment lining the wall behind the bed. Green monitor lights flashed. Soft beeping struggled unsuccessfully to fill the void.

"Why wasn't I told this before? Why was I not in on this? I'm your husband, for Christ's sake!"

"No one but the doctor and the medical team are aware of the plan. In fact, I have ordered them to keep it a secret. No one is to know. That is why the procedure will be performed here in the infirmary at 9 p.m. this evening."

"This is insane!" Rocky, his face reddened, turned back and faced Nick. "You are making one fucked-up bad decision after the other. You may be the goddamn president, but you are still part of a family that loves and cares for you. You are careless and selfish! We should be included in these decisions."

"I agree. I am all those things. I need you. This is the only way I know to regain my health in a timely manner and lessen the risk of Goulet permanently usurping the presidency."

"Is Goulet being acting president really that important? More important than your life?"

"I am the president, Rocky." He swallowed. "And you overestimate the risks involved with the operation."

Rocky ignored the tired glazed look crossing Nick's face. "Well, I beg your pardon. Someone tried to kill you and they came awfully close to doing just that. Now, you are unnecessarily tempting fate."

Nick blinked away tears. "I love you, Rocky, you and the children more than anything on earth. But I have a duty to hold on to the office to which the American people have elected me. I owe it to the nation."

Rocky thought back to the early days when he, Nick, and Sheila had run full force, arm in arm, the Three Musketeers, hellbent on getting Nick elected to one office after the other. First as a young congressman, then as a man maturing, the personification of character, courage, and purpose, the ideal senatorial candidate. That was the dream, at least it was Sheila's dream.

Without her, Nick might never have been elected senator. Unfortunately, she had not lived to see Nick elected to the Senate, as her passing had occurred only days before the election.

It had never really been his desire to be president, but he was caught up in events and armed with a burning desire to serve the nation. Rocky had often wondered if his own zeal as a LGBT activist, always pressuring Nick to use his political influence to advance gay rights, had propelled Nick into running for higher office. Was he doing it in large part for Rocky? Maybe Nick really just ran for president for him, to be supportive, empower him and his diversity agenda. Give him what he wanted, needed. That was true love. Rocky felt his stomach turn. Light-headed, he sat back down on the bed.

Nick reached for Rocky's hand and squeezed it, pushing the past from Rocky's thoughts, bringing him back to current events. "None of us, you, Brooke, or Rick went into this blindly. We knew there would be risks associated with my running for president. But we all agreed, right?"

"It's not that simple." Rocky said as he glared at Nick. "You are intentionally increasing the risks."

"Yes," Nick replied. Then, looking into Rocky's eyes, he said soulfully, "But it's my decision, and I feel, my constitutional duty."

∞

Twenty minutes later Rocky sat in the East Wing.

The offices of previous first ladies had been transformed into an operations center. It was now manned by two dozen personnel previously working in the corporate offices of Chambers Enterprises in Boston.

The worldwide conglomerate that was Chambers Enterprises had been founded as a minor trading company in colonial Massachusetts over two hundred years earlier. The name had changed over the years. But the family had remained in control and deeply embedded in running it. Fortunate to have wise steady hands at its helm, the burgeoning company had increased its trading ventures to include shipping, railroads, chemicals, oil, technology, pharmaceuticals, and eventually Information Technology.

The multibillion conglomerate, headed by Rocky and Rick Chambers-Jeffries had unlimited resources. The most significant of these, at this juncture, being the company employing many of the world's leading Artificial Intelligence (AI) engineers.

After Sheila had died and Nick had been elected to the Senate, Rocky returned to the helm of Chamber's Enterprises. In the course of events, he directed the AI department at Chamber's Enterprises to research the role AI might play in anticipating the direction narratives might take in corporate marketing. It wasn't long before he expanded the research to include narratives relative to political campaigns.

Subsequently, the AI engineered under the direction of Rocky was utilized to help the President Nicholas Chambers-Jefferies campaign anticipate and take the lead setting the campaign narrative. This led to the election of the underdog, a gay Republican, President of the United States.

∞

Rick had returned from Boston with Buck Gerard and a select team of the best and brightest AI types Chambers Enterprises had in its employ. After settling them into the operations center, Rocky asked Brooke and Rick to join him in the infirmary.

Rocky, Brooke, and Rick sat in three cushioned metal chairs placed around Nick's hospital bed. Rocky sat crossing and uncrossing his legs, his arms folded on his chest. Brooke and Rick were curious as to why they had been brought to the infirmary. Their queries as to why everyone was gathering remained unanswered.

Nick sat upright in the bed. He smiled and nodded when the three had taken their seats. "Hi, everybody."

"Hi, Dad," Brooke and Rick said in unison.

Rocky inhaled and exhaled and said nothing.

"How are you feeling, Dad?" Brooke asked.

"Pretty good. I am getting my strength back. Looking forward to getting my operation over with, later today."

Leaning forward, Rick said, "What do you mean, operation? Isn't it too soon?"

Rocky remained stone faced.

"They are going in to remove the bullet, relieve some of the pressure, and if all goes well, they will patch me back up and I will soon be good as new."

Brooke stood up and sat on the edge of the bed. "Are you sure? Why the rush?"

Taking her hand in his, patting it, he smiled gently. "Not to worry, honey, it will be just fine."

"I don't understand," she said.

"I have a job to do and am eager to get to it." He paused. "Now. sweetheart, there is something Rocky and I need to share with you both."

Rick entered the conversation. "Are you sure, Dad? Are you strong enough to undergo such an invasive procedure?"

Brooke and Rick turned their attention to Rocky.

He looked at Nick and swallowed hard. "It appears your father has something to share. Something we should have told you about years ago. We both regret not having told you. While I believe this is neither the time or the place to go into it, he insists, and under the circumstances, I support his decision."

Nick's eyes moistened, and looking at Rocky, said, "Thank you. I love you."

Rocky sat expressionless.

Beeping monitors punctuated the tense mood.

Nick motioned Rocky over.

Rocky and Rick stood and went over to Nick and Brooke. Not a word having been said, they worked together adjusting the bedding, propping him up.

Both men then returned to their seats.

Nick blew out through his mouth and began. "Years ago, when you were both infants, we had, Rocky and I, had a DNA test run on both of you."

"What?" Brooke asked.

"What on earth for?" Rick asked.

Rocky cleared his throat. "Because we suspected there was some doubt as to who your father was."

Rick stood up. "Why did you think—?"

Nick held up his hand. "Please, take your seat and we will explain. Give us a chance to explain."

Brooke and Rick exchanged bewildered looks. Both their faces had taken on a ghost-like pallor.

Rocky stood. "Before your mother and father had married, the three of us were in Brussels. Your mother was visiting while we were on assignment. It was three weeks prior to their marriage."

Nick said, "Rocky and I had been intermittent lovers since we had met at the Naval Academy. We loved each other then as we do now."

Brooke had returned to her seat, her hands now caressing her downturned head. "This sounds like this is going to go in a weird direction. Why didn't you tell us before now?"

"It was between the three of us," Nick said, "your mother, Rocky, and me, before you were born. So very long ago."

Rick and Brooke exchanged solemn looks.

Sh+aking, Rick asked, "Did Mother know you were lovers?"

"Yes, I told her," Nick said. "Told her that I could not marry her, because I was in love with Rocky."

"This can't be happening. This is just too weird," Brooke sighed.

"Yes, it is. But it is what it is," Nick said.

"How did she react? Why didn't she just call it all off?" Rick asked.

Brooke looked up and into Nick's eyes and then into Rocky's, and in a deep modulated voice she said, "I know, or rather I knew my mother very well. She wanted —," Looking at Nick, she said, "she wanted you, and she would rather live in denial than give you up, right?"

"Brooke!" Rick exclaimed. "How could you know this?"

In a defiant tone, she said, "I am my mother's daughter."

"Ridiculous," Rick insisted."

"But correct," Nick said. "Now, back to the DNA test. We need to get through this."

"I told you, Nick. This was not a good idea," Rocky said.

"You're worried about the operation, aren't you?" Rick guessed. "And just in case, you need to get this off your chest. Just in case you don't make it. Who is this really all about?"

Rocky stood up, thrusting his index finger at Rick. "Don't you ever speak to your father like that again!"

Rick's jaw tightened. "I'm sorry. It's just that this seems so surreal." Then facing Nick, "Certainly not what I imagined happening with you recovering from someone trying to assassinate you, Dad. And now this DNA thing?"

"It seems," Brooke said, "as if the family is unraveling, going in directions none of us could have imagined. Look around. We are in the White House having this sordid conversation and . . ." Focusing first on Rocky, then Nick, she said, "You are asking too much to expect us, to act, respond, as if we are members of some audience watching some god-awful play. We are part of this craziness, dragged in, center stage and haven't a clue what will broadside us next!"

Brooke sat back in the chair and crossed her arms, tears cascading down her face.

Rick stood and paced the room, his hands clasped behind his back, and in a matter-of-fact tone said, "The DNA thing. The three of you were lovers. Mom got pregnant. You felt there was a need to find out who was the father."

"I think I am going to be sick!" Brooke said.

Rocky went over to Brooke and placed his hands on her shoulders.

Brooke escaped his touch and slipped over to stand next to Rick. She took his hand in hers. "What, what was the verdict. Who is the father?"

Nick said, "I am your father, Brooke."

Brooke stared at Nick and then, jaw agape, looked at Rick. "And Rick?"

Rocky looked at Nick, then Brooke, then Rick. "Rick is my son."

Rick looked up at Brooke and said in a muffled voice, "But we're twins."

"Heteropaternal superfecundation, twins," Rocky said.

Brooke stood, took Rick by the hand, and they both walked out of the infirmary.

CHAPTER 5

Viral Headlines:

PRESIDENT CHAMBERS-JEFFRIES SEEN UP AND ABOUT!

PRESIDENT ON ROAD TO RECOVERY!

PRESIDENT STRONG ENOUGH TO USE WHEELCHAIR

GOULET ASKS CABINET TO MAKE HIM ACTING PRESIDENT WHILE PRESIDENT MAKES SPEEDY RECOVERY

CABINET VOTES TO ASK CONGRESS TO DESIGNATE GOULET ACTING PRESIDENT

PRESIDENTIAL COUP IN THE MAKING!

∞

"No, that is ridiculous," Vice President Goulet insisted, stand-ing on the Senate steps of the Capitol Building. "This is not a coup, it is part of the process. Laid out by the 25th Amendment when the president is unable to perform his duties."

A CNN reporter shouted, "But Mr. Vice President, the presi-dent is obviously recovering! We have seen pictures of him wheeling himself around the White House! Are you overreach-ing, sir?"

The vice president, his forehead beaded with perspiration, re-sponded above the din of questions being shouted at him, "Absolutely not! We don't know if those pictures are real! Any de-cent graphics person can manipulate photography! I am here to do what is best for the country! To protect the American people!"

A FOX correspondent thrust a microphone in the VP's face. "Are you accusing the White House of releasing fake photos of the president? When was the last time you saw the president?"

"Go to hell!" Goulet said under his breath, then turned his back to the throng of reporters and onlookers and climbed the remaining steps to the Senate Portico and entered the building.

∞

"It looks as if the VP's emotions are wearing a bit thin," Trish Smart said, grinning at Rocky.

Rocky kept his eyes on the live newsfeed contemplating the day's events. *What would happen next? Would the public fall for the staged photo-op? Would Congress think twice before voting to officially designate the VP acting president? Then what? The operation only hours away. How would Nick come out of the operation? Good as new, not likely. Sooner or later, it would come out that the president had risked his own life for political purposes. And the kids, God, the kids. Man, we really fucked up!*

"General?" Trish asked. "Where are you?"

Shaken from his thoughts, Rocky forced a smile. "Just thinking, thinking too much. Everything is so convoluted and tenuous."

"I was really surprised to see he had finagled that picture of him in the wheelchair. How is he, anyway?" She folded her hands in her lap. "The truth please."

Rocky adjusted himself in his chair. "Not as well as one would hope. Besides, you saw him for a few minutes, so I heard. What do you think?"

"I understand he is going to have major surgery in a matter of hours."

He sat up straight, his face dazed. "How did you know?

"The question is, why wasn't I informed earlier?"

"I wasn't informed either. Not until just a couple of hours ago. I asked him not to do it. But he insisted. There is no convincing him otherwise. I am concerned. That is one of the reasons I'm here. To give you a heads-up."

"You will recall, General, I asked for this meeting."

"If you hadn't beat me to it, I was going to ask for one. You can imagine how caught up I have been in . . ."

She sat up and looked Rocky in the eyes. "If it does not go well, we may lose any credibility we have, and the vice president will have a carte blanche to do anything he likes. Regardless of how the president's health may improve in the future, we will have lost all credulity. That will be it."

"Yes, I know."

Trish shifted her weight in her chair. "Let's change the subject, if you don't mind, General."

He nodded. "Please do."

"The investigation, it is moving along quicker than I had imagined. But before we go into that, I understand you have set up some sort of team in the East Wing."

Rocky broke out of his funk and offered a sly grin underneath raised eyebrows. "Yes, that is true. I have marshalled corporate assets to delve into this clusterfuck. I beg your pardon, Trish."

She chuckled. "That's all right, I've heard worse. Hell, I've said worse."

He widened his grin. "I have recruited some of the best and the brightest from Chambers Enterprises to dig deep into what's been happening around here."

"Buck Gerard, I've heard of him," Trish said.

"Interesting!" Rocky said, leaning forward. "So, you've been keeping an eye on me."

"It's my job to know everything that is going on in the White House. Including that thing about the vice president's missing computer." She smiled. "He didn't make a big deal out of it. Odd, though. It was found under the desk. Hm."

Rocky did not acknowledge what she had said.

"But I almost missed the planned surgery." Glancing at her watch, she looked up. "Happening in a couple of hours."

"Yeah, still sorry about that. It's a little hard to keep all the plates spinning these days." Rocky sighed.

"What can I do to help with the 'East Wing' investigation, General?"

"I don't know, haven't thought that far ahead."

Trish sat back and folded her arms. "What if I make arrangements for Dr. Parsons to get assigned to the White House for a while?"

He jerked his head back and touched his fingers to his lips. "Surprised?"

"Uh, um, yes, I am."

"What do you think?"

"I think it's, it is super, uh, great. When can she start?"

"She has."

"What?"

"While you and your family were meeting with the president in the infirmary, I personally escorted her over to the East Wing and made the introductions. Not to worry, no one has supplanted your chain of command."

Rocky shook his head side-to-side.

"I just wanted to make sure that we didn't lose any time. They are waiting for you there now."

In view of the assassination attempt, the White House was closed to the public. Rocky had gathered the key players in the East Wing.

"Hello, General," Buck said. "Good to see you again. Well . . . ," Buck shrugged. "Well, I mean but not so much under these circumstances, but good to see you, sir, regardless." Sticking out his hand, the six-foot-four-inch red-headed, freckle-faced, lanky Buck Gerard smiled broadly.

Rocky shook Buck's hand and said, "I guess you've met Dr. Parsons and you remember my daughter, Brooke?"

He smiled and nodded facing the middle-aged Dr. Parsons. Parsons returned his smile.

Brooke inhaled and stared in awkward silence.

"I was just introduced to Dr. Parsons," Buck said, "and know her by reputation. And of course, how could I forget Brooke?"

Brooke shifted her weight and nodded hello.

Rocky motioned everyone to join him around the table. Brooke found a seat between Dr. Parsons and Rocky.

"Rick, Brooke, Dr. Parsons, Buck, I am so grateful for everyone being here. I think we are all aware of the momentous task at hand. We've a great team assembled, and I can say for myself and the president that we are counting on all of you to spearhead getting to the bottom of the assassination attempt."

Everyone nodded soberly.

"General," Dr. Parsons said, "Brooke and I, along with Rick, have briefed Buck on all we know, and I think we can begin organizing a plan of action to delve into the assassination attempt."

"Excellent," Rocky said. "It goes without saying our activities are highly confidential, and that I can trust all of you to keep it that way. I believe that what we are about to discover will shake the nation. There is no doubt that whoever has perpetrated this atrocity is well embedded in the government. When they get wind of our investigation, and no doubt, somehow, they will, all our lives could be in danger."

All sat silent and expressionless.

"Let's get started then," Rocky said. He removed a pile of papers from a satchel and distributed individual files to the other four.

∞

Unable to sit still, Rocky paced the hallway outside the infirmary. *What was taking so long? They've been in there for four hours. It was a complicated procedure, but we've been here sitting, waiting, and none of us speaking to the other. Would Brooke and Rick ever forgive us for not telling them who their real fathers were? If I were to do it all over again, I would have told them long ago. But so much has happened over the years. Our lives have been full. There was no right time. This silence is killing me. Please say something. Yell at me or something. Maybe Nick doesn't survive or is brain damaged? What then? What if he comes through with flying colors, would it make a difference to them? Would they forgive Nick and me? Why did Nick have to tell them? Why couldn't he have left well enough alone? God, I hope he makes it. Not just makes it but thrives. Gets back to normal, the good old Nicky. I miss that, Nicky.*

Rocky shuddered.

Brooke sat, her head in her hands one moment and the next minute sitting back, arms crossed staring at the wall. She had alternated the two positions saying nothing, not a sound for over four hours.

Rick had occasionally reached over to her and patted her shoulder, whispering something inaudible to Rocky. He would then return to a thick file that lay in his lap, scribbling notes. The same file Rocky had given him earlier.

Rocky decided to quell the screaming silence. "Um, uh, I know the two of you are very angry with us, but all the same, we ought to be of the same mind when the doctor gets here." He paused, no response other that Rick looking up and nodding. "It would be very helpful to let him see we have an uplifting and positive demeanor. Show him we are a family united."

Brooke glared at Rocky and then returned her gaze to the wall.

Rick closed the folder and folded his hands on top of it. "Okay, I can see that, I can do that." He turned to Brooke and took her hand.

Rocky spoke softly, "Can you do that Brooke?"

She remained silent.

The infirmary door opened. Out stepped Dr. Samson dressed in a fresh set of scrubs. His manner betrayed nothing.

"Hello everyone. Finally, we've finished. It took a bit longer than we had anticipated."

"Is he okay? Is he going to recover?" Brooke asked.

Rick and Brooke exchanged looks and glanced at Rocky. And then focused on Dr. Samson.

The physician inhaled. "Only by the grace of God, or luck." He took a moment and then continued, "He lost a great deal of blood. Removing the bullet fragments from his brain was difficult, and as you can tell by the hours the president was in surgery—" Dr. Samson paused. "From what we can tell we got all of it. It was a small bullet, which does not make sense. Maybe a .22 caliber. Not a lot of damage was done, thankfully. If the bullet had been a higher caliber, say a .30 or .33, things would have been so much worse."

Brooke muttered, "M-F."

Everyone looked at her.

"I beg your pardon?" Dr. Samson asked.

Brooke swallowed, shook her head, and replied, "Nothing. Really, nothing."

Rick hurriedly interjected, "What is the prognosis, Doctor? You mentioned loss of blood. Any brain damage? Any permanent injury?"

"Yes, a great deal of blood, four pints. It will take several days, maybe a week for him to regain the strength he had going into the operation. As far as damage, permanent disability of some sort. Only time will tell."

"Thank you, Doctor. When do you think we might see him?" Rocky asked.

"He remains under sedation, and we have rewrapped his head in ice to keep the swelling down. Maybe tomorrow. It is too soon to tell when he will be cognizant enough to see anyone, much less even know you are in the room."

"Can we take turns sitting with him?" Brooke pleaded.

"Maybe tomorrow, but not now, we have a physician and a nurse with him 'round the clock. I am happy to provide updates. I'll see that you are kept informed of any changes as they develop."

Rocky stood and extended his hand. "On behalf of myself and the family, please accept our greatest appreciation for what you and your team have and are doing."

"Yes, thank you Doctor," Rick said. "But what about updates for the press?"

Brooke sighed. "Oh God, not that."

Rocky folded his arms. "Yes, that could be a problem. The nation, the world thinks he is rolling around the White House in a wheelchair."

"Tests," Brook said. "Which is what we can say. You and your team are conducting invasive tests, and he is being forced to—"

Dr. Samson cocked his head. "But that would be a misrepresentation of the facts and would not represent his true health status."

"So, what you are saying, Doctor," Rick said, "is that we should tell the public that he has had another operation, albeit successful, but that his health condition remains tenuous?"

Rocky raised his hand to slow the conversation. "I can see your position, that of not being ethical. Correct?

Doctor Samson shifted his weight. "Essentially, yes."

"Well, we certainly do not want to put you in that position," Rocky said. "May I suggest you leave the updates on the president's health to the White House Press Office?"

"Very well, General. But please note that I disagree with not being totally transparent about the president's health."

"Noted," Rocky said and turned to Brooke and Rick. "Do either of you take exception to letting the Press Office handle this?"

Following a moment of silence, Rick said, "Perhaps we should discuss that amongst the three of us."

"I agree," Brooke said sitting back and folding her arms.

"Very well. Thank you, Doctor. Brooke, Rick, let's meet in the Residence in an hour. Brooke, I would like to see you in the Diplomatic room first."

Brooke cocked her head. "What for? I have work to do."

"Yes, I understand, but I have something of an urgent and personal matter."

As the doctor moved toward the medical office's door Brooke said stiffly, "I am not comfortable with having that discussion at this time."

Dr. Samson looked at Brooke and then Rocky. "Excuse me, I have to check on the president." He left the room.

"I know, Brooke, neither am I. I will meet you there in ten minutes."

∞

Brooke sat opposite Rocky. They were alone.

"Thank you for meeting with me."

"I really don't have a choice, do I?"

"We need to have this discussion so that we can move on with our relationship and proceed clear-headed into the investigation of your father's attempted assassination."

"I am not sure we have a relationship anymore, certainly not one of trust."

Rocky looked down at his lap, lightly drumming his knees with his fingers. He looked back at her. "I get that."

"Do you really, Dad? Or do I call you Dad? After all, you are not my real father. How could you possibly understand? You have deceived me!"

Rocky grimaced.

"I have called you Dad ever since you and my father married, and now, you deceived me. I don't feel you deserve to be called Dad anymore."

He felt his heart sink and thought, *how could this be happening? Happening now, of all times, when we need the family to support one another more than ever. But she's right, we have deceived her, horribly.*

"And furthermore, what do you expect me to think? You know I am right and have every reason to feel the way I do."

"Yes, Brooke, I agree. You have every reason to feel the way you do. I am sorry your father and I did not tell you and your brother years ago. We did what we thought best."

Sarcasm dripping from her lips, she said, "Half-brother."

"He is still your brother, and as full a brother as anyone could be. You're twins, so that makes it a special bond. You have been through so much together. Your comment, though made in the emotions of the moment is unkind and unfair. I am disappointed in you, Brooke. He deserves better."

Brooke hung her head. "Yes, you're right. I didn't mean it."

"Thank you." He paused. "Brooke, you are the stronger of the two. You know that. You have always been there for him. I pray you would consider that. This is not just about you. He needs you more than ever at this moment. I hope you will be there for him. He loves you beyond words."

She sniffled and looked up with tearing eyes. "Don't worry, we are, regardless of whatever is going on, here for each other." She sat up straight. "It's just that he was deceived as much, even more than I was." She raised her voice. "He is the one more wronged in this whole thing! He has always thought we had the same father and mother. Imagine just what he is going through!"

"I can't. I can only be the supporting and unconditionally loving parent I have always been to both of you."

Brooke wiped her eyes. "And there is Nick, my real father."

Rocky responded in a whisper. "I would like you to take a moment to think how difficult it has been for me through the years being in some sense an outsider, a father who has never been acknowledged as one."

Brooke ignored him and said sternly, "My father, he has as much responsibility in this as you do."

"He does; we both do."

Brooke stood. "I don't want to talk about this anymore, ever again."

Rocky disagreed, "You know that will be impossible, not until the four of us work it out, come to terms with it, reconcile."

"I don't know if that will ever happen," Brooke said. "Now we need to go to a meeting with Rick to discuss even more deception. Which apparently, deception, seems to suit you."

"For Christ's sake, Brooke!"

Rick, Brooke, and Rocky sat in the West Hall of the residence, a sleeting rain beating against the large half-moon Italianate window. Brooke wrapped in a gray woolen blanket sat next to Rick on the sofa opposite Rocky. Both Rocky and Rick held crystal tumblers of scotch. Brooke's hands caressed a cup of piping hot chocolate.

"Precisely, why are we not being transparent about Dad's health?" Rick asked. "It seems to me things could go way wrong here. Is it worth it? What do we gain? We know what we can lose, all credibility and potentially fuel the vice president's goal to unseat the president."

Brooke summarized the situation. "If Goulet becomes acting president, it will be hard for Dad to get Congress to make him president again. Goulet will do everything he can to hold onto power. It is conceivable, regardless of good health, that Goulet will do everything he can to block him from being reinstated. That is not what the voters said they wanted when they elected Dad president. But that won't matter to the acting president."

"I could not have said it better," Rocky said.

"The wheelchair photo is the problem," Rick said. "People think he is much healthier than he really is. Now he's unconscious and will remain that way for at least a day or two. Then he has to recover and get back to where the public thought he already was, and having made progress, healthier."

The three sat silent absorbing the reality of where they found themselves as it related to Nick's health and what appeared to be a very cloudy future for his presidency.

"Getting his strength back will take time, days, weeks," Rick said. "In the meantime, Congress could vote anytime in the next three weeks. Dad sure as hell can't make a public appearance the way he is now. It won't be long before people get suspicious."

Taking Rick's hand in hers, Brooke said, "You're right. But there is one thing we can do. There is a picture of Dad talking to Trish Smart in the Oval when he was in the wheelchair. He had a different jacket on than the one he wore in the picture fed to the press. Use that one."

"What the fuck? I didn't know about that picture," Rick exclaimed.

Rocky sat up straight and placed his glass on the coffee table.

"It was my idea," Brooke said. "You didn't know about that one either, did you?" she asked looking at Rocky.

"No, I did not."

"We could provide the photo to the media and accompany it with something along the lines that he has been going through a battery of follow-up tests and procedures, or something along those lines. That should hold them off for a couple of days. Maybe even long enough for him to make an appearance the day before the vote. Depending, of course, on when the vote is anticipated. We need all the time we can get."

Rocky thought, *this girl is brilliant, has foresight and cunning. She is definitely her mother's daughter. Nick and I can't hold a candle to her.*

"When does Congress vote?" Rick said.

"We have a day," Rocky added, "maybe two, for us to send our remarks to Congress stating our case justifying why the 25th should not be enacted."

"He won't be up to making an appearance by then, Dad." Rick said.

His sister looked at him and then Rocky. "Congress won't act immediately. Remember, they have twenty-one days to take the vote. We can reach out to party members and get them to postpone the vote for as long as possible. Maybe hearings. That would slow down the process."

Rocky picked up on what she had said. "That gives us maybe three weeks for the president to regain his strength and take back the duties from Goulet. Remember, if Congress has not voted, the president can take his powers back at any time. Congress could still vote, but it would be much harder to get two thirds vote if he appears to be healthy enough to assume the duties."

Brooke leaned forward. "Now the hard part. He has to be healthy enough to address the American people when he takes back the office. And if Goulet insists on moving forward with the vote, well—"

"The Dems have the majority in both houses," Rick said, "but it takes seventy percent of the House and the Senate for the vote to pass. It will require a lot of our members to cross party lines to enact the 25th."

"If Nick does not present himself as totally healthy and able to serve," Rocky said, "he would lose a lot of party support. It just makes sense to ensure the president, any president can do the job. Remember, Republicans don't often vote strictly along party lines. They cross all the time. Dems are much more loyal to their party. Politics."

"Yep," Brooke said, "It doesn't help that he's gay. A lot of Republicans would take any opportunity they could to dump on Dad."

∞

"Did you see that goddamn White House photo release?" Vice President Goulet shouted. "I haven't seen the president since he was shot, that was five days ago! They're fake. Gotta be! I know the first photo and the one with the chief of staff are bogus. They gotta be! Who approved the media releases? Get rid of them!"

Merrill Spaulding stood stunned in front of the vice president's desk. Another tirade. "Sir, um, uh, I beg your pardon, but—.

"Out with it! What?"

"I hate to say this, but you approved the White House Press Office updating the media."

"I didn't think they would show another picture! This is healthier looking than the last. It actually looked like he was doing business. I sure as hell haven't seen him wheeling around the White House. This is garbage!"

"Yes, sir," Spaulding said.

"Tell the doctor, whoever he is, that I want to see the president as soon as I get back from the Hill later this afternoon! I've got to wrap up the votes for the 25th now!"

"Yes, sir."

The vice president stormed out of his office.

Spaulding removed her cell phone from her pocket and called Trish Smart.

∞

Spaulding entered the chief of staff's office and closed the door.

"Your call sounded urgent," Trish said. "What is it, Merrill? Please, sit down." She motioned to a chair opposite her desk.

"The VP is livid about the press release."

Trish smiled. "You were so clever getting him to sign off on sending out a release."

Spaulding chuckled. "Well, it helps he was ten sheets to the wind late last night after lobbying Congress all day. I had a pile of documents for him to sign. Too many cocktails on the Hill with his cronies. I really doubt he remembers initialing it."

"What's next? What brings you here?"

"He demands to see the president later this afternoon."

"That could be a problem."

"Oh?"

"Not to worry, Merrill. But it would not be a good idea."

"What are you going to do to hold him at bay?"

"I have an idea, let's see if it works. Why don't you tell the vice president that the president is not seeing visitors, and let's see what happens."

"Sounds like our only option," Spaulding said. "I'll get on it."

"Thank you and good luck," Trish said.

Merrill stood, turned and left the office.

The chief of staff picked up the phone.

Holding the handset to her ear, "General, Trish Smart here. I just finished speaking with Merrill Spaulding. Do you have a moment to come to my office?" She paused. "Thank you, sir. See you shortly."

Rocky entered the chief's office and took a seat in front of her desk. "Must be important, how can I help?"

"Vice President Goulet is incensed with what he saw on the news release. He demands to see the president this afternoon when he returns from Capitol Hill."

His mouth dropped. "We didn't plan on that. Gotta find a way around it. I guess he didn't like the photo op with you and the president."

"Apparently not."

He smiled. "Don't know why, that was a good pic of you!"

Trish smiled. "Yeah, I thought it was pretty good myself. Pure jealousy, no doubt." She laughed and settled back in her chair.

"If he finds out the shape Nick is in at the moment," Rocky said, "He will fly back up to the Hill and start making the rounds claiming we are not to be trusted. He'll get them to vote as soon as possible. Nick will not be able to recover in time to convince Congress to vote in his favor."

"I agree. We must stop him. But I am not sure how to do that. He probably has the right to see the president." Trish sighed.

"Not if the family tells the doctor he is to have no visitors."

Trish shot up in her chair. "Do you really think you can get away with it?"

"We'd better. Dr. Samson is a reasonable man. He certainly does not want to be implicated in some sort of medical misinformation. Through no fault of his own, he is caught in the middle. It is in his interest to keep things on the down low. Besides, he's gotta recognize that the role of White House physician demands discretion, whether political or not. No one asked him to misrepresent anything, but he didn't exactly get in the way of the press release. I will speak with him."

Two uniformed armed Marine Guards stood at attention outside the door leading into the infirmary.

"I'm sorry, sir, but no one is allowed inside the infirmary except the medical staff and family."

"I am the acting president and I order you to let me pass!"

"We are under orders not to let anyone except the medical staff and family inside the infirmary."

"I am the acting commander in chief! This is insubordination! Get me the goddamn doctor!"

One of the guards pushed a button on the intercom next to the door.

"Yes, may I help you?"

Goulet shouted, "This is Vice President Goulet, let me in!"

"Just a moment, Mr. Vice President."

The vice president, arms clasped behind his back, paced around the anteroom.

Several minutes later Dr. Samson emerged from the infirmary.

"Good afternoon, Mr. Vice President."

"What is all this nonsense? What do these Marines mean by telling me I cannot speak with the president? I am the acting president of the United States!"

"Sir, we are so terribly sorry to inconvenience you, but the patient's right to privacy takes precedence. Without his or the family's permission you will not be able to see him. He has not given permission and the family has specifically requested, under my advice, not to receive visitors."

"Doctor, he has been photographed galivanting around the White House in a wheelchair. What are you hiding, Doctor? I want a full report on his condition, now!"

Dr. Samson folded his arms across his chest. "I am sorry, sir, but that will not be possible until I am authorized by the president or the family to release that information. The family have released what updates they feel appropriate."

Goulet wagged his finger at the doctor. "This is ridiculous! It is in the interest of the United States government and the American people that I have this information. I have a need to know."

"Sir, again, the Privacy Act applies to everyone, including the president. I am forbidden by law to divulge what the president and his family have requested be kept private."

"Doctor, you will be sorry as hell you have not obeyed my order to see the president."

"Yes, Mr. Vice President."

∞

Buck Gerard stood in front of a wall-sized holo display/projection, utilizing a laser pointer to zero in on a map of Washington, DC. The White House and the location of the Inaugural Parade reviewing stand figured prominently in the center of the display.

Rocky, Dr. Parsons, Rick, Brooke, Director Hamilcar, Special Agent Hunter, and six ASI—Super Artificial Super Intelligence—scientists sat at a crescent-shaped table in the East Wing, facing Buck.

"For purposes of this graphic, as you can see, the White House and grounds are represented to scale. This figure super-imposed on this particular tree is what is commonly referred to as a Robot Bird, affectionately referred to as MF for Maltese Falcon."

"A what?" Special Agent Hunter said.

"Robot bird. Not a real bird, but a technologically advanced type of drone, if you will. The science is not all that new.

"Just as a side note, the first robot bird was believed to have been invented by Archytas, a mathematician, about 350 BC. He may have used compressed air or an internal steam engine of some sort to power its flight of 100 meters. Certainly, all of you are familiar with Da Vinci and his interest in flight. But back to the present. In the last few years, robot bird technology has grown exponentially. Essentially, we are talking about a flying robot made of light weight, hollow carbon material, much like the bones found in birds. The feathers are artificial and made of ultra-light material that overlaps just as they do on bird's wings."

"Oh my God," Hunter said. "This is incredible, like for surveillance and who knows what."

"That is absolutely correct. It is something that we have been keeping an eye on. We believe the Chinese are developing such surveillance techniques. These robot birds are a lot less detectable than their balloons they've been using for surveillance. We have no connection, as of yet, between the Chinese and MF, but we believe surveillance was, at least, part of MF's mission," Dr Parsons said.

A couple of snickers followed her comment reference to MF.

"Air filters through the wing during the downstroke to propel it forward," Buck said. "I could go into greater detail but suffice it to say that the advanced AI contained within the bird's programming controls the positioning of the feathers and wing movement so as to perfectly imitate that of a real bird. These robot birds can do anything a bird can do: dive, soar, change altitude and direction, even barrel roll!"

All eyes remained fixed on Buck. "Up until now they have been used to scare other birds away from crops and airports. As you can imagine, new uses are being devised, and thus the technology continues to advance. The most significant advancement is a recent development, that of being able to perch."

"Perch, like on a tree," Sandy Yoe, one of the SAI scientists, said.

"Oh, interesting, very interesting," Hamilcar said.

Buck continued. "Another limitation has been its size and weight. Until now it was thought they could weigh no more than a golf ball and still remain airborne. It is estimated that our bird weighs two, maybe three pounds." Buck paused. "A robot bird with that weight can be weaponized."

Stunned silence permeated the room.

"This is just touching on the surface," Rocky said. "These robot birds are controlled and manipulated just as are drones. But they are more maneuverable and almost impossible to detect from the real thing. And except for the flapping of wings are virtually silent, battery operated."

After allowing for what had been said to sink in, Buck pointed back to the holo display and the tree on the screen. "It appears that MF fired the small caliber bullet that struck the president from within the bird's body."

An uncomfortable silence hung in the air.

Dr. Parsons caught everyone's attention when she said, "As Buck . . . that is Mr. Gerrard, said, we believe that MF is the murder weapon. And as the General said, we are just touching on the surface. I would like to draw your attention to where we hypothesize MF came from and from where it may have been controlled."

"DC is divided into four quadrants." Buck used the laser pointer to designate each quadrant. "The Northwest, Northeast, Southwest, and Southeast. The nexus of the four quadrants is the Capitol Building. As you can see," singling out the White House, he continued, "the White House is in the Northwest

Quadrant, just barely. But our focus originally took us to the eastern end of the Southeastern quadrant."

"Why there?" Lynn Elle, one of the young female engineers, asked.

"That is the route the MF initially took when it left the White House grounds hours after the assassination attempt," Dr. Parsons said. "It took us a while to figure out where MF went. We matched up what we thought was MF's trajectory with satellites that had been overhead in the area at the time. It required a great deal of processing, and thanks to the General's and Buck's efforts, we were able to triangulate its location and get a visual on MF from Chambers Enterprise's satellites."

"We have committed Chambers Enterprises assets to this effort," Rick said. "By necessity, we have established our own investigative team outside the US Government. For obvious reasons."

"Okay," Director Hamilcar said, visibly uncomfortable. "Someone, please state the obvious, where is all this cloak and dagger going?"

Everyone in the room exchanged blank looks.

Rocky stood. "I have asked that we not use any government communications assets, including computer hardware, moving forward."

Hamilcar breathed in, closed his eyes, and exhaled. "I get it, I really do. But this is complex and—"

Lynn rose from her seat and went over to a side table and picked up a stack of white boxes, each approximately 12" x 14" x 3". She distributed one box to each attendee.

Lynn spoke while distributing the boxes. "Each of these contains a laptop configured to an individual. If the individual is not within inches of the unit, it will automatically shut down and require a log in via retina scan. I know this can be annoying, but it will restart as soon as the person is facing the screen and remains no further away than 24 inches. The camera detects eye movement. That being said, we will need each of you to undergo a retina scan, and then we will get started."

The next fifteen minutes was spent setting up everyone's computer. Rick, Brooke, and Lynn assisted the others.

Dr. Parson's said, "I have advised the General to keep the investigation's files and data as far away as possible from the government's IT system. We have reason to believe the guilty parties, rather those we suspect are involved in the assassination attempt, are embedded in the government at some level. We simply do not know who and where they are."

"Thank you, Dr. Parsons," Rick said. "Importantly, we are also providing you with burner phones that will in addition to voice communication between all of us on the team, will serve as hotspots for the laptops accessing the Internet. We have our own servers, etc., dedicated to this network. While you can access the dark web, your phone and computer cannot be detected. We ask you to not conduct any research or communicate on any other computer or cell device when working on this investigation."

"Now," Rocky said, turning his attention back to Buck, "Let's pick up where we left off."

"This is where MF lighted or landed after leaving the Executive Mansion's grounds." Buck pointed to one of the most northeastern parts of the Southeastern quadrant. The holo projection map was then changed and replaced with an enlarged satellite image of a nondescript warehouse backing up against a thicket of trees and an alleyway. "Now take a look here." He enlarged the image further so that all could see an obscure dormer at the back of the building; its single hung window standing wide open. "The entire building is battened down as if a severe storm was on its way. But why was this window left open? So conveniently positioned so as not to be seen from the street."

"Well, what did you find?" Special Agent Hunter asked, leaning forward in his chair. "Did you send a team to investigate?"

"Well, sort of," Dr. Parsons said.

Everyone shifted their attention toward her.

"We decided to play with them at their own game. Adopt their strategy of hide-and-seek. The problem we faced was acquiring the equipment we needed. We certainly couldn't work inside the government. So, Buck and I got ahold of a drone of our own. Please do not ask for details, they will not be forthcoming."

She grinned at Buck and placed her hands in her lap. "We flew our own drone, 'Cuckoo,' into the building." She paused. "Guess what we found."

"Ahem," Rocky said. "Cuckoos are known for raiding other birds' nests, am I right?"

"You found MF," Rick said. "Where is MF now?"

"Where we found it," Buck said and added, "We put Cuckoo to work."

"Which of course makes sense, as we do not want to let our adversary know what we know, correct?" scientist Sandy Yoe asked.

She rose from her seat and walked up to the holograph screen and stood on the side opposite Buck. "Please open the file on your laptops titled MF. It has a robot bird icon there for your convenience."

All attendees shifted and centered themselves in their seats. As if it had been choreographed, they all simultaneously opened their laptops, waited for the facial recognition to engage, and tapped the MF logo on the desktop page.

"Our drone cozied up to MF," Sandy said.

"Sounds a bit creepy," Hunter said under his breath.

Sandy let go a slight snort. "After thoroughly analyzing images taken of MF and finding an external data port, we got to work. We found a way, using Cuckoo, to physically tap into MF. We then transmitted the hacked data via Cuckoo." She paused and directed her next remark to Hunter. "Getting even creepier, isn't it, Special Agent?"

Hunter looked up at Sandy, more intrigued with her attentiveness than the topic at hand. "Yes ma'am, it is. You have my attention." With a straight face and sensuous eyes, in a flat voice, he said, "I'm looking for the happy ending."

Rocky sat beside Nick's bed. Nick wore a much smaller version of the previous head bandage. He was clean shaven and had just finished breakfast.

"You look so much better than you did before you went in for the operation two days ago. Doctor Samson says you are doing well."

Nick smiled and motioned him to come closer.

Rocky moved in close. Their lips pressed together for a moment. Not pulling away, Rocky said, "This is so nice. The first time I have not had to compete with a tube, a bandage or some such thing . . ."

Sighing, Nick said. "Yeah, it's nice, isn't it?"

"Uh, huh." Rocky kissed him one more time, chancing a little pent-up passion. He then sat back in his chair and took hold of Nick's hand.

They looked into one another's eyes. They yearned to hold one another, to feel each other's bodies pressed one against the other.

Nick blinked away the moisture pooling in his eyes. "I'm really surprised how well I feel, stronger. But not to worry, I won't be running out and about in a wheelchair for a few days at least."

"Good, my darling. That will make all of us rest a bit easier."

Nick positioned himself more upright. "Has Trish put together my letter to the Senate and the House? It's due tomorrow, right?"

"Today," Rocky said and reached down and into a satchel resting on the floor next to his chair. He removed a black, leather bound, portfolio embossed with the presidential seal.

Nick raised up a bit more, a puzzled look on his face. "Today?"

"Yes, my dear. It appears you may have missed a couple of days recovering. Are the days all flowing together?" He handed Nick the portfolio.

Nick opened it. Inside he found a single-page letter typed on the presidential letterhead. He read the letter through three times and placed the open portfolio on his lap and looked up at the ceiling. "It doesn't really say much, does it? It won't convince anyone I am healthy enough to assume my responsibilities."

"No, it doesn't. It is a historical document. It must withstand microscopic scrutiny."

Rocky reached into the satchel and took out a pen embossed with the presidential seal. "It is a placeholder, putting Congress on notice that you are prepared to fight to keep the office. We only have three weeks before Congress must vote. It is our plan to spend the next weeks fending off a vote for as long as possible. We need time for you to recuperate. Recuperate enough to go to the Hill and lobby on your own behalf. In the meantime, we will be meeting with every member of Congress in an effort to slow down the process."

"Do you think I'll be ready?"

"Of course, I do. I have no doubt you can do it. I know you can."

Nick swallowed. "Please tell me the truth, Rocky."

Rocky stood and leaned over Nick. Resolve in his eyes, he said, "If I did not have total faith in your being fit for office within the next three weeks, I would not allow you to pursue this course of action. I love you and would never encourage you to engage in a fruitless effort. Particularly one of such proportions that it will require every ounce of physical and mental courage you possess."

"You are doing this for the nation, Rocky?"

"No, for you. Only for you."

Nick used the bed's controller to raise him up to the point he sat nearly upright.

Rocky sensed an aura of strength and hope in his posture.

Nick reached for the pen. And with a flourish, he signed the document, closed the portfolio, and handed it and the pen to Rocky.

Rocky returned the pen and folder to the satchel and stood. "If I had my druthers, I would haul you out of here and take you away, never to return."

$$\infty$$

"Brooke, what are your thoughts on how the meeting went today?" Buck asked, handing her a glass of chardonnay.

Not looking at the glass, she took it, twirled the stem with her right thumb and index finger and placed it on the residence's kitchen table. Forcing a shallow smile, she said, "Fine."

"Fine?" He shook his head. "Just fine?"

She looked up and raised her glass. "Here's to you, the team and the task at hand." She leaned forward and pushed her glass towards Buck's not yet raised glass.

"Thank you." He clinked her glass with his. They both drank the contents in one fell swoop.

Brooke took in his well-formed chest covered by a crisp white T-shirt. She extended her glass. "Another one please, a member pour! Don't be stingy."

"Yes, ma'am!" he grinned. He took a seat at the table cross-corner from Brooke.

She smiled and looked him straight in the eye. He returned the smile. They then focused on their wine, taking sips and remaining silent.

"Brooke?"

"Yes?"

"Something is bothering you, and I don't believe it has anything to do with what we are investigating."

She rolled her lips and nodded slowly.

"What is it? How can I help?"

"What is done, is done. There is nothing that can . . . Time will lessen the pain, only time. But—"

His hand found hers resting on the table.

Brooke swallowed and then in a feigned coquettish flair said, "It's Top Secret."

"My clearance is higher than Top Secret. Top Secret/Sensitive Compartmented Information."

"That may well be, but you don't have the 'need to know.'"

He furrowed his brow.

Brooke squeezed his hand. "I'm sorry Buck, but it is deeply personal. It could also make my family's life even more difficult than it already is. Let's just let it be."

Buck patted her hand. "Okay. Just let me know how I can be there for you."

She leaned over and kissed him lightly on his cheek.

He sat up, grinning broadly. "Fine, now that's fine!"

She laughed. "Glad you approve. Now, back to that meeting you wanted to talk about."

Rocky sat in the residence looking at his watch and suddenly sat up. *Jack! What the fuck! Why is he texting me? Jesus, a blast from the past!*

JR STRAYVE JR   128

            —Hey Rock. Remember me? NYC?
Thought I would reach out. It's
been decades. Been keeping an eye
on you for all these years.
Thought you could use a friend
about now.

Rocky thought, *What the hell? This is weird. All these years. Now. Why is he texting me? Better not touch this. Who knows who is monitoring my phone?*

He sat for a few minutes wondering *if maybe, just maybe it would be okay. Sure, would be nice to catch up. God, he was good to me and so hot. No good can come of it. If the press got ahold of this, that would be it.*

He put the phone down and tried to concentrate on the files he was reviewing.

Thirty minutes later his phone buzzed with another incoming text.

            —Listen, I would really like to
see you. I just lost my husband of
thirty plus years. I could use a
friend. I know you could too.
Let's meet for a drink.

Wow, I didn't know he married. Thirty years! Poor guy. I could use a friend. Maybe if we're discreet. How can I be discreet, I live in a fish bowl?

            —Hey, Jack. Thanks for reaching
out. It's really good to hear from

you. Sorry to hear about your
loss. Discreet. Of course, you understand. People, always suspect
the worst. Just saying 'Hi' would
get them speculating. I know you
understand. No one knows about our
past and we gotta keep it that way.
Just friends now.

Rocky buzzed open the townhouse's front door.

He'd turned off the outside porch light. Having entered from
the rear of the house, he'd left the Secret Service in the government SUV out back. He told them he'd be in the house for a
couple of hours meeting with a corporate associate.

A tall figure stepped into the dimly lit foyer and closed the
door quietly behind him.

Rocky swallowed and thought, *What am I doing? This is crazy.*
"Hi, Jack, long time no see." Rocky felt a surge of excitement
course through his body. *Nothing good can come of this. God he still
looks great.*

Jack removed his Boss winter leather coat and watch cap.
Dressed in a tailored long sleeve lavender polo shirt and skinny
jeans set off by tan snake-skin cowboy boots was just too perfect.

Rocky remembered him being taller, but now they were the
same height. Back then Rocky had been just eighteen years old,
and Jack, well, maybe thirty. *I must have grown an inch or two.*

His physique defied his age. He looked as fit as ever. Broad
shouldered, a well-formed chest and strong looking legs. *If he'd*

only turn around, I could see if his ass is still as good as it was. No doubt it is. This is crazy. He still turns me on. He's old, I'm almost old! Jeez!

"Yes, Rocky, a long time."

They stood staring at one another. Rocky stepped forward; hand extended.

Jack rushed toward Rocky, ignoring the outstretched hand, and wrapped himself around Rocky.

Rocky returned the embrace, their heads resting on the other's shoulder.

"I've missed you," Jack said.

"And I you, Jack."

Rocky gently pulled away and took Jack by his hand and led him into the paneled study.

The drapes were drawn shut. Two low-light lamps rested on tables at the end of a large leather sofa facing the lit fireplace.

Rocky released Jack's hand and walked toward the carved mahogany bar. "Scotch and soda?" He turned back toward Jack and smiled. "The usual?"

Jack grinned. "You remembered."

Mixing the drinks, he said, "I remember everything about the short but life-changing weekend in New York. It was the beginning of my new life, certainly a very important chapter. You were there when I desperately needed someone. My family had forsaken me, and I was careening headlong into my new life."

"I remember. We were both in a dark place. With the loss of Umberto, well, we were—"

"Here." Rocky handed him the cut crystal glass. The scene was set, the fire's flames dancing through the amber cocktail, refracting off the room's walls.

"Thank you, Rocky." He lifted his glass. Clink.

"Let's sit, my friend," Rocky said motioning to the couch.

They sat inches apart in the center, sipping their drinks and gazing into the fire.

"So, Jack, tell me a little 'bout what has been going on with your life. What was your husband's name?"

"Sure, but first, before we get into all that, aren't you a little concerned people might not like the idea of us meeting up?"

"Yeah, I am." Rocky sat up. "I've taken precautions."

"I hope so. I was a little nervous texting you."

"Not to worry, it comes in on a secure phone. The messages are AI-encrypted."

"I'm not sure what that means, Rocky, but on both ends, right?"

"Pretty much. Auto encrypts both ends. And then destroys the message. Didn't you notice that there's not a trail on your end? Both messages disappear as soon as they're read."

"Come to think of it, I did. What's that all about? Your phone got into my phone?"

"Kinda like that. Millions of encryptions back and forth and deleting the text on both our phones and their servers. Any time my phone is contacted the process automatically happens on both phones. You texted me on my personal phone, and it was forwarded to another phone. It's seamless. All three phones are protected. Now all your texts automatically go to my new *secret squirrel* phone. No one can trace shit."

"Holy crap. Wow. Anyway, that makes me feel a lot better. Hope it's foolproof."

Rocky smiled. "I'm counting on it. Now back to your guy."

"Roberto. He was a great guy." Jack sat back on the couch and continued sipping his scotch and looking into the fire. "When I found your note, when you left New York, I was devastated, but not entirely surprised. You needed to get on with your life, and I realized then that there was no place in it for me, especially as you were entering the Naval Academy. I just wish we would have had more time together."

Rocky inhaled and stretched his neck side-to-side. "I had to go then, or I never would have left."

"I get it. You did the right thing, but it hurt, nonetheless. I was in somewhat of a daze for months. I took a leave of absence from the airline. Eventually I pulled it together and threw myself back into the party circuit. It was stupid, but that was all I had after losing you and Umberto."

Rocky turned from the fire and looked into Jack's eyes. "We were both badly cut up by Umberto taking his own life. I was numb until I met you. You helped pull me out of it. For that, I am eternally grateful."

Rocky patted Jack on his knee. He took Jack's empty glass from his hand and stood up. He smiled. "Tell me about Roberto while I make us another drink." He walked over to the bar. "Throw another log on the fire, will ya?"

Jack returned Rocky's smile and set about stoking the fire placing a large piece of wood on the flames and returned to the sofa.

"Roberto was a kind sensitive kid, a little older than you. You know I like the young Hispanic boys. He was born in Spain. Gorgeous and equally beautiful on the inside." Jack chuckled. "So that was good." He paused. "He was a med student, looking for an older guy. He needed me and I needed him. I got back into flying, and he eventually finished med school and took a residency in the Bronx. We spent the next thirty years together, happily married. We had both been thinking about retiring." Jack choked up. "And then—"

Rocky handed him a drink and sat down next to him. "What, what happened?" He took a sip. "You don't have to tell me, Jack, if you don't want to."

"I want to." He set his drink down and put his head in his hands. "He had a blood disorder. SCT, sickle cell. We couldn't believe it. It is incredibly rare in Hispanics, so it never crossed our minds. Even him being a doctor."

Cocking his head, Rocky said, "I had no idea that was possible."

The men moved closer to one another.

"It got so bad; he was forced to quit work. I retired eighteen months after his diagnosis. He was unable to care for himself, and I refused to let anyone else do it."

Rocky placed a hand on Jack's shoulder and pulled him up against himself. "I'm so sorry."

"Thank you. He's been gone for a year now."

"This kind of feels like when we first met," Rocky said, "consoling one another over the loss of Umberto."

Jack rested his head on Rocky's shoulder. "Yes, it does."

Several minutes later Jack sat up, reached for his drink and downed it. "I'll have another please."

When Rocky returned with the refill, they changed the subject. Rocky regaled Jack with the story of his life. They laughed and commiserated going back and forth exchanging stories.

"You know, Rocky, I had so much fun showing you the seedier parts of the gay underground!"

"No doubt. You were quite the host." Rocky grinned mischievously. "And so hot in bed. The things I learned from you in a matter of those few days."

"Remember the fountain?" Jack asked, "when we stripped naked and washed out the filth from our clothes, put them back on, and headed for the Barracks?"

"Hell, yeah! That was hot. I think I surprised you with that fountain thing, stripping down in the park." Rocky laughed.

"You sure as hell did! I was really concerned I'd shown you too much too soon. I thought you might have been diving too deep, too quickly, into the gay world's underbelly."

Nodding his head, Rocky smiled. "So did I. That's why I left."

Rocky's last comment sobered them up a little.

"If you'd have stayed around, I would have protected you." Jack lightly punched Rocky's shoulder,

"I believe you would have," Rocky said, clinking their glasses.

"So, when are you going to show me around this magnificent house?"

Rocky's stomach flipped. He thought, *I know where this is going. We'll end up in bed. I can't let that happen, but I want him. Someone to hold me close and relive our time together. To get my mind off what's happened to Nick, to Brooke and Rick. I can't do this to Nick, it's not fair. He deserves better.*

Jack stood up and pulled Rocky to him. "Let's go. Show me around this place! C'mon!"

The warm masculine touch of Jack's hand aroused Rocky and almost took his breath away. He felt himself getting hard.

They looked into each other's eyes. Rocky thought, *fuck it*, and placed a gentle kiss on Jack's lips, passion having wiped out his better judgement.

Jack smiled. "That's a welcome surprise." He reached down and adjusted himself. "You kinda got me goin'.

"Me too," Rocky said and kissed Jack on his neck. He inhaled and moaned. "I remember this musk-like smell."

Rocky pulled away, walking backwards and motioning Jack out of the study and to the bottom of the stairs.

Rocky stepped behind Jack and placed his hands on his shoulders. He kissed the back of Jack's neck. "Up you go." Following him, he admired the firm ass stretching the jeans with each step. "You still gotta nice ass."

"It's yours if you want it, hot man."

They entered one of the guest bedrooms.

Rocky and Jack, holding the other's hands, stood facing each other.

God, I want him. I shouldn't, but I do. Should I? It's just sex, and I need it bad. It's temporary, a fling. Comfort. Someone to hold.

"I'm not sure about this. I'm married," Rocky said, trying to escape the temptation swallowing him whole.

"Yeah, I was too. You and Nick ever play with anyone else?"

"Every now and then, usually together. It was just sex, something different, but we have a solid relation. You and Roberto?"

"Sometimes. He was so much younger than me. Had a huge libido. I wanted to keep him happy."

"So, it worked out okay between you two, having sex with other guys?"

Jack's reply was a kiss placed on Rocky's forehead, then his neck and then his lips.

Rocky sighed and thought, *I want this guy. I really need some flesh, to hold, to make love to, sex.*

As if reading his thoughts, Jack said, "What would Nick think if he found out?"

"I'm not sure." Rocky inhaled. "He's been okay with it in the past, just as long as it didn't get in the way of us."

Rocky pressed his body against Jack and felt all of him press back.

Jack slowly unbuttoned Rocky's shirt and explored his chest with his mouth.

Unbuttoning the top buttons on Jack's polo shirt, Rocky pulled the lavender shirt up over Jack's broad shoulders and over his head.

Wrapping their arms around each other, they fell on to the bed passionately kissing and exploring the other's body.

An hour later they lay naked under a sheet, wrapped around each other, chest to chest, content.

Running an index finger from the bridge to the tip of Rocky's nose, Jack said, "That was nice, it's been a long time." He leaned over and placed a light kiss on his forehead. "Thank you, it meant a lot to me, in so many ways."

"Me too."

Jack raised himself up on an elbow and stared into Rocky's eyes. "This may sound a little out of place right now. But one day I'd like to meet the guy that got to have you in his life all these years.

CHAPTER 6

"Follow the money," Nick, said. He brought his hospital recliner upright. His Mango linen pants, and a white cashmere V-neck sweater gave him a refined, yet casual look. "Diamonds? That is totally bizarre. But come to think of it, Goulet's wife used to wear a lot of them. Not so much anymore, since she's in the limelight nowadays."

"It appears we have two paths, no three, we can follow: money, diamonds, and what you refer to as MF."

The president used the bed's controller to extend the recliner and adjust the leg height. "Can't wait to get out of this room. Are we any closer to finding the origins or location of that MF's controllers?"

"Yes, we are. Slowly, but yes." Rocky said. "Brooke, maybe you could bring your father up to date on this."

Brooke answered without her former enthusiasm, having abandoned it since learning she and Rick were not full siblings. "As Dr. Parson's mentioned in the last meeting, we can't avail ourselves of most of the government's intelligence assets because we do not know who we can trust. That being said, Buck, his scientists and engineers have been able to cobble together what they think transpired on Inauguration Day and after. We got a big break."

"What do we know specifically?" Nick asked, "Where did the break come from?"

"We have been surveilling the MF, roosting in its hideaway for days," Brooke said. "This morning, when I was with Sandy Yoe tracking the diamonds, Buck called Rick and me to the East Wing. Rick headed directly to the East Wing. So, Rick, why don't you share with Dad what you and Buck talked about? After all, these are your corporate folks doing the work, most of it anyway."

Rick's somber mood paralleled Brooke's. "MF came to life around 2:00 a.m. this morning, about seven hours before Buck asked us to come to the East Wing. MF just sat there and didn't do anything. Except erase data. Of course, we had already copied the data. No problem."

"What do you mean, no problem?" the president said.

Rick looked stone-faced at Nick, the man he had been misled to believe was his father for all of his twenty-four years. "Well, we had anticipated something like this could happen, so we'd flown a drone through the open dormer the night before and let it sit there. That is until MF woke up and we hacked into it."

"Congratulations," Nick said. "That was quite an accomplishment. Were those the Chamber's Enterprises folks, Rocky?"

"For the most part. Though Dr. Parsons and Brooke were integral to the process as well."

"Thank you, everyone," Nick said, his facial muscles relaxing into lines of fatigue. "What happened next?"

"Like I said," Rick continued, "we had copied the data that was soon erased, and we also copied new data being downloaded into MF. That was the big break. Immediately, Buck's team, particularly with Lynn Elle's help, was able to correlate IP addresses and ended up triangulated on the signal's origin and located the source."

"No shit!" the president said.

"MF shut down within minutes of firing up," Rick said. "Six hours later it was airborne. It flew in an irregular pattern, much like any bird might have, but toward where we believe the controller is located. Then another big break."

Nick cocked his head. "Oh?"

Rick folded his arms. "Okay, you were not made aware of this, but Chamber's Enterprises Satellites have been repositioned to watch MF's progress. Brooke came up with the idea to have a vehicle positioned nearby on the ground. They started following MF's flight. Fortunately, a tracking device the drone had placed on MF worked perfectly."

"Tracking device?" the president said. "How did that happen?"

"After originally passing through the dormer," Rocky said, "the drone settled next to MF. It then used a miniature robotic arm, one not unlike the much larger ones used by robots to defuse explosives and placed the dime-sized device on MF."

"When the MF left the dormer around eight this morning," Rick said, "we had three drones following at a seventy-five-yard distance on the left, right, and rear, videoing MF in flight."

Rick, his voice and hands animated, said, "Now get this! Suddenly, a huge hawk swooped down out of nowhere and latched onto MF with its talons."

"This is crazy," the president said. "Why didn't whoever is controlling the MF intervene?"

"We have no idea. The only thing we can figure out is that they were not online observing at the time," Rick said.

"Yep, it is crazy!" Brooke said.

"Buck and his team were right on it." Rocky leaned forward. "They sent all three drones after the hawk carrying MF. Friggin' unreal! Think about drones chasing a hawk carrying a robot bird."

"You've got my attention," the president said.

"The hawk was struggling to carry the artificial bird," Rocky said, "so probably didn't notice the drones bearing down on it. These big drones aren't battery operated and are not particularly quiet. But then, just as the drones came within fifty feet of the hawk, they each cast their nets. The first one missed the hawk entirely. The second one landed on its tail causing it to stumble midair. Thank God the third drone's net completely encased the Hawk and MF!"

The president sat up straight in his chair, ignoring any discomfort the movement caused him. "This is like sci-fi! Nets? Are you kidding me? What's all that about?"

"Yep, it is." Rocky said. "These interceptor drones have been used for three or four months now at stadiums and other at-risk locations vulnerable to drone attacks. They are semi-autonomous radar guided. Drones bringing down drones with nets might sound primitive, but the technology certainly is not."

A pause in conversation followed.

"The hawk," Brooke said, interrupting everyone's thoughts, "tangled in the nets, fell thrashing from about one hundred feet, landing on some marshy ground adjacent to a distribution center. Our team tracking MF quickly located the grounded pair. The hawk was tearing at the nets with its beak and lashing out with its talons. All the while, MF was tossed about inside the nets."

"Did this mayhem attract any attention?" the president asked.

"Fortunately, not," Brook said. "It was late in the morning and the yard was relatively empty. The team surmised the trucks and their drivers had departed on their routes earlier in the morning. They felt vulnerable to being discovered by MF's owners and tried to figure out a way to detach the tracking device from MF. One of them came up with the idea to cover the hawks head with a piece of canvas they'd found discarded in nearby brush. I don't know exactly how they did it, but they covered its head with the canvas. It wasn't long before the thrashing subsided, and they were able to hold down the hawk and extract MF from the nets and detach the tracking device and shut down MF."

"And the hawk?" the president said. "Wasn't the bird injured in the fall, 100 feet?"

"Not that they could tell Dad, er, uh, Nick," Brooke said, "Not that we know of."

Brooke's slip calling him Dad brought a hint of a smile to the president's face.

"No! Dad!" Brooke said, visibly annoyed with her faux pas. She shook her head, then laughed.

Rocky sat back in his chair, grinned, and folded his arms.

Rick formed his hands into pistols, pointed at Brooke, "You go girl!"

Brooke shook her head. "Okay, get over it."

"Okay," the president said. "So where are we now?"

Still smiling, but serious, Rocky said, "Trying to figure out our next move while we are analyzing the data. Now that we think we know where the controllers are, or were . . . before the pair hit the dirt, we directed satellites to surveil the vicinity. We now have eyes in place, on the ground."

"Sounds good," the president said. "Now let's get back to the diamonds. We haven't seen money, but we have seen diamonds. I would like to speak with Director Hamilcar." Looking at Rocky, he said, "Have him meet me in the Oval in two hours. I need a couple of hours to rest up. Thank you everybody, love you! Now get out of here and let me rest."

"Ca, Ca, Ca, Can, ya, ya, ya, you believe that?" Brooke's words stumbled out of her mouth as she entered Buck's temporary office in the East Wing. She closed the door behind her and took a seat opposite Buck who sat at his workstation scanning three computer screens.

Hands out, palms up, he said, "Believe what, Brooke?"

"Believe that my dad is going to meet with the Director of the Secret Service in the Oval?"

"Really? When? Is he up to it? I thought he was still bedridden."

"Yes, really. In less than two hours. And no, he is NOT up to it, and he SHOULD stay in bed!"

"Wow."

Buck came from behind his workstation and pulled a chair up beside Brooke and took one of her hands in his. "I understand why you are upset."

"I'm more than upset." She swallowed. "I'm scared to death he could suffer a setback and maybe even worse, die in the process. Why is he being so reckless?"

"Well, you know him as well as anyone else. Why do you think he's acting this way? After all, it's not sheepish and risk adverse people that become president of the United States."

Tears pooled in her eyes. "I am so afraid we could lose him. It's not necessary for him to do this. We have everything under control." She slammed her fist on the arm of the chair. "He should be resting!"

Buck moved his chair closer to hers, leaned over, and wrapped his arm around her and pulled her in close. Brooke's head rested on his shoulder.

"Your dad must know what he's doing. Remember, he is always full of surprises. Just be as supportive as you can. That's all you can do. And if you are the praying type, pray."

Trish Smart and Dr. Parsons sat in the Oval facing Rick and Rocky. A low table separated them. Lazy flames danced above the waning embers in the fireplace.

"General," the chief of staff said, "when you told me the president would be meeting here with Director Hamilcar, you could have knocked me over with a feather."

"Me too," Dr. Parsons said.

"I am sure that makes four of us. You should have been there when he said it. Right, Rick?" Rocky said.

Effusively nodding his head, Rick said, "Absolutely, Dad. But he said it. And here we are." He shrugged. "I guess the director and the president will be here in thirty or so minutes. How do we prepare for this? You know, we weren't exactly invited to this meeting. From what I can tell, he only invited Hamilcar."

"There are some things that all chiefs of staff must do now and then to protect presidents from themselves," Trish said. "This just might be one of them. We can apologize later if he is not happy with us being here."

"Sound thinking, Trish," Rocky said. "I have been doing that kind of thing all his political life. He's fortunate to have always been surrounded by people that have had his best interests at heart and have never been afraid to confront him on things he need consider or reconsider."

"A good sign that he is a good leader, being willing to work with a staff having his back, you would have to agree." Dr Parsons said, "The thing is, how do you prepare for a meeting with the president when you have not been invited and have no idea what he has in mind, other than diamonds? Where is he going with this? I don't know what he wants or expects from us."

Trish reached toward the table to refill her coffee cup.

The fireplace popped and startled everyone.

Rick, amused, let out a light snort.

Rocky said, "I guess we have thirty minutes to start second guessing as to what this meeting will be all about!"

Despite a far-reaching discussion, thirty minutes later they found themselves no closer to resolving their dilemma. When the phone next to the chief of staff buzzed, she pushed the speaker button.

"Director Hamilcar here to see the president."

The four exchanged *okay, here we go* looks.

"Thank you, please send him in," the chief of staff said.

Director Hamilcar entered the room. The four stood.

"Please come in, Director." Rocky pointed to a vacant wing chair at the end of the sofas facing the fire.

As the director moved toward the chair Rocky thought, looking at the president's desk, *how odd it is that they were in the Oval Office without the president being there. When would he arrive? Would he be in a wheelchair?*

"Please have a seat, Director. The president should be here shortly."

"Yes, thank you, General."

The director shook everyone's hand and took a seat in the wing chair. The others returned to their places on the couches.

"I was certainly surprised to hear the president is recovering so quickly. I guess I should have anticipated it though, after seeing the pictures." He looked directly at the chief of staff.

She smiled and nodded. "Yes."

"It's good to see all of you," the director said. "I am not sure how I should have prepared for this meeting with the president. Any ideas what this is about?"

"Diamonds," Rick said.

The other three nodded.

"Here we are discussing something that has no real intrinsic value," Dr. Parsons said. She paused. "Diamonds, by themselves, excepting of course, industrial diamonds, have no real practical use. They look pretty." She paused once again, as if in deep thought. A moment later she went on to say, "They are the object of myths. In the Middle Ages they were thought to have healing properties and could instill courage and protection for those wearing them. As a scientist, I find any preoccupation with diamonds surreal. But forgive me, I digress."

"Let me digress!" Rick said, "What about those legends? Curses and the like? Think of the Hope Diamond, the Black Orlov, the Koh-i-Noor. Talk about over-the-top. With any luck one of those curses will stick to Goulet."

The phone buzzed again. Trish pushed the button.

A voice on the line said, "The president requested the conversation be placed on speaker phone so all five of you can participate in the conversation."

"All five of us? Trish said"

"Yes, ma'am."

The five exchanged looks of surprise.

"Very well." Trish pushed another button on the phone console. "Hello, Mr. President, we are on speaker phone."

"Hello, everyone, thank you so much for agreeing to meet with me on such short notice," the president said. "Sorry I cannot physically be there, but my wheelchair has a flat."

Bewildered looks were combined with muted laughter.

"The reason I asked for the meeting is to discuss the diamonds found under my desk in the Oval. As you are aware, it wasn't me in the Oval." He chuckled. "By the way, has the vice president moved his things out of there?"

"Yes, he has, Mr. President," Trish said.

"Good."

Rocky looked around the room thinking it had only been nine days since he had walked into the Oval and been overwhelmed with having found Goulet's personal affects in boxes and on the shelves and desk.

"Director, I have concerns," the president said, "the legality in all of this. We need to get to the bottom of this thing about the diamonds. It is imperative everything be done in a way that can stand scrutiny by a court of law. No illegal searches. We must utilize investigators, a district attorney, and judges that are above reproach."

"Yes, Mr. President," the director said.

"Rick," Rocky said, "from what you have shared with your father and me, have you been able to trace the diamonds?"

"Yes, Dad, sort of. By that I mean, we know where they were cut. They were sold to diamond brokers in Dubai. But after that, we really do not know in whose hands they ended up. We hit a dead end."

"Nefarious. That is the crux of things," Director Hamilcar said. "Our research shows the sellers and buyers concealed ownership and the fact that they disappeared only two months ago is cause for alarm."

"Uh huh," Dr. Parsons said. "My question is, are these the only diamonds involved? Are there more?"

"We think there are more," Rick said. "We found that the Dubai firm handling these diamonds is known for dealing diamonds to those who demand total discretion. The very rich trying to secure part of their wealth in something that will hold its value in case of inflation, currency devaluation or banking issues. Sanctions, that sort of thing."

"Regardless," the president said, "we need to find out if these beauties lead anywhere. Will they take us to the why and who tried to kill me? Director Hamilcar, what do you think we ought to do?"

"Sir, I am not sure. Find the source, the trail. Who mined them, cut and marked them, and subsequently sold them to whom, I suppose."

"How do you propose we do that, Director?" the president asked. "We know it has something to do with Dubai. But we need to find something closer, geographically closer. Are there more and where are they? Whoever had them in their possession will know where they came from. It's that simple. Wouldn't you agree?"

"Theoretically, Mr. President. But practicality is the problem. I am not certain. We need to know where to look and then get a subpoena."

In an impatient tone, the president said, "We know where to look! Wherever Goulet is and wherever he has been since the inauguration. If there are more . . . Just think. The diamonds Brooke found probably fell out of a bag or package of some sort. Where is that bag? Or that package? Most probably with Goulet.

Try his office or how about the Naval Observatory, his official residence? Think!"

"Sir," the director said, "We can't just go in and search his homes, his offices, vehicles, without just cause and a warrant."

"Dealing drugs," Brooke said, entering the Oval.

"Christ, what's next?" Hamilcar said hearing what she'd said entering the room.

"Thank you for joining the meeting, Brooke," the president said over the speaker phone.

"Hi, Brooke," a startled Rocky said.

"Sit over here." Rick gestured to her as he and Rocky made room on the couch.

"The vice president is dealing drugs. There is no way you are going to get me or a judge to believe that," Hamilcar said.

"Good, that is not my intent," Brooke said. She sat up straight, her hands folded in her lap. "During the election, I shared with Dad's campaign that Goulet's son, Gage, an undergrad at Georgetown had been dealing. The next thing I knew, the papers touted Gage being sent off to work with the Peace Corps or something of that ilk in Africa. He returned to the US following the election and is back at GU."

"Back to his old tricks?" Trish said.

"Can't say," Brooke interjected.

"Hm, this has possibilities," Hamilcar said. This kid is living on campus part of the time and at the VP's residence infrequently. My reports say he was there last night."

"Folks, the doctor just arrived," the president said. "I am going to sign off. Keep talking and thank you for what you are doing. Gotta go."

CHAPTER 7

"Director Hamilcar," Rocky said, "we need to find a way into the vice president's residence. And we need to do it legally and, on the QT. Any ideas?"

Hamilcar shifted uncomfortably in his chair. "We can do it, but it could get really messy. If the vice president remains acting president and he finds out he was being investigated, heads will roll."

"No doubt, Director," Rick said. "It's vital we follow every lead. For all we know, MF's interrupted flight might be a dead end. It's vital we follow every lead. With each passing day the trail gets colder. Right now, any hope of finding out who attempted to kill my father rests on a mechanical bird and some diamonds. That's not a lot to go on."

"And let's not forget," Trish said, "this is the first time in US history an attempted assassination has been done remotely. Importantly, it is also the first time the assassin has not been nabbed immediately, with the exception of John Wilkes Booth."

"Strange, isn't it?" Brooke said. "Just how hard are Justice and the FBI trying? It is a national embarrassment. Not to mention,

I have a personal interest in bringing the bastards that tried to kill my father to justice!"

The director cleared his throat. "I can certainly understand where you're coming from. But we need to be careful and follow the law. Things are sounding a little out of control here."

"You know, Director, we can keep the Secret Service at arm's length," Rick said.

"Why and how would you do that? It's the Service's responsibility to protect the president."

"Well, uh, because if the Service gets involved, we have to go by the book. If we go by the book, well, word of the investigation could leak, and we'll be back to square one."

"But I thought we were going to go by the book," the director said.

"Some are. I have other ideas," Rick said. "Ideas some might judge to be murky."

The director sat, looking down at his folded hands. "So, Rick, it is apparent that, and I have no doubt, the VP is involved. And, let me guess, it is likely we have a plant or maybe several moles embedded within the administration." The director looked up and focused on Rick.

Returning the director's attention, Rick said, "Maybe not just the administration. Who knows where the tentacles of this monster have reached? Just the same, many feel, historically, they can't trust what appears to be a politicized Justice and FBI. Christ!"

Director Hamilcar shook his head. "Why has it come to this? I have spent my entire career trying to bring honor and transparency to the Service. Hoping that others were doing the same in their respective agencies. Now, here we are again, trying to insulate ourselves from our own government. I fear it will be never ending. It is a Byzantine nightmare in the making. No one, not even me, trusts the government to be entirely upright and serve the people."

"I agree, sir," Rick said. "Let me take it from another angle. "I assume you have never had to live a lie. A lie that made you feel like your life was a cardinal sin. That you were evil, hated, despised, mentally ill, and would be held with disdain and contempt should your secret be exposed. Living a life where every day you feared you would be discovered and destroyed."

"I cannot say that I have," the director said. "You're talking about living in a closet. This sounds very personal, Rick."

"Yes, it is personal and should be personal for all of us. Not just homosexuals."

"Not to presume anything but may I ask?"

Rick exhaled. "This is not about me, Director."

"Very well."

"Think about it, Director. Not being allowed to openly love someone of the same sex. That lie. Remember, my father was shot protecting the man he loves from haters."

"Yes, I remember. I also recall people making jokes about it or even not caring. It made me sick to my stomach. I felt then, as I do now, very sad, ashamed for those that were so cruel."

Rick stood. "But everyone must play the cards they've been dealt. My father, the president, decided long ago he would survive and protect those he loved whatever the cost. He has fought for his country, my family, and his LGBTQ brothers and sisters.

He will not stop just because cowards lurk in the shadows. If we keep the investigation under the radar and legal. Well, as legal as we can, at least there is some hope we can nail the perpetrators and get some sort of justice."

"You aren't going vigilante on me, are you, Rick?" Hamilcar asked.

Rick smirked. "I have no idea what you are talking about, Director."

"Something to keep in mind, Rick. If things go awry, and the VP and his conspirators survive intact, you, your fathers, and Chambers Enterprises would be easy targets for the VP, an empowered and vengeful acting president."

"I know," Rick said, "but without moving forward and squashing them before they destroy us, they could regroup and attack again. We have a plan."

"Okay, give it to me. Who is we?"

"I can't tell you. I am sworn to secrecy. Secrecy that will protect both you and other parties, Director."

"Secrets usually get out. But what the fuck. What's your plan?" Hamilcar said.

"Gage Goulet is definitely dealing again."

"How do you know this? Any proof?"

"Yes, we have him on video and audio, dealing. On campus, at GU," Rick said.

"How the hell did you get that? My agents run protection on that little snot-nosed coed, 24-7."

"Not really, they really don't," Rick said. "When he is with his group of so-called friends, he is given plenty of room. Especially during class, in the bathrooms, in his buddy's apartments. Ever notice how he always uses public transportation? The service provides him a car, driver, and protection. But he never uses it."

"Yeah, there has been some talk about that," the director said. "He's had protection assigned ever since his father was nominated along with the president. Unfortunately, but true to form, when the jerk was out of the country, he behaved badly. Drank and smoked dope, dabbled in coke and kept our team hopping. Gage acts like a real entitled asshole most of the time. None of my agents want to be assigned to his security team. They'd just as soon kick his ass. The Service concluded he needed space, so we let him have it his way. Agents are taking bets on when one of his stunts will big time embarrass the administration."

"Well, Director, his behavior and giving him room has provided us with an opportunity to search the vice president's residence."

"And once again, who is we? Who obtained the video and the audio?"

"Chambers Enterprises is at the leading edge in surveillance product development. As of two days ago, we have video capability planted in every room he enters on campus, the halls and outside areas. We have four of our men tailing, recording, and always videoing. It is literally impossible for him to be out of sight, accept in the residence. We are going to change that."

"For Christ's sake!" the director said, his jaw tightening. "That's illegal. I feel like I am being compromised knowing all this!"

"We have all been compromised," Rick said. "And yes, illegal for the government. But maybe a little gray as far as the private sector goes. That is exactly why you can't be directly involved. Armed with a search warrant, timed when the residence is unoccupied, we'll get what we need."

"Search warrant? Why bother, you seem intent on doing it your way, regardless."

"A search warrant could provide some wiggle room. You'll see."

"Regardless, done improperly, none of that so called evidence will be allowed in court," the director said.

In a curt tone, Rick said, "You don't think we want this resolved in a court of law, do you?"

"Hey, Nick, feeling better?" Rocky asked. "It's good to seeing you sitting in a chair."

The president extended his arms. "Hey, babe, come over here and give me a hug."

Rocky smiled broadly, leaned over, kissed his husband's lips, then wrapped his arms around Nick's shoulders and held him for several moments.

"It feels so good to have you close, to feel you, to smell you," Nick said.

A tinge of guilt stung Rocky. Jack came to mind. Rocky thought, *I will have to tell him, sooner or later. He'll be all right with it. We've played with others before. Even Sheila. I'm just a guy, like any other guy. Jeez, who am I kidding? Push it out of your mind. It is what it is. Nick knows I love him and that's that. I'd want him to have someone to comfort him if our places were reversed. Just a little sex and companionship. I sure hope this isn't a problem. I hate myself! Fuck it!*

He brushed his agonizing thoughts away. "It sure does. I don't ever want to let go. Love you."

"You okay, Rocky?"

"Yeah, I'm good. A little stressed, nothing, really."

"Love you, too." Nick smiled.

Rocky released Nick and pulled up a visitor chair. "So, I've some things to share with you. But first, you look great. What are you working on?"

"My speech. I'm giving a nationwide speech at 9 p.m. tonight."

"Great! I guess this is about getting your powers back. Letting the nation know you're alive, willing, and able. Goulet will hate that."

Nick chuckled. "Pretty much, but not so fast. I will let them see for themselves that I'm conscious and recovering. But my intent is to make sure that whoever was behind the assassination attempt does not become alarmed, or know we are anywhere near them. I will thank the nation, the vice president, and FBI, etc. for their support. The tenor of the speech will imply that while we are looking for the assassin, our focus is on doing everything possible to heal and move on."

Rocky rubbed his chin and sat back. "Do I understand correctly that it is your idea to give the conspirators a false sense of calm, security? Room to move about, let their guard down? Then they'll either shut everything down and go away or continue to plot."

"Hopefully," Nick said.

"That could prove dangerous, babe. What if they try to kill you again?"

"That is the chance we have to take if we are going to find them. They've had time to cover their tracks and disappear. We need them to feel emboldened. I may even pardon them in abstentia."

"You have got to be shitting me! You would do that? 'The Unknown Assassin's Pardon.'" Rocky paused and smiled broadly. "You never cease to amaze me! An interesting option. Not sure what you're up to, but no matter."

Nick grinned. "It would start the healing, get the nation back on track, and hopefully facilitate our finding the conspirators. There are many ways to deal with people like this. Just not now."

Nick's face hardened. He stared at the ceiling. "When we do find them, they will never see the light of day!"

Rocky's jaw dropped.

"Thought I would take this lying down?" Nick asked. "Never! This is the second attempt on my life. They shot you the first time because you jumped in front of the bullet. This time they succeeded in shooting me."

Nick's eyes widened as he continued speaking focused on the future. "But unlike last time, I have the power and position to make things happen. And so does Rick. These bastards will pay with their lives!"

"I don't understand!" Rocky said, eyebrows furrowing, "Rick? What are you talking about? What can he do?"

"What can he do? He has already started. He is using all of Chambers Enterprises resources to surveil and hunt down the bastards."

"What the hell? I brought in Buck Gerard and his team. What else is going on? Have you been going behind my back?" Rick asked, folding his arms.

"No one has been going behind your back," Nick said, tempering his tone. "I called Rick in and told him to use company assets, private sector assets, to do what the government cannot do. Because, obviously, the people who want me dead are entrenched in the government."

"Nick, you don't know this for sure. We've suspected it. But have no proof."

"And we will never have proof," the president said, "if we leave it up to the Justice Department and the FBI. Remember, those agencies couldn't stop former President and Mrs. Tanner from getting assassinated. Remember, the haters turned on their own and shot him and Josephine because they supported me for president. Where were these agencies two weeks ago when I was cut down? Where are they now? They've found nothing. It's not unlike AIDS. When tragedy strikes the gays, well, it's not a priority. What makes any of us think that they will ever really be there for people like you and me?"

"Hey, honey, I think you need to calm down a little. I don't disagree with you, but you are getting angry, a bit hysterical, worked up. You should rest."

Nick sighed. "I agree. I should rest. But you know I'm right. I will rest and I will fight back. I will rest some more, and I will fight back until gays and those of us who live our lives as we choose can do so with dignity cloaked in the same mantle of safety afforded all Americans. The bigots can hide behind lip service and continue to corrupt our government and a jaded society, but we will find them. We will rout them from their insidious lairs and strike back!"

CHAPTER 8

"Buck," Brooke said, "I'm just not sure how long we can keep the surveillance on the ground without getting discovered. Whoever is in charge of that robot is sure to have outward looking cameras and their analytics will be monitoring the camera feeds. What happens after we're discovered? Another dead end or worse?"

"You're right, but homeless encampments spring up all over the place at odd times. As long as our people do what homeless folks do, which isn't really all that complicated, they should be okay. The best part about it is that as they scrounge around the area looking for stuff that will help them set up camp, our pretend homeless people can thoroughly check out the building. They can find the location of the escape routes and vulnerabilities in the building without arousing suspicion."

Brooke pointed to Buck's monitor. "Look, one of our guys. God, he looks mangy. He's actually looking in the door window, trying to get in. Ballsy!"

Buck chuckled. "He's also checking out any surveillance assets they may have in place and planting a listening device of our own while rattling the door. Look here," Buck continued, pointing to another video feed provided by a camera from across the street. "While the guy out front is distracting whoever might be inside, this woman is checking out the back, doing essentially the same thing. She's also looking in the dumpsters. I doubt the guys inside are stupid enough to put incriminating evidence in the trash, but there are always things you can tell about people by analyzing their garbage."

Brooke laughed. "God, I hope no one goes through my trash. They'll discover I have no life and am boring as shit."

"I bet several sets of characters have been mining your garbage ever since your father started his run for the White House. No doubt all sorts rummage through your garbage, wherever you are, for the next four years or more."

"Damn, that's gross! Are you serious?" She paused and thought a moment. "Of course, you are. Damn. Fuck! It will be almost impossible to date anyone without being discovered. That sucks."

He looked at her, with one brow lifted and a mischievous grin.

"Don't look at me that way. And don't read anything into it. Crap!"

"I'm just listening, relax."

"You're doin' more than just listening. You've fired up that imagination of yours, I can feel it."

"Feel what, Miss Brooke?" he said, cocking his head to the side.

Her cheeks flushed. "You know what. The heat, the hormones."

"Yours or mine?" he asked, lips parted.

"I'm not so sure we should be doing this," she said.

"This? Me? You?" Buck asked.

"Yes, you. Me too," She replied.

He turned toward her and caressed her face with both hands.

Brooke's eyes closed. She said, "I can't do this."

"We can and we will." Buck pulled Brooke close and stroked her cheek with his thumb. Slowly he pressed his lips to hers.

The kiss deepened into a passionate embrace.

Rick walked into the office through the open door. He froze.

Through one half-opened eye, Brooke caught sight of her brother watching them.

Rick slumped up against the door frame and pressed his fist to his mouth.

He caught his sister's look, spun around, and left the room.

Brooke pulled away and gazed directly into Buck's eyes. "Is there something going on between you and my brother?"

The media lights in the Oval Office switched off, and the nationwide broadcast was over. President Chambers-Jeffries slumped in his chair behind the ornate Theodore Roosevelt Desk. "This feels a bit odd. I hadn't anticipated it happening this way. That's for sure. Had no idea I'd have spent my first weeks as president in the infirmary before getting here."

The president straightened his shoulders, sat up, and transferred himself to his wheelchair. The video crew continued dismantling the lights and removing their equipment.

One of the cameramen said, "Good job, Mr. President. That's what the nation needed."

Nick smiled. "Thank you!"

"Mr. President," Trish Smart said. "I think your—"

He held up his hand.

"Thank you, I am sure, but please give me a moment. Let's chat once the office is cleared."

"Yes, Mr. President."

Rocky beamed at his husband from the other end of the room but remained in place when Nick asked Trish to hold her comments.

Rocky watched Nick look around the Oval Office.

Rocky felt his heart tighten thinking about all Nick had been through. *What a momentous moment this must be for him. One minute inaugurated, hours later shot and no longer able to function as president. Then the days and days spent in a hospital bed and the multiple surgeries. All the while searching for his would-be assassins and fending off an ambitious conniving vice president. And, at last, able to address the people in the hope that Congress will not strip him of his office. How is he enduring all this?*

The room emptied, leaving only the president, Rocky, and Trish.

"Thank you, Trish. I appreciate your masterminding the speech."

"You are very welcome, Mr. President. But it was your idea, and you wrote the speech. A very good one I might add. Social media comments and reactions are running in your favor. It looks like the tide is turning in your direction."

"I am not sure I follow you. I think popular opinion was and is on my side. The tide? Tell me precisely what you mean. I thought the nation was behind me."

"Nick," Rocky said. "The people are definitely behind your recovery. But as far as your resuming your duties, that is another matter."

The president's jaw slackened, and his head tilted. "And?"

"The picture of you lying face down on the White House lawn shocked the world. No one anticipated you surviving, much less resuming your duties as president. Most people, reasonable people, were grateful that days later it appeared that you might survive. However, resuming your duties as president was more than most could imagine. With the vice president running around as if he was not only the acting president, but more than likely the president, for the long term, people got used to him. It was a security blanket of sorts. Now the blanket is being pulled back. Here you are, an enigma. You survived. You are alive and well, and fully competent. Very few expected to see what they saw tonight."

"Trish, you stated my speech was successful," the president said. "Okay, real time, what feedback are we getting online? From the networks?"

"Mr. President, the polling is in your favor. We are seeing some very positive feedback. Generally, very good. Of course, there are those expressing caution, a wait-and-see sort of attitude. This means we must continue to work toward garnering more support. Your speech was the first real concrete step in that direction. We have one week until Congress must vote. It could happen sooner, but we are doing our best to hold them off until we can be assured of enough support to carry the vote in your favor. And one more thing. Your encouraging people to bone up on the 25th amendment has gone viral. Negative comments regarding Goulet pushing it through the Cabinet are gathering steam."

"Interesting," the president said.

"Ultimately it is Congress that decides," Rocky said. "But public opinion might help push a couple of votes our way. Our efforts need to focus on the Hill."

"I agree," Trish said. "Three days from now you are expected to motorcade up to the Hill for a meeting with the leadership from both parties. If all goes as planned, you will return two days later to address the House and the Senate."

"Sort of an impromptu State of the President," the president said, "as opposed to State of the Union."

Rocky and Trish grinned and nodded.

"Has Simon been advised that I will be moving from the infirmary to the residence tonight?"

"Yes, over your doctor's objections," Rocky said. "Our bedroom looks more like a hospital room than a bedroom."

Nick asked, playfully, "Aren't you looking forward to sharing our bed?"

Trish blushed and covered her mouth. "You both will excuse me, won't you?"

Rocky and the President laughed as the chief of staff headed toward the door.

"Hold on, Trish," the president said.

She turned back. "Yes, sir?"

"Goulet, where was he this evening? I mean, he said hello when I arrived, but I didn't notice him in the Oval when I finished speaking ten minutes later. Did he have something more important to do? Politic? Plot?"

"It appears that there was some sort of domestic incident at the vice president's residence. My guess is his son got in some kind of trouble again. Maybe throwing a raucous party while his parents were here at the White House. I'll look into it and get back to you with details as soon as I have them."

CHAPTER 9

"So, what did your teams find?" Rocky asked.

"As everyone here knows," Rick said, "I am heading up one team, the clandestine team, supported by my sister and Buck Gerard. Director Hamilcar is running the official team made up of his staff and supported by Ms. Smart and Dr. Parsons. My team does not exist. Is everyone in agreement?"

All parties nodded.

"Good. Director Hamilcar, would you please update us on the matter regarding the vice president's son?" Rocky asked.

"First of all, let me set the scene. As you all know, the vice president's residence is located about two miles from here. It is on seventy acres that makes up the Naval Observatory. The property is fenced, secure, and actively patrolled and not open to the public."

The director continued, "Yes. Armed with a warrant, US Marshals augmented by the Secret Service surreptitiously entered the vice president's residence avoiding the staff, as they were watching the president's televised address. As expected, drugs and paraphernalia were found in Gage Goulet's room. Not well concealed and in some instances, pretty much out in the open.

The quantity was such that *personal use* as opposed to selling will not stand up in court. With the videos and audio obtained at GU and the cache from the residence, he will do time if brought to trial."

"And the other team?" Dr. Parsons asked. "Any success there?"

"Excuse me, Director," Trish said, "but what was done? Did they remove the compromising items? Seize them as evidence?"

"Yes, they did, all of it, and more. The drugs, paraphernalia, $54,000 in cash, two computers, and three burner phones. This guy is into fetish, some wild stuff. Got that too. Lots of toys." The director smirked. "Bound to have some piercings and bruises on that young bod."

Parson shifted in her chair. "Sex toys?"

Buck nodded.

"Christ, they learn early these days," Hamilcar said in a stage whisper. "Bet that boy could teach all of us some tricks!"

The tension broken, everyone exchanged OMG looks.

"We'll try to keep this as professional as possible," Dr. Parsons said. "Let's take a break."

Ten minutes later everyone had returned to their seats still high from their shared amusement.

"My team did not have nearly the fun yours did, Director," Rick said.

"I doubt they did," Hamilcar replied.

"We went in with another objective entirely," Rick said. "We used US Marshals from a unit that is far removed from those utilized by the director. The director's team purposely confined themselves to the VP's son's bedroom and sitting room. Once the director's team had vacated the residence, and using the same warrant, my team entered the residence."

"Warrant?" Trish asked, incredulous. "Doesn't a warrant have to be specific? Going back into the residence? Why would you do that, I mean, go back into the kid's room?"

"Yes, warrants are specific. However, we find a lot of times the rules are stretched," the director said.

Rick said, "This effort was very time consuming. We'd used twenty people to conduct the search. We brought in people from other jurisdictions and used forensics experts, IT consultants, safe crackers, both robotic and human, a cleaning crew, dogs, and interestingly, four expert gemologists."

I must beg the question, Trish said, "How did you get that army in unseen?"

"There is a two-hundred-yard escape tunnel leading from the residence. I didn't think the family was aware of it, at least not yet. I was mistaken. Too much has been going on since the president was shot. More on that later."

Trish tried to suppress a scowl.

"Sure enough," Rick said, "the team found diamonds, lots of diamonds in a safe in the library. The safe was not difficult to open. The challenge was the volume of diamonds. We had brought about six hundred lab grown diamonds of varying sizes to switch out with the real ones. We only had enough correctly sized stones to switch out half of what was in the safe."

"Why were you switching them out and not just taking all of them?" Trish asked, eyebrows raised.

Rick stood, his hands in his pockets, rocking back and forth on his heels. "Because we had two objectives. First, to make sure the diamonds belonged to Goulet. Second and quite Machiavellian, if I do say so myself, to disrupt the camaraderie amongst the conspirators. By that I mean, if Goulet thinks he's been hoodwinked, he might inadvertently show his hand."

Dr. Parson's inquired, "Why would he bother to check the authenticity of the stones at this juncture? He has a lot going on as acting president. My guess he expected to have been ratified as acting president by now. If I was in his position, some diamonds in a safe wouldn't be a high priority."

"I agree with you Doctor," Rick said. "That's why, once we're certain where the stones originated, we will start planting false information in the media and within the Gemological Institute of America and international gemology organizations. The idea is to create doubt about the authenticity of all stones originating from certain sellers."

"Also, like father, like son," Rick continued, "Apparently the apple doesn't fall far from the tree. The safe contained six burner phones."

"What?" Brooke asked. "Did you leave them in the safe?"

Rick said, "Had to, didn't want him to know we had been there."

Both Brooke and Trish shook their heads.

"Now get this," Rocky said, "One of our tech gurus made sure we will be in on every call on all six phones."

"Nice!" Brooke said.

"Yeah," Rick said. "We removed nothing else, but we did plant video and audio devises in every room. Every single room."

"That removes any semblance of privacy," Trish said.

Dr. Parsons nodded her head. "It does, indeed."

A moment passed and Trish said, "Now that you have the goods on that rascal Gage, what are you planning on doing with the evidence?"

"Nothing, at the moment." Rick said. "Just hold it for safe-keeping and leverage if necessary. No real reason to complicate things and embarrass the administration. It remains in our back pocket. Might be useful. We got what we wanted gaining access to the safe."

All nodded in agreement.

"The president noticed," Rick said, "as did several of you that the vice president left the Oval before the end of the address. It turns out that he had received a call from his son that his room had been ransacked."

"Thank God search warrants remain sealed in DC," Trish said.

Dr. Parsons looked at Rick. "And the tunnel, you said that you thought the family was not aware of the tunnel. Why did you say that?"

Rick inhaled. "We found some paraphernalia in the tunnel. We ran prints. They belong to Gage Goulet. He can come and go as he pleases, unseen. Just like we did."

The following day, Vice President Goulet sat at the desk in his residence's library with Director Hamilcar opposite him.

The vice president, avoiding eye contact, face flushed with anger, said in a cadenced tone, "Director, I have a rather sensitive matter to discuss with you. One that I do not want to leave this room. Is that understood?"

"Yes, Mr. Vice President. Understood."

"Last night, someone broke into the residence," Goulet said.

"This residence, or the White House residence?"

The vice president slammed his fist on the desk. "This residence! This residence, my home! Damn it!"

The director opened his mouth to speak, paused, appeared to think better of it and said nothing.

"What are you and the Service going to do about it?"

"I beg your pardon, Mr. Vice President," the director said, "but nothing, sir. I do not see how anything could be done. You told me this was not to leave the room. This is the first we have heard of it. No one called it in to the local police, the FBI, or the Service. We would have known, had someone done so."

"Don't be an idiot, Hamilcar! Of course, we didn't call it in. It's private. Besides, you are certainly aware my son has a checkered past. I am about to be made president. We can't have this shit getting out. Something must be done. Quietly." Goulet's eyes threw daggers at Hamilcar. "It just doesn't make sense. Your people are watching the place 24/7. In fact, I thought Gage was at home. He should have heard something. Christ! They were in his room!"

Feigning ignorance of the break in, Hamilcar said, "Yes, sir. Can you tell me about the break-in? Was anything stolen, missing?"

"My son's rooms, only his rooms, appear to have been searched. He admits things are missing. I am not sure what exactly. He hasn't been one hundred percent frank with me. He never is. He mentioned a computer and gaming stuff. And some cash."

The vice president wrung his hands, looking out a window, then back down at his desk. "I asked him if drugs were involved. As I am sure you must know, he has a brief history with recreational drugs. Like all young people these days. We, by that I mean his mother and I, helped him get over that by sending him away for a while. He seems to be okay. But you never know."

"We will need a detailed description of all the items your son thinks were stolen. It would help if we had the sales receipts etc. so we can get serial numbers and the like. Some of the info we need might be listed on the valuables rider on your insurance."

"Not likely, Gage is very private and never shares anything with his mother and me. Hell, I don't think either of us have spent time in any of his rooms here or at home for several years. Everyone is too busy."

"We will do everything we can with the information you provide us to locate the items and deal with the perpetrators."

Calmer, the vice president said, "Thank you. My family is eager to hear what you find out."

"One more thing, sir."

"Yes?"

"Have you checked to see that your and Mrs. Goulet's valuables are secure? Could there be anything else in the residence that could have gone missing?"

The vice president thought for a moment. "I'm not sure. I haven't noticed anything. My wife is pretty upset about Gage's room . . . but hasn't mentioned anything missing."

"Sir, objects of value, jewelry, art? Have you verified none are missing?"

"Like I said, Director. Nothing appears to be missing."

"You may be surprised to learn, Mr. Vice President. Valuables such as paintings and the like are sometimes replaced with fakes. I hope you can appreciate my asking."

The vice president shifted his weight and ran his tongue over his teeth. "Uh, sure. I understand, Director. No offense taken."

"One more thing, sir. The matter of national security."

Goulet sat for a moment; a blank look crossed his face. He cleared his throat. "Exactly what do you mean? I, I'm, uh, um, a lit'l confused here. What exactly are you saying?"

"Sir, sometimes one action might be a decoy, a distraction. One created to conceal the real purpose and ensure that it is not discovered. In this instance, one might be concerned that you have private papers, classified documents. I recommend you check one more time. Private papers, collectables anything of that nature. Again, national security could be at risk here, sir."

Goulet said, "Fuck! Just what I need!"

CHAPTER 10

"Thank you for filling us in on your meeting with the vice president," Rocky said, addressing the director. "It sounds to me like he is feeling pressure from several directions, his son, his nefarious activities, and oh yes, being acting president. Not surprised he got agitated. Good job!"

"You're welcome, General."

Brooke said, "It was brilliant tweaking him to make sure his artwork and personal papers were safe and sound. Nice!"

"So smooth, so 007," Rick said.

The director acknowledged the kudos with a smile a shake of his head. "Video? Let's see the video, Buck. Put it up on the 3D holo screen. I am anxious to reap the fruits of our labor."

Everyone turned to face the screen.

Buck stood, remote in hand, dimmed the lights and started the video. The first clip showed the vice president speaking with Director Hamilcar when Goulet began slamming his fists on the desk. The audio caught the reverberation of the desk being struck and the ensuing conversation. The hologram showed the facial and body language of both men simultaneously.

"As you can see," Buck paused the hologram. "We have a bird's-eye view of the conversation, and the audio is excellent. I have trimmed the various scenes highlighting Goulet's activities once the director departed. Here you go."

The hologram resumed. Goulet could be observed jumping up from the library desk and rushing to the other side of the room. He grabbed a painting off the wall and tossed it carelessly to the floor, revealing the wall safe. They watched as he fumbled three times unable to open it.

"The safe is programmed to lock down after three failed attempts," Buck said. "As you can see here, this really ticked off Goulet. This segment lasted for thirty minutes. I'll fast forward so you can see how he starts tearing up in the office. Whoops, watch this, there goes a lamp, a decanter, and wow, all those books at the same time!"

The onlookers watched, transfixed, first silent, then murmuring to themselves, and were soon cheering Goulet on. Several different voices from those watching the video sounded off, "Yo, go Baby!" "Tear it up! Destroy the place!" "That'll open the safe you dumbass!"

"Okay, okay, settle down," Trish said. "This isn't a football game! You guys!"

Buck skipped ahead to where Goulet successfully opened the safe and retrieved a black velvet sack. The vice president then walked over to his desk, sat down, and removed a jeweler's pad from the center desk drawer and emptied a pile of diamonds onto the pad.

"Jesus, just like a Sherlock Holmes mystery," Rocky said. "Black velvet bag and a mountain of diamonds. Look at that, he's using a jeweler's loupe!"

Dr. Parsons said, "It looks like he knows what he's doing. There must be hundreds of diamonds. But he's going through them fast . . . Interesting, he's making two piles."

"He doesn't like what he is seeing," Buck said. "Again, I'll skip ahead because it lasts for hours. See here, he is so agitated he has gone looking for the decanter he'd tossed earlier. Ha! Look!"

They all watched as Goulet found the decanter, turned it end up, and drank whatever hadn't spilled.

Buck returned to his narrative. "You can see he goes to a cabinet, pulls out a bottle of Macallan 25, and took a swig right from the bottle. Then listen to this!"

Goulet said, "Goddamn it! I checked every one of these stones and I was sure they were fuck'n real. What the Sam Hill happened?"

"This guy is out of control," Rocky said.

They watched Goulet pick up the phone and call someone by the name of Hammerschmidt, demanding that they make a house call, immediately.

"Hammerschmidt arrives a couple hours later, as you can see by the time stamp. There was no point in showing you Goulet spending all that time separating the diamonds into different piles, one considerably larger than the other. In the meantime, he has given instructions to his staff he is not to be disturbed unless it is a dire emergency. So, the nation's business has been pushed aside for the time being, while the acting president examines diamonds."

"Dad was right," Brooke said, "in pressing us to go after the diamonds while we wait for something to happen elsewhere."

"Yep, his hunch about looking into the diamonds paid off," Rocky said.

The video resumed and a tall, lanky, gray-haired woman entered the library. Goulet explained to her that he thought he had some fake diamonds mixed in with real stones. He thanked her for coming on short notice and asked her to verify what he thought he'd discovered.

Buck time-lapsed the video.

The inspection took place over several hours according to the holo's spinning timestamp. All the while she made notes on an iPad. Once the woman had completed her task, the large pile had grown a little larger. "Mr. Vice President, I must commend you on the quality of work you did differentiating the authentic stones from the others. Most amateurs, please forgive me for using that term, it is not a pejorative. Most would not have been as thorough, as accurate as you. My compliments, sir."

She opened her large purse, withdrew a maroon velvet bag from it and placed the large pile of diamonds inside. "These are authentic. The others, are not."

Goulet shook his head side-to-side.

The gemologist continued. "The lab stones are very good quality and have serial numbers on the girdle. However, they are not authentic. The numbers are forged. In that I mean they have been duplicated, copied from authentic diamonds. You only missed a couple of lab diamonds. Like I said, good job for an amateur. What else can I help you with?"

"Perhaps you know where the authentic and the lab diamonds originated. Who's the seller? Where did they come from?"

She paused. "I do not know how or why you obtained these stones, but I would be very careful in going down that road. You don't know who you may be dealing with."

"Can you be more specific, madam?"

"I will, but only as specific as I consider prudent."

Scalping his hand through his hair, he asked, "Why? What could be the problem?"

"The authentic stones originate from a firm in Dubai that has a reputation of dealing with rough trade. I would not transact with them. It concerns me that you, in your position, may somehow be connected to them. I advise caution."

The vice president took a deep breath. "I hope you can keep this between you and me."

"One has to be discreet in my business. As far as the lab diamonds, it is difficult to say where they came from. So many places are making them these days. The process is relatively simple and not expensive." The woman folded her arms. "You realize, I will have to let certain people in my industry know to keep an eye out for lab diamonds having stolen serial numbers. Particularly the numbers on these. I recognized them right away and have noted them. Duped numbers used to identify authentic individual stones have been duplicated on lab stones. This is going to cause all kinds of problems worldwide."

The vice president, looking down at the floor, shuddered, then nodded. He looked at the woman, extended his hand and thanked her again.

Buck took up the narrative. "The vice president ushered her out and returned the diamonds to the safe. He removed one of the burner phones and placed it in his pocket. He locked the safe. He picked up his briefcase and headed for the Executive Office Building. We believe he is there as we speak."

A few moments passed in silence, then Rocky said, "I think what we need to do now is wait for the vice president to take some action that might lead us in the direction of his conspirators. My guess he is very upset that he appears to have been tricked by his associates. As he said, he thinks that all the diamonds were real. Now many are fakes. This has gotta be driving him nuts. He knows someone is jerking him around."

"Interesting, isn't it," Dr. Parsons said, "He has no idea who is yanking his chain."

Rocky stood, placed his hands behind his back as he scanned everyone in the room. "We are at a crucial juncture. Congress will vote any day now on whether or not Nick regains his powers. The vice president has a coke head drug dealer for a son and has been compromised. He thinks someone has double-crossed him. So far, the assassination that would have made him president has failed. There are so many dangling loose ends. It's like some sort of flailing octopus with deadly tenacles having the potential to wrack holy hell on anyone and anything they strike. We really have no idea ultimately with what or with whom we are dealing.

"The scariest part is the man in the center of all of this, Goulet, a man who we know has never been totally in control of himself.

His emotions and his ambitions are unraveling. One step in the wrong direction and who knows what could happen."

CHAPTER 11

Rick and Buck sat in a back corner booth facing one another in an obscure bar four blocks from the White House. It was late. The lights were low. The half dozen mostly male patrons were scattered around the shabby dark room. Madonna's, *Like a Virgin*, played in the background just loud enough to muffle conversations.

"Why didn't you want to meet in the White House? Say the third floor, shoot some pool, push back some brewskis in the lap of luxury?" Buck asked.

Rick leaned in. "Maybe Brooke would find us and before you know it, we would be in a menage a trois."

"Fuck! You saw us?"

"Damn right, I did!" Rick said loud enough for a couple of people to glance their way.

"Hey," Buck said, "Keep it down. Besides, you and me, we, well we never said anything about monogamy. We both play, and you know it."

"Me, not so much! And shit! She's my sister, asshole!"

"Importantly, she's not my sister."

"I should knock the shit out of you right now for saying that."

"Give me a break. You know I swing both ways. It's not my fault you don't."

Rick stiffened; anguish crossed his face.

Buck said, "Sorry, didn't mean it, damn. You know I didn't."

Rick rolled his lips and pressed his knee against Buck's leg. "That's not the point here. Brooke isn't the real point either. I thought we had something."

"We do, so please don't fuck it up," Buck said.

"You're the one fucking it up."

Both men took a tug on their beers.

"Buck, do you really think you can have it both ways?"

"Yes, I do. I do have it both ways. I see other guys and women. Again, I was straight ... uh, bad choice of words. I was honest about this from the first time we played together. You didn't seem to mind then. What's the big deal now?"

"I guess, well, I just said, I thought we had something. Is it too much to hope that it be, be just you and me?"

Buck squeezed Rick's inner thigh under the table. "You know the answer to that. I want it all, and you, you are a big part of my all."

Rick swallowed as he gazed into Buck's eyes. "I don't get it. Aren't I enough?"

"Sweetie, even if I'm seeing other people, I want to be with you too."

"I don't know if I can handle that. I thought we might come out together after everything blows over with the assassination attempt. Make our relationship public and live openly."

Buck said, "Whoa! That's not going to happen now, if ever! I like my life just the way it is. I've a career to keep intact. I'm not like you. I don't run a family international conglomerate. I can't have my colleagues think I have my position 'cause I'm fucking the CEO."

"Knock it off, Buck," Rick said, narrowing his eyes. "About cred, bullshit. That hurts, Buck. You know that's not true. You've worked hard and earned your position. Everyone knows that!"

"They might know it now but sure as hell would rethink it if it was public knowledge, we were an item. I don't need the distraction and neither do you. You haven't been CEO long enough to establish yourself as credible. And I'm relatively new to the executive suite. I gotta lot to prove."

"You're wrong about that. You've plenty of cred, Buck."

"Besides, Mr. Chambers-Jeffries, I want to know something."

"What?"

"Does your family know you're gay?

"No."

"Why not?"

"I didn't want to be a cliché. You know, my dads are gay. It's the apple doesn't fall far from the tree kind of thing."

"See what I mean?" Buck asked. "We both have our reasons. And another thing, I've always felt that you come across professionally as more of a hard ass than you really are. I think you're compensating, overcompensating, trying to make sure no one suspects you're gay. Get a girlfriend. That will work better. Ever had a girlfriend? Ever been with a woman?"

"You know I date girls for show, just show. Beards. And no, I don't think I could ever have sex with a woman, ugh."

Rick's countenance darkened. "And no, it's not overcompensating. I am not really a nice person sometimes. Sometimes I can be an asshole. I admit it. If I'm overcompensating, maybe it's because I got my job handed to me. At least that's what my shrink thinks. But most of all, I work and play to win. You should know that. It's in my DNA."

Buck sat back, then raised his glass, Rick raised his. "Thought so! Well, good luck with that, homo!"

They smiled at one another and sat silent for a moment.

Rick looked up from his beer. "Are you going to marry a woman one day and raise a family. You and I could do that. My dads did. Do you love me?"

"Do I love you? Yes, I love you, but in my own way," Buck said, mouthing a kiss.

Rick's cock twitched.

"As far as getting married, I don't know. You don't have to nowadays to be in a long-term relationship. Will it be a woman? I imagine so, but I don't know for sure, that's too far off, anyway."

"Okay, thanks for answering my question."

Buck ran the palm of his hand alongside Rick's cheek. "You are very welcome, and yes, I love you."

"I love you too, only you."

Buck leaned forward and placed a hand on Rick's knee. "Hey, Rick, wanna play some?"

Rick looked around the room. "What, here?"

Buck said. "There's a discreet room in the back. I bet it's not crowded."

Rick returned the invitation with an encouraging smile.

Buck rested his hand on Rick's cheek. "But what about your protection? They're waiting outside. That sucks."

"Why? They won't say anything," Rick said.

Buck placed both elbows on the table, clasping his hands, and said, "Don't be naïve, my boy. The Secret Service keeps files on wherever their protectees go."

"Those aren't Secret Service."

Buck sat back. "What the fuck?"

"I declined protection. Those guys outside belong to me. I've been under corporate security's protection since I was in college. They belong to me, and they'll tell no one. They're compensated extremely well. Not even a book and movie contract would cover what I pay them."

"Damn, you're good," Buck said.

Rick grinned. "Thank you, hot man. There is a lot we could learn about and from each other."

"Enough of that! Let's go have some fun!" Buck said and took Rick by the hand and led him toward the back of the bar.

CHAPTER 12

Darkening clouds hastened the early evening twilight. The president, a blanket wrapped around his shoulders, sat with Trish Smart in the residence, each holding a cup of coffee.

"Well, Trish, how is the count going? How does it look?"

"It doesn't look too bad, Mr. President. From what we can tell, we have all but one or two of our members in both houses. We can't lose. We have forty-six percent in the House and at least that much in the Senate. And that doesn't include the Dems. You know we'll get a bunch of them. It's a done deal."

"Yeah, that's not too bad," the president said. "We need to get as many votes as we can from both parties. Have to have a mandate to squelch all doubt. I think it's doable. More so now that Goulet is apparently occupied with some, shall we say, personal matters, ahem!"

Trish spewed the coffee, she had just sipped, back into her cup.

He smiled. "We'll cover that after the meeting with the team in the East Wing."

"Thank God he has decreased the pedal to the metal. His not prowling the halls of Congress has left somewhat of a void. Your visit up there today, Mr. President, with the leadership of both parties garnered a lot of good press. Let's face it, the press can make or break us."

The president sat for a moment thinking, then said, "Not sure how to get those needed votes for a mandate in time for the vote. And fortunately, the pressure to hold the vote has eased, as I said, since the vice president has backed off. Who knows when and if he'll get back on track. I have got to get rid of my wheelchair and take advantage of his being sidetracked."

"Well, again, you did a good job doing just that today, sir."

"Thank you, Trish. I think I will use tomorrow to make phone calls and rest. I would like you to pin down who is voting for and who is voting against us. Provide me with the list first thing in the morning. I will personally reach out to each one of those who are either on the fence or set dead against us. And arrange to meet with them individually over the next couple of days."

"Sounds like a plan, Mr. President. Is there anything else?"

"No, thank you."

The sound of freezing rain beating against the windows mixed with the murmur of crackling wood in the Treaty Room fireplace.

"Hey, Dad, how are you feeling? Long day, huh?" Brooke asked.

The president's fallen face perked up hearing Brooke's upbeat tone.

"Yeah, Dad, good to see you," Rick said. "You look pretty good considering your trip to the Hill today."

Nick turned to Rocky sitting next to him. "Reminds me of when they were kids and they wanted something. Now after graduating college and getting access to their trusts, they don't talk like that to us anymore!"

Rocky smiled and pointed to Brooke. "He's right. Don't think we haven't noticed. You could humor us old guys every now and then and make us think you need us, at least a little."

All four broke out in laughter. For the first time since it had been revealed Brooke and Rick were not full brother and sister, the family appeared to be moving towards reconciliation.

Rocky got out of his chair and walked over to the side table opposite the fireplace. "Anyone want hot chocolate?"

"I do! I do!" Nick, Rick, and Brooke said simultaneously, causing more laughter.

"Thought so! I'll pour and grab each of us a cookie or two!"

After serving everyone and back in his chair, Rocky said, "If you want more feel free to slurp and dip, this is a family meeting."

"Gee, thanks, Daddy," Brooke said in a feigned little girl voice.

"You're welcome, baby doll," Rocky said.

"Oh my God!" Nick exclaimed.

Rick whimpered, feigning anguish, "You two always liked her best."

"And why not?" Brooke asked, lifting her chin and looking down her nose.

"For good reason," Rick said, beaming at his sister. "Love you!"

"Love you more," she said.

The four sat quietly enjoying their beverages and cookies and the familial closeness.

Nick placed his cup in its saucer and said, "I hate to change the topic but need to be brought up to date on all that has transpired over the last couple of days."

"Sure, Nick. Let's go. Each of us have areas where we are intimately familiar with the details. I'll start with the overview and the kids . . . sorry, kids. Rick and Brooke will fill in the blanks."

The three spent the next fifteen minutes bringing the president up to date.

Nick sat back, nodding slightly, and said, "Thank you everyone. It is absolutely amazing what has transpired. All of you have accomplished so much over the past several weeks. It feels like we are now on more of an even playing field." The president rose from his seat and retrieved the thermal coffee pot and refilled everyone's cup. "See, I can be useful."

The family chuckled.

"Thank you, again," Nick said. "But there is one area that seems to be bothering me. A major dangling end left untied. That is, who is behind all this? Goulet could not possibly put this together by himself. Who and why did they want him to be president? Also, what the hell is happening at that location, the place the mechanical, err, drone went to?"

All eyes focused on Brooke.

"Actually, Dad, I was saving that for last. I haven't had the opportunity to share the latest with anyone but Rick. So, this is the latest. Buck and I have been working closely the last couple of weeks."

Rick shifted his weight and chewed his lower lip, then said, "Our focus has been keeping an eye on the building to see if any of the bad guys show up. No one has come close to the building, but there are a couple of vehicles that have cruised by now and then, obviously checking out the area. They never stop, but just seem to be interested. The vehicles are late model and don't appear to fit in to the run-down surroundings. We checked out the plates, but they came up as stolen. So, no help there."

After making sure everyone was still following the train of thought, Rick continued. "Every now and then skaters come by and taunt what they think are homeless people. Occasionally we get some ruffians panhandling for cigarettes or booze. Nothing significant. Except once a cop, well, we think it might have been a cop, came by and harassed our people and told them to move on. Our guys paid him lip service. He left and the team remained in place."

Nick asked, "As anyone been inside? The team?"

"Yesterday," Rick said. "Sorry, Brooke, this is your—"

She said, "Our biggest concern has been some sort of alarms or surveillance on the building. Every evening our people have been poking around the exterior. The first thing we established by monitoring the electric meter on the side of the building . . . Easy to do, just affixed our own device so we monitor and analyze remotely. The meter runs consistently and does not fluctuate much. Something is drawing on it. The load is certainly more than should pull in an abandoned building. Because we haven't seen inside, and the electric use is consistent, we suspect there may be appliances such as a refrigerator or a HVAC system. Nevertheless, electricity is powering some sort of equipment."

"We have debated all along," Rocky said, "whether or not we should just enter the building. But because we don't know who may be watching, we didn't want to tip them off and lose an opportunity to catch those involved red-handed. It's been almost two weeks. It is time to act."

"Have you determined who owns the building?" the president asked.

"Yes, well, not exactly," Brooke said. "It is owned by an offshore company. We are digging into exactly who owns the corporation. So far all we get are dead ends."

Rick said, "Offshore entities are very tight lipped. They respond best when interrogated by the US government. But we aren't in a position to ask the State Department, CIA, the FBI, or Justice to assist. We can't risk compromising our investigation. Layers and layers of ownership and secrecy have slowed us down. But eventually, we will get to the real owners."

The president nodded. "Brooke, honey, keep going."

"Rick has given our team access to all of Chambers Enterprise's best surveillance detection equipment. We've employed it in every way imaginable. Mostly at night and in inclement weather, so as to obscure visibility. You'd be impressed. These guys, the people on the team, can be real ninjas. They covered every inch of the building's exterior, top to bottom. We assume that physical movement and sound are monitored from inside the building. Maybe not, but we aren't taking any chances.

"Over a twelve-hour period, a small hole was drilled into the side of the wood building. The drilling had to be undetectable, that is why it took so long. Then a cable was inserted through the hole and into the structure. This cable is unlike anything we have ever seen."

Rick chuckled. "Not so. Chambers Enterprise's surveillance R&D department has been developing it for years. This item will go into full production next month."

"The entire length of the cable sees and videos everything around it," Brooke said. "It is also night-vision capable. Objects do not have to emit heat to be seen. And the resolution is uncanny. When you look at the videos and pictures, it's like they were taken in full daylight." She paused, shaking her head, then said, "I was dumfounded to learn it also has stealth capabilities."

Rick smiled broadly, as if congratulating himself.

The president leaned back in his chair and interlaced his fingers behind his head. "This is truly absolutely amazing. I am so impressed with what has been done, but could we move it along just a little faster?"

Rocky said, "What have you surmised or found from your omni-visual snaking cable?"

"Nobody is home," Rick said.

Rocky snorted a laugh.

The president sat up and smiled. "Got it. But what's in the building? Forgive me, but I'm getting a little tired."

"I'll keep it brief, Dad," Brooke said. "First of all, it is one large open space. No walls. The place is definitely an operations center, containing everything you can imagine. Computers, modems, satellite communications equipment, a generator, living accommodations for at least a half dozen people and maybe a week's worth of food and water. Everything in perfect order. And to top it all off, we were able to snake the cable up into the attic and locate where the MF had nested and find Cuckoo still there."

"Awesome! Well done! And worth the wait!" the president said.

"Thank you, kids," Rocky said.

"What's next?" the president asked.

"We are currently using the snake to help us figure out how to get into the building undetected. Buck said they have analyzed the alarm and video systems and should be able to override them any day now."

The president stood up and made his way to his wheelchair. Rocky rose and followed Nick. "Thank you. See you tomorrow."

"Good night you two," Brooke said.

"Love you both," Rick said. He turned and smiled at his sister, "You too, Brooke."

Brooke grinned.

"Love you more," Rocky and Nick said as they left the room.

CHAPTER 13

Goulet left his office in the Executive Building as he did almost every day and crossed the street onto the National Mall. The towering Washington Monument loomed overhead. He looked down the mall to the right and admired the Lincoln Memorial and then to the left he viewed the Capitol Building atop Capitol Hill.

His Secret Service entourage followed behind out of ear shot as he had instructed. The vice president dressed in running attire set out on his customary power walk. He soon withdrew a burner phone from a zippered pocket and punched in a number.

Brooke and Buck, wearing headphones sat at the oversized workstation in Buck's office.

"This should be interesting," Buck said.

"I certainly hope so," Brooke replied.

They stayed silent as they eavesdropped on Goulet's conversation.

"This is number two. I've been trying to get hold of you for days. We've got a problem. Or maybe it's just me. I need some answers."

There was silence on the line.

Brooke said in an anxious voice, "I can't hear anything, only garbage, on the other end."

Buck surmised, "Obviously encrypted. I was afraid of that. We're lucky our device hears Goulet."

"Even half of any conversation is better than nothing," Brooke said.

Buck nodded.

Goulet's voice started again. "First of all, my home was broken into."

Garble.

"What do you mean you heard? What did you hear?"

Garble.

"That's bad, no one else knows about it. I didn't report it. Yes, my son's room was turned upside down. Nothing of mine or the wife's was touched."

Garble.

"I don't know exactly why. You may be right, it could be drugs, but nonetheless it makes no sense that someone was able to get into the residence. Something is definitely up. I think it may be some sort of sleight of hand. That is why I called. I found out something that concerns me. It may impact our agreement. Our deal."

Garble.

"Hey, I'm the one that has the problem here. Don't go telling me what to do. I gotta live with whatever is going on here."

Garble.

"You're damn right we need to close this down. It should have been closed down when you didn't fulfill your end of the bargain!"

Garble.

"You were supposed to take out the target! There's nothing else we can do. You fucked it up!"

Brooke and Buck both sat back in their chairs, mouths agape.

"I'm the one standing here with my pants down. I have no idea if they've figured anything out or if they're coming after me. I've got something to discuss."

Garble.

"I don't know anything about the location. I sure as hell can't go anywhere near it. Aren't you keeping an eye on it? Isn't it dismantled?"

Garble.

"Sounds like you guys fucked that up too. And no, there is nothing I can do about it here. What would you expect me to do, nuke it? That's your job. You said you would take care of everything. That was a load of bullshit. Now, something else. I checked on the items you gave me as part of my compensation. I was screwed. Half the stash are fakes! I got fucked!"

Garble.

"What do you mean you don't know anything about it? They came from you! Besides a handful of the stones are missing. I don't know where they are. I had a precise inventory; just trusted you and never really verified authenticity. Never should have trusted any of you. It's either you or those Dubai guys. I wonder who else they screwed. Better inspect your own inventory."

Brooke and Buck waited during an extended garbled period.

"For Christ's sake, why do you think I'm going to do anything stupid. Again, I'm the one that has everything to lose. As far as

I'm concerned, it's done, closed down. My biggest concern is the break-in. I can't get anyone involved. Who knows what that could lead to."

Garble.

"I want the real thing not the fakes. I need you to make it right. Most importantly, close down the location."

Garble.

"Don't give me that. When you were in charge, things went bad. Now, I'm telling you and your international cabal to fix this!"

The call ended.

Brooke said, "That is one hell of a lot of information, even if we only heard half the conversation."

"We have him dead to rights," Buck said. "The question now is, what do we do with this information? This is high treason and conspiracy to commit murder and a host of other crimes."

"Are you surprised?" Brooke asked.

"Not really, but like you said, where do we go next?"

"I suggest we meet with my dad, the president dad, and get his advice."

"Yeah, well, he's on the Hill and when he gets back will be exhausted. We don't want him overtired when we present this to him. It's a lot to take in."

"He's stronger than you think," Brooke said. "We need to speak with him as soon as possible. Let's share it with Rick and Dad first."

Buck took her hand in his. "Agreed."

Brooke smiled and squeezed his hand. "Thank you for everything, Buck. I truly appreciate what you are doing for my family."

"I'm doing it for you and my country as much as anything."

Brooke blushed.

"Hey," Buck said, "there is something else I wanted to ask you. Let's run down to the mess, get something to eat and bring it back here so we can chat."

"Sure, while we do that, I'll reach out to the guys to ask them to meet us here in an hour."

Buck leaned over and kissed Brooke. "Sounds perfect."

CHAPTER 14

As the motorcade departed the Capitol Building and headed down Pennsylvania Avenue to the White House, the president said, "It feels odd not only riding in the Beast but having a wagon train of vehicles in front and in back. Did you know that one of the code names for this armored behemoth is *Stagecoach*? It weighs 22,000 pounds."

"Mr. President," Trish said, "you certainly sound like a typical man. It's always all about cars with you men if you don't mind me saying. But right now, talking about cars sure beats what we should be discussing."

Nick said, "Did you know that these windows are five inches thick? That it's got run-flat tires? It also is equipped with weapons, tear gas cannisters, grenade launchers, even a supply of my blood type?"

"Gee. Mr. President, isn't that grand!" The chief of staff grinned and shook her head.

The president slapped his knee. "Yep, you're safe with me when we're in the Beast!"

"It looks like we are making progress on the Hill," Trish said, changing the topic and tacking back to business.

"That's the feeling I'm getting. Other than being wheeled around, I don't believe I showed any physical or mental impairment. Thank you so much for scheduling breaks during the meetings. I needed that. The ten-minute rest and our debriefs between sessions helped a lot. That may have appeared to some as my being tired, but it is what it is."

"I hope you are right, Mr. President. The leadership agreeing to not make a decision either way until you meet with the undecided members works in our favor." She paused. "The vote, by law must be taken in three days. The next two days are going to be a grind, sir."

"I know. Early to bed tonight. Let's not schedule anything else over the next few days."

∞

Buck and Brooke had returned to the East Wing with their meal and sat together at a table.

"This is one of the best perks working in the White House," Buck said, digging into his oversized Salade Niçoise. "It's like you can get anything at any time of day. And you know me, I'm a big eater."

"Yes, you are a big boy, and you work twenty-four hours a day." Brooke smiled, then dug into her salad.

Buck's cheeks flushed. He forked a large portion of the salad and shoved it into his mouth.

He chewed slowly, appearing to be contemplating what he would say next.

"What is it that you wanted to speak to me about, big eater?" Brooke asked.

His eyes sparkled above a toothy grin.

"Well, come on. Out with it. Salade Niçoise got your tongue?"

He reached across the small worktable and removed her fork from her hand and placed it on her plate. He then took both hands in his. "Brooke, I don't know if this is unprofessional or not, but I wanted you to know that I like you a lot. I have been doing my best to keep it cool, but after thinking about it and speaking to someone I value as a good friend, I decided to get it out there."

Expressionless, Brooke stared at Buck.

Wearing a quizzical look, he asked, "Am I wrong about this? Do you like me at least a little?"

"Wow, you've caught me by surprise. Yes, I do find you attractive."

"Attractive? Is that all?"

"I find you interesting.

"Just interesting?"

"Well, actually," Brooke said, "kinda hot too." Sporting a flat grin and wide-eyed, she said, "Really hot!"

"Thank God! I was nervous there for a minute." With a dramatic swipe of his brow he said, "Whew!" He smiled, blew a kiss, released her hand and returned to his salad.

"But you're not going to be playing patty-cake with both me and my brother! Got it?"

Buck spat out his mouthful of food all over the table and onto Brooke's blouse.

∞

Buck was cleaning up the mess on the table when Rick entered the office. "Where's sis? She said you were going to have lunch together before our meeting." He looked down at the splattered table. He chuckled. "Did you guys have a food fight?"

"Not exactly. She went to change her clothes. I had a mouth full of food and she came out with some crack and caught me off-guard. And as you can see, my food shot out all over the table. Oh, and onto her. Damn that was a good salad. C'est la vie."

Buck hid his grin and kept cleaning up.

"Yeah, she used to pull that stunt with me when we were kids. I'd have too much food in my mouth, and she would come up with some real off-the-wall shit and I'd spew it everywhere. The last time that happened I purposely aimed it at her. God! It was awesome! She didn't try that again."

Without missing a beat, Buck said, while wiping the floor, "She asked about you and me."

"Shut up! No fucking way!"

"Yep, apparently, you haven't been fooling anyone."

"Christ! What did you say?"

Buck gestured to the food lying about. "You see it here. That is as far as it went. She simply looked at the table, her clothes, used her serviette to wipe her mouth, rose out of her chair, brushed off the food with her napkin, placed it on her plate, and said, 'I have to go change.' I suppose she will return brandishing a new outfit shortly."

"Hell, that sounds like more drama than we could have seen in any drag bar."

"It was something else. Not so sure where to go from here."

"What do you mean, Buck ole' boy?"

"I had just told her that I liked her. She indicated she had an interest in me, then hit me with 'what about you and my brother.'"

"That is one for the ages. She must be really proud of herself. Buck, it was you who relegated us to friends with benefits. At least until you make up your mind. I won't be available forever. I certainly won't be pining away for you. You? Me? I'm out to make more friends. You can work your thing out with my sister." He paused and picked up a piece of carrot off of a plate; and before chomping down on it said, "Be careful not to put too much food in your mouth when you are eating anywhere near Brooke. She can be very calculating."

Rick stepped over and placed a quick peck on Buck's cheek.

Buck said, "Me and you? Are you over us?"

Rocky, who had been listening at the door unseen, stepped away and headed back down the hall. He decided to give Rick and Buck time to move forward with their conversation. He walked toward the West Wing.

He thought to himself, *this is an interesting development. Known it for a while now. Guess I tried to avoid thinking about it. Hm, wonder how that, rather those relationships will work out. Gotta stay out of it. So sorry for all involved. It won't be easy. Rick is great at internalizing. Always has been. He's hurting. If Buck doesn't see it, that's bad. No doubt there is a volcano bubbling up inside Rick. Hope he controls it.*

I wish he had come to me. Quite the family dynamic. Crap. Maybe I should have gone to Rick when I initially suspected, when I knew for sure. I sure could have used supportive family when I was his age—

Trish Smart ran into Rocky just outside her office door.

"Hello, General. How are you? Looking for me?"

"Not really, but uh, how did things go on the Hill?"

"Pretty well, all things considered. Do you have a moment?"

"Sure."

"Thank you, let's go into my office," she said, gesturing toward her door.

They settled themselves at a work table nestled in the corner.

Trish said, "The leadership indicated they would be openminded and said they would hold off taking the floor votes until the president had time to meet with individual members."

"That will certainly take some effort on my husband's part. As you and Nick have, I'm sure, discussed, there are a number within our party that haven't fully committed. We also need members on the Democrat side to go along to ensure we win a mandate. Would hate for Nick to be a lame duck president."

"Yes, General, that is why I asked to see you."

Rocky's head flinched back slightly.

"You see, General, the president is exhausted and needs to conserve his strength. He is resting now."

"Really? Not surprised, but he looked pretty good when he left this morning. But I can only imagine the toll it has taken." Rising, he said, "Maybe I should go check on him."

"Again, sir, which is why I asked to speak with you. He expressed his wish that he is not disturbed this evening."

"By anyone?"

"Anyone, sir. I hope you understand."

"Hm. I guess that puts me in the guest room tonight."

"I suppose it does, General."

"No problem, at least it's for health reasons and not a disagreement."

"I guess everyone regardless of sexual orientation goes through that," Trish said.

Rocky said in a flamboyant manner, "I guess so, Surprise!"

He stood and heading out the door, he turned serious. "Time to macho it up, gotta get to a family meeting. One that was planned to bring him up to date on the investigation."

"Would you like me to attend that meeting on the president's behalf?"

Rocky thought for a moment. "I don't think that would be a good idea. Some of what we need to discuss is of a nature that would conflict with your responsibilities as his chief of staff. Frankly, you may need plausible deniability at some point. Things are evolving rapidly, and it's best we not risk putting you in a compromising position."

"I understand, thank you. Oh, and General, the president has asked Gene Smithers to meet with him and accompany him to the Hill tomorrow. You may want to join them for that meeting prior to their leaving for the Hill tomorrow morning."

The dumbstruck look on Rocky's face signaled surprise and concern.

"Excuse me." Rocky took out his phone and texted Rick that he would be a few minutes late to the meeting. "Why Gene?"

"The president feels that his political acumen and history with their previous working together might prove useful. He has worked members before on the president's behalf, as you know, when the president was in the Senate."

"I can see that," Rocky said. He put his hand in his pocket and took a turn around the office. "Do you think that he might put off some of the more conservative members with him being transgender?"

Trish looked at Rocky, then thought for a moment as she turned toward the window. Without facing Rocky, she said, "I hope that sort of mindset is in the past."

"Trish, it will never completely be in the past. Even giving people the benefit of the doubt, unintended bias and all that. You know it will always be there in some form. It's kind of like living with alcoholism or drug addiction. Not sure transphobia will ever go away. It has to be fought day after day. Only brave souls and their continued commitment to making it right will make it go away, if it ever does."

She turned from the window and faced Rocky. Her face fell, her eyes pooled.

Rocky stood resolute, until a wave of self-consciousness swept over him.

She wiped her eyes. "We need to pull out all the stops. Do whatever we can to get every single vote. We need Gene."

"I'm certainly not against it," Rocky said searching for a way to flee his previous comments. "Gene is a dear friend of mine. It was Sheila and I that convinced Nick to hire him in the first place, years ago. We go way back to when I was advocating for Human Rights before Nick eventually came out. This whole thing gives rise to roiling emotions and stokes the memories of many ugly events."

"Yes, it does," Trish said.

Rocky exhaled. "I am happy to embrace whatever you and Nick decide to do. Gene is indeed qualified and has been a valuable and an effective asset."

"Thank you, General. I think your participating in their meeting will bolster Gene's and the president's confidence moving forward."

"Excellent. Count me in. Now I must head to the East Wing."

CHAPTER 15

As Rocky passed by the Cabinet Room he ran into Brooke. "Hi, Brooke! Headed to the meeting? You've changed clothes. You look lovely as ever."

"Very funny, Dad. Thank you."

Rocky smiled and put his hand around her shoulders.

She looked at Rocky. "You know why, what happened. I can tell. Don't you?"

He drew her toward the Cabinet Room. "Let's go in here for a minute."

She cocked her head. "Why? They're waiting for us."

"Just for a moment, dear. Humor me, please."

Rocky pulled the door shut. "Yes, I accidentally heard Buck replay the events for Rick."

"So, you overheard they have a past and a present."

"Yes, I did."

"Were you surprised, Dad? Did you know Rick is gay and that Buck and he are an item?

"I have suspected your brother is gay for some time."

"Half-brother."

"Whatever, Brooke, that's a different matter, and we can discuss that at some length whenever you would like."

"How did you know he was gay?"

"I have suspected it since he was in high school. I don't think others did. Then, when he came under the protection of Chambers Industries security, well things happened. I saw the reports of where he went, and who he spent his time with. It was obvious."

"Did that bother you, Dad?"

"Certainly not that he was gay, but as any parent I was concerned for the challenges that he would face because of the sexuality which he was born with."

"Does my father know?"

"Yes."

"Is he cool with it. I mean he should be."

"Totally. We both are. I hope you are as well."

"Of course, I am. I just don't like the idea that it could interfere with how I feel about Buck and the way I think he feels about me. Buck, the bisexual thing, is troubling, it complicates things."

Rocky placed his hand on her forearm.

"Brooke, I understand, as best I can. You will remember there was a similar situation that existed between your mother, father, and me."

"Unlike my mother, this is not okay by me. It apparently worked for you guys. But it's not the way I want to live."

"That is your decision. I respect it. Set your boundaries and stick to them. It's much healthier that way."

Brooke said, "I'm frankly a bit overwhelmed over this and everything else that is going on around here. I don't need to be distracted. Too much is at stake."

"That's true. So how do you think you should handle it?"

"Stay the course, the investigation. Then after this is all over, spend some time thinking about things and if I am interested in seeing if it can work, I'll talk to Buck."

"Sounds like an excellent plan," Rick said, reassuringly. "I am proud of the way you are handling things. You've had a lot on your shoulders with your father's campaign, being elected, the transition to the White House, the assassination attempt, the investigation, and now learning your possible love interest is involved with your brother. A brother you didn't know was gay."

Brooke teared. "I think I knew, Dad. We're very close, twins, sort of. I knew. I just didn't want it to be true. I hope I haven't failed him.

Rocky pulled her close and placed his arms around her. "If he needed or wanted your help, remember you have always supported each other. He would have reached out. Not everyone is the same. And I am sure you would have been there for him. Don't beat yourself up, honey. You have been a wonderful and supportive sister. He loves you just the way you are."

"Okay, thanks, Dad." She pulled a tissue from a nearby box. "And by the way, I have always thought and will continue to embrace you as my father."

"Thank you, darling. That means everything to me."

Brooke wiped her eyes. Rocky took her hand and the two walked towards the East Wing.

∞

It appeared to everyone present that recent personal events had been tucked away and would not interfere with the topic at hand.

"A lot has happened since our last meeting," Buck said. "Brooke and I listened in to a conversation Goulet had with at least one of his fellow conspirators this afternoon."

Rocky and Rick sat up straight and leaned forward.

Buck and Brooke took turns replaying the part of the conversation they had overheard.

Rocky and Rick were at a loss of words and said nothing as the vice president's conversation was recounted, alternately staring at Brooke and Buck as they spoke.

When they had completed their story, the four remained silent for several minutes, no one moving, each in their own thoughts.

Rocky broke the silence. "We have a lot to think about."

"Dad should be in on this right now," Brooke said.

"I agree," Rick said.

Buck nodded.

Rocky said, "Nick needs to conserve his energy, emotions, and thoughts for his work on the Hill. Let's finish our discussion and figure out if and how we can brief him."

"Are you kidding, Dad?" Rick asked.

"No, I am not."

Rocky went on to share the recent conversation he had had with Trish.

Again, silence filled the room for several minutes.

"I suppose there is no real immediate need to get him involved, even though all of us would really like him to know," Rick
said. "It's international, and that certainly makes it high treason."

Everyone shifted their weight.

"Unless something happens that absolutely requires his attention, I vote we wait," Rocky said.

"Okay," Rick nodded.

"I'm okay with it, but don't like it," Brooke said.

"Whatever the family says," Buck agreed.

There was a sharp rap on the door and in walked Sandy Yoe.

Everyone turned toward her.

"I beg your pardon, but this is urgent," Sandy said.

Rocky's brow furrowed. "What is it?" He turned and faced
Rick and Buck. "She works with you both, right?"

"Yes, she works with Buck," Rick said.

Rocky motioned her in. "Please come. And close the door behind you if you don't mind."

"Thank you, General."

Buck grabbed a chair and made a place for her.

Sandy took her seat and folded her hands on the table.

"I apologize for the intrusion, but this is vitally important."

"Not to worry Sandy" Buck said. "I am sure you wouldn't have
come if it wasn't. Please, tell us what you've got."

Sandy gave an uncomfortable smile. "Thank you."

She inhaled, her voice and demeanor more confident, as she
said, "We're in MF's lair!"

"We're what?" Rick said, leaning forward.

"Rick and Buck gave the go ahead yesterday to go inside as soon as we could come up with a strategy that would not compromise our team and its purpose. We worked fast."

"That was fast," Buck said. "How was it executed?"

"After surveilling the interior and taking inventory of its contents, our team entered the rear of the building under the cover of darkness. They set a fire in a corner of the building where the generator was situated. The propellants used to start the fire targeted the electrical control box on the generator which was placed against an exterior wall. The idea was to disable the generator before it could engage when we cut the power. A vacuum hose pulled the smoke from around the control box and out of the building so that the smoke detectors wouldn't go off."

Brooke asked, "Didn't the noise from the hose sucking the smoke set off the alarms?"

"The suction motor was well away from the building. We calculated that the sound of the air and smoke being pulled out of the building would not create enough noise to set off the alarm. Fortunately, we were right. As soon as the generator was disabled, we cut the power."

Rocky said, "Wouldn't the power drop alert the alarm system? Surely it has its own power supply. My guess is they would have had some sort of defenses, booby traps, in place to blow up the structure, or something like that if the alarms were compromised."

"General, sir," Sandy said, "we had that same concern. Fortunately, the system, we discovered, when reconnoitering the building, did not have that capability, and we couldn't find anything that indicated the location was wired to self-destruct." She paused for a moment. "Nevertheless, the team members were well away from the building."

Rick said, "Apparently when they thought the coast was clear, they entered the building."

"That's correct," Sandy said. "The first thing the team did was gather up the computer equipment and communications devices and remove them from the site. All the while the fire was growing in intensity. The team had to use protective clothing and oxygen as the structure went up like a tinder box."

"Was anyone injured during the operation?" Rick asked.

"A couple of minor things, scrapes, nothing serious," Sandy said.

"When did the fire trucks arrive?" Buck asked. "Had the mission been completed?"

Sandy said, "If I may, let me take this play by play. The equipment removed from the location was replaced with like equipment. The team vacated the premises and let it and the faux homeless encampment next to the structure burn to the ground. The firemen arrived minutes after the team had vacated the area."

"What about onlookers, witnesses?" Rick asked.

"Since we entered and exited from the back of the building and used the cover afforded by the wooded area to conceal our activities, we feel reasonably sure no one saw anything."

Rocky asked, "What about other homeless in the surrounding area and the woods?"

"They had been chased away days ago by our homeless look-alikes. Unfortunately, they had to rough up a couple of the more belligerent ones to get them to move on."

"Sounds a little messy," Brooke said.

"Not so much," Buck said. "People can be territorial. Particularly in that community, the homeless community."

Brooke asked, "What's happening there now? Did you replace the equipment to make sure no one familiar with what was inside would be suspicious?

Sandy answered, "The fire department is extinguishing the hot spots. There really isn't much there but ashes, large burned wooden beams and half disintegrated metal shells. The area has been cordoned off."

"Did your surveillance team see any suspicious looky-loos?" Rocky asked.

"Yes, they think they did. The two vehicles that cruised the neighborhood days earlier drove by separately, a half hour apart. They couldn't get close to the building because the fire equipment was in the way. One of our guys said people inside the vehicles were taking pictures. They drove off. We still have people in place to keep an eye on the surroundings."

"Did anyone follow the vehicles?" Rocky asked.

"Yes, both of them. But we lost them in traffic."

Rocky grimaced. "That's not good. Bad break. I'm surprised we didn't have alternative ways to tail them in place."

Sandy did not respond.

"One more thing," Rocky asked. "Where is the equipment removed from the building, and what arrangements have been made to have our people clean up the site after the fire department leaves? Before someone else gets to it."

"The equipment is on a Chambers Enterprises corporate jet on its way to your analytics lab," Sandy said.

"Excellent!" Rocky said. "Good work. And the clean up?"

"We are going to continue to surveil the area," Sandy said, "and we'll use a third party to clean up the site after the fire department and the police have completed the investigation."

"But the owners and their insurance company usually handle that sort of thing," Brooke said. "How will we get around that?"

Rocky said, "Rick, Chambers Enterprises has people in place with the insurance companies and fire and restoration companies, as well as hazmat companies. Is that right, son?"

Rick nodded. "Yes. I'll take care of it. Consider it done."

"That's all I have," Sandy said.

Rocky stood and stretched out his hand. "Thank you so much. You were right in immediately bringing this to our attention. Please let the others know that their hard work, diligence, and success is greatly appreciated."

Sandy rose, shook Rocky's hand and said, "You are welcome. And I will pass on your remarks."

She turned and left the room closing the door behind her.

Rocky addressed the group. "It will be very interesting to see what comes out of those computers that are winging their way to Boston. In the meantime, we need to keep a very close eye on Goulet. His band of conspirators must be apoplectic. That means things could get very dangerous. No man or animal is more unpredictable and relentless than when feeling backed into a corner."

"Can you imagine," Rick remarked, "what is going through Goulet's mind about now. I mean, if he even knows about it."

Buck's phone chirped. He looked down at the phone and then at Brooke. "We gotta go, Goulet is headed out to the Mall."

Rocky nodded. "Go for it."

CHAPTER 16

"This can't be a social call," Trish said as Merrill Spaulding and Dr. Parsons entered her office and shut the door. "You never arrive unannounced."

"Exactly, Chief."

"Merrill, it's good to see you. I appreciate all you have been doing to keep us apprised of the vice president's goings on. And ladies, please call me, Trish."

Merrill nodded.

"Sure. No problem, my pleasure," Dr. Parson's said. "We've been following some chatter on the international scene. The vice president's name has shown up a couple of times. These aren't diplomats talking, it's corporate types and even a blurb or two out of Dubai. We haven't been able to piece anything together, but someone or several people are agitated."

"How are you getting only part of the conversation?" Trish asked. "I thought our assets can pretty much untangle most of the encryption codes out there."

"It's getting harder and harder to do that. In fact, my guess is we'd not know anything if a couple of those calls hadn't got a bit careless. Our people are working on it. We may learn more over the next few hours."

"So, what've we got so far?"

"Mostly words and phrases. Of course, mention of Goulet caught our attention. We feel it's not political, because the communications are short. Then Dubai came up alongside the mention of diamonds."

Trish sat up straight. "How? How did this happen?"

"NSA has been working overtime listening to domestic and international traffic following the assassination attempt. We have also been able to ascertain that these same words are being used in conversations amongst at least a half dozen multinational corporations. Again, there is no sign that any governments are involved."

"So, you think," Trish said, "the NSA, CIA, FBI, and like agencies are trying to figure this whole mess out? That we may have misjudged their commitment to getting answers?"

"Not at all, Trish," Dr. Parsons said. "Sometimes things slip out during briefings from someone who might be trying to stonewall their having missed something for which they might be held accountable. Remember, these are bastions of personal empire builders. They won't say a word if doing so does not serve their purposes and if they can't share something valuable that will aggrandize them and lead to expanding their power. If they aren't sure of what they've got and how they can control what happens, they keep it to themselves until they know they can profit from sharing the information. It's insidious and does not serve the nation well."

"That means we may not hear anything more about it."

"Precisely. That is why we wanted to see you," Merrill said.

"Okay, Merrill. It must be good, out with it," Trish said.

"Dr. Parsons and I have been trying to sort out what to do with the information, both from a scientific/intelligence perspective, her bailiwick, and from a political vantage point, my area of expertise."

Trish folded her arms. "That makes sense, please go on."

"We agree," Merrill said, nodding toward Dr. Parsons, who in turn returned the nod, "that we would like to take this information and turn it over to Buck Gerard and his team. They are the only ones I know we can trust and have the capability to dig deeper and perhaps learn something from those transmissions."

"Wow, I'm afraid that goes above my pay grade. I am not certain that the president or acting president can authorize that without NSA review."

"That's unfortunate, Trish," Merrill said.

"But not insurmountable." Trish walked over to a window and rested against the sill, facing Dr. Parsons and Merrill. "The vote happens day after tomorrow. The president is headed to the Hill to press the flesh with members. He'll be there the rest of today and return there tomorrow. In the meantime, we can start laying the groundwork for getting his permission after the vote. When he wins, and he will, of that I am certain, no problem. He signs off, making them available to Gerard. If he loses, what the hell. Congress thinks he's incapacitated. He didn't know what he was signing. It was a case of misjudgment. He can apologize later. In the meantime, we continue investigating."

"That's a bit bold, Trish," Merrill said.

She smiled. "I've never been accused of being timid. In the meantime, get me those transmissions and anything else you think the Chambers people can use. I'll take care of the rest."

They said their goodbyes and set about completing their tasks.

Trish returned to her desk and texted Rocky.

Ten minutes later he entered her office.

"Hey, Trish, what's up? I'm meeting with the president and Gene in a couple of minutes."

"Thanks for responding so quickly, General."

Rocky nodded.

Trish briefed Rocky on her meeting with Spaulding and Parsons. When she had finished, she asked, "What are your thoughts, General?"

"As soon as Dr. Parsons sends you whatever they have, we pass them over to Buck. I'll brief him ahead of time. Also, I suggest you have two documents drawn up. One dated today and the other dated three days from now releasing them to Chambers Enterprises for analysis and asking them to do their own investigation on like traffic."

"You do know, General, these documents most likely have no basis in law and national security?"

Rocky grinned. "And your point?"

"I thought as much. I'll take care of it."

"Oh, and thank Dr. Parsons and Ms. Spaulding on behalf of the president."

∞

That afternoon Brooke and Buck found themselves sitting once again at the computer center in the East Wing, headsets on, waiting for the vice president to start his power walk and pull out his burner phone.

"I can't imagine this conversation being as dramatic and revealing as the last one we heard," Buck said.

"I can. Look what's just transpired. He's an hour early for his sojourn on the mall. I give you two to one it'll be big. Someone must have signaled him to call. An hour earlier than normal and Dr. Parson's just texted. It happens that he abruptly left a staff meeting after taking a call mid-meeting. Let's buckle up!"

Buck put his headset down and laid it on the console and looked at Brooke. "When are we going to pick up where we left off?"

"You mean where you threw up all over me?"

"You made me do it!"

"I made you do it? It was a simple question. I said— Wait, he's on the line!"

Buck grabbed his headset and popped it on his head.

"What's the emergency, I had to run out of a very important meeting. The diamonds? Is Dubai pushing fakes?"

Garble.

"What are you saying? What? Location? I don't know anything about that. I have no idea what you're talking about."

Garble.

"What do you expect me to do. Call the DC police department about some fire I heard about? Hey, the place burned down. It's done, right? I can't risk getting caught up in more shit.

Remember my house getting broken into? Something's really fucked up here."

Garble.

"Your guys are going to have to take care of anything that goes on around here. My influence will be useless to all of us if anyone even thinks somehow I am involved in anything related to anything with you guys. Christ! This is out of control. All this shit has taken me away from getting the votes we need to can the president."

Brooke slammed the console with her fist.

Buck patted her shoulder. "Sorry you had to hear that, Brooke."

"I'm not," Brooke said. "Now we've got him dead to rights."

"Only if this tap is allowed in a court of law . . . you're the lawyer. Is it?"

Brooke shrugged.

Garble.

"I'd really like to help with this, but it's not gonna happen. I am the fucking acting president of the United States! If shit hits the fan, me, you, your corporations, and everything else are down the toilet. Fix it. I can't!"

Garble.

"Okay, I'll bring what I got, the fake ones only. You guys deal with it."

Garble.

The line went dead.

Buck and Brooke removed their headsets.

"Sounds like they're coming unraveled," Buck said.

"In a big way. I hope things don't take a nose dive so fast we are unable to figure out who is out there working with Goulet. We need to rethink what we are doing. Better have this discussion with my dad, ASAP."

"I agree, but maybe not until he gets done working the Hill."

"That's for sure, I'll update Dad, er Rocky, that dad, and Rick."

"Okay," Buck said and turned his chair toward Brooke and settled back. "Now, what were we talking about before we were so rudely interrupted?"

She got up from her chair when Buck reached over and took her hand. "Please, take a seat, give me a moment."

Brooke pressed her lips, looked past him. "All right, just a moment or two, that's all." She returned to her chair.

"I know it is kind of confusing and I'm sorry you are in this position," he murmured.

"What position? I haven't committed to anything."

Still holding her hand, he said, "But you were thinking about it, right?"

"Maybe, but not now."

Buck bit his lips. "I never had the opportunity to answer your question."

"I know the answer. You and my brother are involved. It's as simple as that."

"That doesn't mean things can't change," Buck said looking deep into her eyes.

Brooke pulled her hand back and folded her arms. "There is no way I am going to live a life like that. It's too hard. I'd always be second-guessing. Wondering if you were with some guy. I won't live like that. And besides, you and I, well, we're just getting to know one another. It's time to break whatever it was off and move on."

"I don't want that to happen, Brooke," Buck said.

"Of course, you don't. You want to have your cake and eat it too, as the saying goes." She paused. "By the way, which one of us, Rick or me, is the icing?"

"That's not fair."

"Perhaps it's not, but that's what it looks like to me. When was the last time you hooked up with my brother?"

"Come on, Brooke!"

She glared and him. "Sorry, not sorry."

They sat saying nothing for a few minutes.

"I like you, Buck, but I will absolutely not share you with anyone, male or female."

"I get that," he said.

"Buck, there is so much chaos around us right now. Neither of us really know how we feel. Let's just cool it. Keep it professional."

Buck gave a slight nod. "Friends?"

"If you don't push it and make it uncomfortable for me, or Rick." Brooke stood, pushed her chair under the console, turned, and walked out the door.

CHAPTER 17

The next morning Rocky stood at the bottom of the stairs leading to the residence.

"Hey, Rocky," Gene Smithers said, drawing him into a bear hug.

"So good to see you, my friend. It seems like forever, but's only been a little over three weeks since the inauguration."

"Yep. You and Nick and the kids have been on my mind a lot. The operator hasn't been putting through my calls. Must not know who I am. Dumb fucks."

"That'll change as of this meeting, Gene. So sorry."

"Good, can we use that elevator? This old body is allergic to stairs."

"Sorry about that, old man. Even I'm not allowed to use that elevator unless the president is on it."

"Damn."

"There are two elevators. Take the stairs or walk down the hall to another elevator."

"Closest elevator," Gene said.

"Closest elevator it is."

Rocky wrapped an arm around Gene's shoulders and walked him down the hall.

The men soon joined Nick in the residence kitchen. An aroma of eggs, sausage, and fresh baked biscuits wafted through the air.

"I'm starved, let's eat," Nick said when Rocky and Gene walked in.

"Didn't anyone every teach you how to dodge bullets, you dumb ass? Oops, I mean *your highness* or some such shit," Gene said, and stuck out his hand, "Hi ya, Nick, glad to see you up and about. I'm hungry too, time somebody fed this queen!"

They shook hands and embraced.

Gene grabbed the closest chair. "I knew you could cook. We've shared a hundred meals." He looked around the kitchen. "When are you going to finish cleaning up? This is the goddamn White House. You can't leave pots and pans lay'n around. This is the people's house, not your pig pen!"

Nick and Rocky burst into laughter.

"Just like old times, you old fat fuck," Nick said.

Holding his stomach with both hands, Gene said, "I'm not an old fat fuck. This here is a sign of prosperity and power! And from the looks of things, I'm going to get more of both eating this awesome grub. Honestly, you cook this?"

"No, chef did. I asked him to prepare it here so I could smell it cooking. Reminds me of Sunday mornings at home in Charlottesville with Rocky and the kids. Told him not to clean up. Didn't want him around so you could embarrass me."

"Smart thinking. I guess not everyone that gets elected and into the White House gets a case of the stupids."

Rocky and Nick, still standing, grinned and joined Gene at the table.

"Thanks, Gene, for agreeing to come on board and help us out," Rocky said.

"Yeah," Nick agreed. "Once again we need you to work your magic to get us out of another jam."

"That's what I'm here for, not just decoration, boys!"

"So, what do ya' think?" Rocky asked, placing a napkin in his lap.

"First of all, I want to make one thing clear. I don't want to get involved in whatever is going on regarding the assassination attempt. Let me say I'm sorry for what happened to you, but let's keep on topic. Doing what we need to do to get you reelected, so to speak. Can't believe we find ourselves in this spot. But what the hell, it gives me job security. Nevertheless, things don't look that bad. My folks tell me that the vice president seems to have gone to ground. My sources say he is holed up in his office. Except for these long power walks on the Mall talking." He wagged his finger at Rocky. "If you know, don't tell me, I don't need to be distracted. You either, Nick, err, Your Holiness, or Mr. President or whatever it is your sycophants call you around here."

"We're on it. Not to worry, Gene," Nick said quietly.

Gene shrugged and nodded his head. "I've been on the phone with some of the leadership and the malcontent members, Republicans and Democrats alike. I think we can do this thing. We just need to do some cajoling."

He pulled folded papers from inside his jacket and unfolded and placed them on the kitchen table. He picked up one of the pieces of paper. "This here page on the top lists those we have confirmed are on our side. On the face of it, you appear to have the votes. The problem is, if you don't want to be a lame duck, you need no less than the majority of both parties voting for you. It can't be a saved by a," Gene made air quotes, "couple of votes kinda thing. It must be an overwhelming mandate to have the support of the people and Congress. Hell, you're not even started, and you have a crisis. Christ!"

Nick reached over and took the second sheet from the stack.

After perusing it, he returned it to the pile.

"Those guys you just looked at, Mr. P, are the ones you need to see. I put the low hanging fruit on the top of the list. See these guys first. It'll warm you up for the tough sons-of-a-bitches."

"I can see that," Nick said.

"Now," Gene said, "What are you going to do about that wheelchair of yours?" He looked around the room. "I see the walker, where's the chair?"

"It's in the other room, at the ready," Rocky said.

"Well, get rid of it. Don't use it anymore. Terrible optics. When I see you in it, I want to vomit. Terrible optics. These guys on the Hill need to see some progress. That being you getting better, stronger. A miracle! You don't have the option FDR had keeping the press from photographing you in the chair. Gotta tough'n it up. You showing up at these guys' offices on the walker instead of the chair speaks volumes. Besides, ever notice how people make way for folks on walkers? It's weird. People in wheelchairs don't get as much courtesy as people busting their ass mov'n on walkers. You figure it out."

Rocky looking down, shook his head.

"Damnit! Don't do that, Rocky!" Gene said, wagging his finger. "Pump ole' Nick up. He can do it. He has to!"

"You're asking a lot, Gene," Rocky said.

"I am. But not more than is required. Not more than he can do."

Gene and Rocky looked at Nick.

"I'll give it a try, my best try. Got to," Nick said.

"We can take breaks during the day so you can recoup your strength, but no chair!"

"Any ideas on how to approach those sitting on the fence?" Rocky asked.

"Nick knows exactly what to do." Then Gene, still focused on Nick, "Right?"

Nick nodded.

Gene picked up the pages and turned them around so Nick and Rocky could read them. He pointed to the list. "On this side I have made a list of each member's hot buttons. Go in there, and after you've made nice, talk about things that interest them. Keep away from your agenda. Get them to talk about what they want. Everyone wants somethin'. Then ask them precisely how they and you can work together as a team to help them lasso their hearts desire. Of course, you will have to couch all this in politico speak, but you're no stranger to that. Promise them nothing but get them to commit to getting back to you with their answers. Then, before you leave, reminisce a little bit with them about how everyone worked together when you were their colleague in the Senate. You're known as a moderate and a deal maker. Use that to your advantage. Be upbeat. Give them a vision, their vision, making it sound like a team vision."

Rocky asked, "Do you think he can get out of there with their votes in hand? Ask them for their vote up front?"

"Hell no, Ricardo Jeffries-Chambers! God, it's obvious you're not the politico here. Go back to running your empire. Jeez."

Rocky scowled.

"OMG, Gene, go easy on him," Nick said.

Nick reached over and patted Rocky on the shoulder. "Don't listen to him, he's on a roll."

"When have I ever gone easy on you two dreamers."

"Never, obviously," Rocky said, not amused.

Gene said, "Do not ask for their vote. Walk out of there like you are best friends with these guys knowing they have your support, and you have theirs. Hell, you've just given the impression you have handed them their wish list on a silver platter. Promise nothing! Got it?"

"Got it!" Nick said.

"By the way, I ain't going in the members offices when you meet with them. They have to know that it's all you. You are the president and don't need support from anyone or anything other than that damn walker. And one more very important thing, don't mention Goulet. If they bring him up, say something positive about the schmuck and change the subject. Most of those folks don't care for him much or aren't all that comfortable with him. Hell, the Dems really have their doubts about him. But they can count on him to maintain the status quo. Can't say that about you. We campaigned on you wanting to shake things up. That's always popular outside the beltway but causes indigestion and panic inside. You won as a gay Republican. They're scared you'll mess things up. Transparency and draining the swamp is like the plague to them. You must make them think you are one of them. Remember? Promise the electorate everything and when elected, join your fellow politicos at the trough. That's what they want to believe. Make 'em believe it, be their security blanket."

Rocky and Nick exchanged hard glances then stared down at their uneaten breakfast.

"Cheer up, play the game." Gene smiled and dived into his breakfast. Between mouthfuls, he said, "But remember, they've seen Goulet oiling his way through the Senate and House office buildings erecting a case against you. They don't think much of his loyalty. Some smell a rat."

Nick and Rocky pushed their food around their plates, eating little.

Three mouthfuls later and sopping up the remaining food on the plate with a piece of toast, Gene popped the bread into his mouth and clapped his hands once. "Gentlemen, think about it. The guy is slippery. People see it. Deep down, I believe all of them would feel much better keeping you in the White House, particularly if you come across as a team player."

He pushed back his chair. "Now, let's go show 'em! You da' man!"

CHAPTER 18

The afternoon of the president's second consecutive day on the Hill, Rocky walked into Trish Smart's office. She sat reviewing a stack of papers and didn't notice him enter.

"You look focused and exhausted, Trish."

She jumped.

"Uh, oh, General." She rubbed the back of her neck. "Please, sit down," she said gesturing toward a chair.

Rocky took a seat opposite her desk while she arranged what appeared to be classified papers into a neat stack, then covered the pile with a thin binder.

She removed her glasses and rubbed her tired eyes. "So, how's it going? Anything from up on high, the Hill?"

"Yes, most of it's good news, according to Gene. I just got off the phone with him. Nick is a little ahead of schedule and may finish today's meetings early."

"I sure hope so," Trish said. "With those meetings and the press packed in the passages like canned tuna, I'm surprised he's able to navigate the walker. Should have used the chair. It's all over the major networks and social media, him walking the halls. Getting worldwide attention. He'll create a fad. People will be digging out walkers and using them whether or not they need 'em. Look out, Halloween!"

Rocky smiled and shook his head. "You may be right!" He steepled his hands under his chin. "Nick appears to have a good chance of winning most of the members over. One more day, and then the vote."

"Have you heard anything from the vice president, General?"

"Nothing directly. As you know he has basically absented himself from everyone; working in his office during the day and going straight to his residence every night."

She said, "After all, he is the acting president. There's a lot to do. I've been sending piles of work over two or three times a day. I've offered to help him with it, but he says he needs no one's help."

"At least he's not prowling around here trying to make himself at home in the Oval."

"Yeah."

"I thought he'd grab every opportunity to work with you! Surprised he didn't ask you to move into his office."

"Not really, we're not exactly buddy-buddy."

"Has he reached out?"

"No, he hasn't. Just the opposite. Unfortunately, there are a lot of time-sensitive items that are not getting done. He's even let the nominations he sent up to the Hill go unattended. He may be in his office, but I don't see much work getting done. Not the country's work, anyway."

Rocky shifted his weight and tapped his foot.

"What can I do for you, General? I know you didn't come in here to just chit chat."

"Uh, you're right. Um, we, rather Nick and you, obviously, need to be thinking about how to proceed whether or not Nick gets the votes. I suggest we assume he'll get his powers back and we can move forward." He paused. "But what will that look like? He'll be president and saddled with a turncoat vice president. At least that's how it appears."

"General, I've been thinking long and hard on that." She paused and removed a notepad from a desk drawer and took a moment to review what was written on it. "The first thing we need to do is have the president address the nation and let them know he is in the saddle attending to the people's priorities. He then needs to sit Goulet down and give him a list of to do's."

"Don't you think they need to clear a few things up, first?" Rocky asked.

"Yes, I suppose that is inevitable. We, rather the president and the vice president need to have that discussion," she said pondering the notepad. "But other things have a priority, such as the president placing personal phone calls to world leaders. Demonstrate leadership, leadership of the free—"

A rapid knock sounded on the door followed by Rick entering the office. "Sorry to barge in, but we just lost track of the vice president!"

"What do you mean?" Trish exclaimed.

"Vanished! He returned to the VP's residence and ten minutes later the Secret Service said he was nowhere to be found. Vanished!"

Trish stood. "Damn. We need to move fast and locate him. Maybe he's taking another one of his strolls. This could turn into a national crisis if word gets out, he's vamoosed. We're talking about the acting president of the United States disappearing! It will look to everyone like we're nothing more than a Barnum and Bailey act."

"Check the tunnel," Rocky said. "Get someone to get a visual on the exit site."

"It's been under surveillance ever since the break-in." Trish said, catching herself. "Rather the kid's search warrant."

"Good. I'll get back to the team in the East Wing and see what we can find." Rick left the office closing the door behind him.

Trish said, "I bet Director Hamilcar calls shortly to let us know they have eyes on him leaving the tunnel. It exits under Massachusetts Avenue and into Woodland-Normanstone Terrace Park."

The phone rang.

Trish gave Rocky an *I told you so look* and pressed a button on the phone console.

"Hello," Trish said.

"Director Hamilcar here, Chief. We have a problem."

"Yes, Director, it appears you do. Any eyes on the tunnel exit?"

"Yes, and he just exited. I'm watching him on screen. Looks like he is headed towards a grove of trees. He'll be out of sight any moment. Damn! He's gone. But not to worry we have eyes on him on the ground."

"Director, the first thing we need to do is ensure his safety."

"I know, ma'am, it's our fault if anything happens, regardless of what he is up to, including slipping away from his protection detail. We're on this. Either way, we'll have to grab hold of him and take him back to his residence ASAP."

"Not so fast, Director, I suggest you keep your distance for just a little while. He may lead us to something or someone." She paused, then said, "His safety is our number one priority. Use your judgment."

"Will do, Chief."

The phone line went dead.

Rocky folded his arms and sat back in the chair. "I sure would like to be perched somewhere close to whatever he is up to."

She said, "I hope we don't find ourselves explaining why something bad happened to him, especially since we have eyes on him."

There was another knock on the door.

"Yes," Trish said.

Buck walked in. "Sorry to disturb you, but there's been a development I thought your folks might want to be made aware of. I tried to reach Director Hamilcar, but he's not available."

Rocky and Trish said simultaneously, "What is it?"

"Goulet is going to make a drop. I think it's the faux or lab diamonds."

"What the fuck!" Trish said.

"Yeah, and he admitted everything to whoever he is talking to on the burner. He's in the middle of all of it. He is definitely part of the conspiracy to assassinate the president!"

Rocky's mouth gaped.

Trish's nostrils flared and eyes widened. "As soon as we find the son-of-a-bitch, we'll arrest the motherfucker!"

Rocky stood. "We can't, not yet!"

Both Trish and Buck stared at Rocky.

"The evidence we have will not stand up in court, probably won't be admissible. The warrant, the one searching his residence, might not stick. Couldn't trust NSA, the FBI, or anybody, so we have nothing. No federal agency support. Hamilcar's Secret Service is involved in this not-so-legal investigation. We need to bide our time. Get something that doesn't violate his constitutional rights."

"I sure as hell hope Hamilcar and his folks catch him in something soon, something that would hold up in court."

Trish brought Buck up to date on the vice president having used the tunnel to *run an errand*, unprotected.

"We have no idea what he is up to," Rocky said.

Buck said, "He's making a drop."

The phone beeped. Trish pressed a button.

"Hamilcar here again."

"Yes, Director."

"He's up to his old tricks. While he was walking through an open grassy area, talking on his phone, he suddenly looked up and tossed some sort of bag or something into the air. A bird, or rather a drone bird swept down and snatched the bag mid-air and flew off!"

"You're shitting me!" Rocky said.

Hamilcar said, "Um, uh, are we on speaker phone? Who's present there with you, ma'am?"

"Buck and the General. Sorry, should have told you. Buck had just told us he thinks the vice president was making a drop. Guess he was right."

"How would he know that? What kinda drop?"

"It's a long story, one you better now know about, Director," Trish said.

Both Rocky and Buck shook their heads.

"What was in the drop?" Hamilcar said.

Trish looked at Buck.

"Diamonds," Buck said.

"Diamonds? Why diamonds? Never mind," the director said, "I'm headed your way and expect to be brought up to date."

Rocky said, "How about giving us some time to round up the other players. Let's meet in the East Wing in two hours. Okay, Director? Trish? Buck?"

"Fine with me, see you in two hours," Hamilcar said. "Oh, and the vice president returned via the tunnel with no assistance from our men. I doubt he knows we were there."

"See you in a couple of hours, Director." Trish pressed the button terminating the call. She looked at the two men, "I have no idea how and where this is going, but we have just opened Pandora's giga-warehouse."

The president had returned from Capitol Hill and headed directly to the residence and asked that he not be disturbed.

Gene, having been told Rocky was in a meeting with the chief of staff, waited outside her office.

"God, Rocky," Gene said as he exited the chief of staff's office, "you look like you have been run over by a train. What's up?"

Buck, exiting just behind Rocky said, "See you in a few," and walked quickly away from Gene and Rocky.

"In a few," Rocky said.

Gene attentively watched Buck walk, around the corner and out of earshot and asked, "Who's that? He looks worse than you, and that's bad! Handsome, though! Play for our side?"

Rocky, slapping Gene on the shoulder said, "Hey Gene, some things never change, do they?"

"Ah, yes, they never do." Gene sighed. "But really, aside from being tall, handsome, and hot, who is he? What is he doing here?"

"Remember? You don't want to know."

Gene stood with his hands in his pockets, annoyed.

Rocky asked, "How's Nick? How did things go on the Hill?"

"Pretty well overall," Gene said looking down the hall where Buck had disappeared. "You were pretty much on point when you said we have the votes we need. Nick is still determined to get as many as he can. Enough for a mandate."

"How is he, health-wise, Gene?"

"As expected, tired, exhausted. Up in the residence. Asked not to be disturbed."

"That makes sense. I'll let him crash for a while. Now, let's you and I talk about tomorrow's strategy."

Rick found Buck in the White House mess, staring down at an uneaten sandwich, sitting alone at a table in a corner.

"Hey, man," Rick plopped down next to him. "Mind if I join you?"

Buck looked up. "Sure."

"Wow, what's the matter? You look like heck. Are you okay?"

Buck inhaled, held it for a moment and exhaled slowly. "It's a bit tough. The reality of it all. If it's confirmed Goulet has been working with others to assassinate your dad and the diamonds are payoff of some sort, it's game over. We've got all the evidence we need to get him impeached and thrown in the slammer. It's like this country has turned into some sort of a banana republic."

Rick reached over and placed his hand on Buck's arm. "Hey guy, this is the real world. We've seen a lot of bad stuff before now. Sure, it's disappointing and everything, but it's reality. What really is bothering you? Is it me? Brooke?"

"I guess it's everything. Mostly the thing with your dad and the vice president and a bunch of other people really trying to kill him. Your dad symbolizes a lot for people looking for change. Who ever thought a gay man would be elected president? It is more than gays, bis, trans, you know, it's all the disaffected could have imagined. Didn't you feel a little safer as a gay man when your dad was elected?"

"I did, and I do." Rick said, hopefully. "But he's still alive! It looks like he'll keep his job."

"But think of the effect this has had," Buck said. "There was a sense of unity and hope when he was elected. Seeing your family walk down Pennsylvania Avenue brought tears of hope to the eyes of millions. All of us, the LGBTQ community, everyone felt empowered. You could feel diverse communities and their friends growing stronger and stronger ever since the election. Then he was shot! Social media went nuts over people running for cover, feeling like gays were once more under attack. That we'll be persecuted, thrown in prison, killed. Like that hate was starting all over again. You must have seen it. Terror ripped through the hearts of everyone in the LGBTQ community and the hearts of those sympathetic to gays."

Tears threatened. Rick was forced to swallow hard. "I guess, uh, uhm, I guess I really didn't know," er, think of it with everything going on with my dad." He squeezed Buck's arm.

A shallow grin formed, and Buck looked into Rick's eyes. "I can only imagine what you have been going through. I thought of you a lot in the days that followed Inauguration Day. When you reached out and asked me to join the team to find the bad guys, I was really excited, honored. Looking forward to spending time with you and also empowered to think we might get these mother fucking haters . . . But here we are, we've caught them red-handed, and it looks like the evidence is useless, because we couldn't trust our own government to do the job right. It's like the world, the powerful, everything is stacked against us."

"This is, it is beyond surreal," Rick said.

"Then it's the thing between you, me, and me and Brooke. Right?" Buck said.

Rick sat back. His face hardened. "Yes, that is a real problem. One that needs to be left alone until after the vote."

"Yep," Buck said.

"Sometimes I hate you, Buck"

"Hate me?" Buck asked sitting up. "For what?" His face reddened.

"For destroying what we had."

"We didn't have so much. We were just getting to know each other."

"Bullshit! You don't remember those rainy Sunday afternoons lying in bed? What was that all about? Long weekends at P-Town? Partying on Fire Island? Really? Nothing?"

Buck stood, glared at Rick, and in a cold voice, said, "You are reading more into it than was ever there, could ever be." He pointed his finger at Rick. "You better get your act together. You're acting scary."

Rick stood, turned, and walked away. "We gotta all meet in the East Wing in ninety minutes."

The team gathered at 3:00. Rocky quickly brought everyone up to date.

"There is one more bit of news," Buck said, turning to Brooke.

"Just after the drop," Brooke said, "the vice president made a call from his burner inside the VP's residence. This is the first call we'd seen him make on the burner phones except for the ones on the Mall. From what I could hear from his side of the conversation, the drop was diamonds, the lab grown ones. He'd insisted that they take them and get them checked, because his people did not believe him. He must be panicky, because he'd made the call to see if they had them."

"Yeah, that seems out of the ordinary. Risky, making unnecessary calls," Dr. Parsons said. "He's bound to make more mistakes."

"I'm not so sure his proving the diamonds were not real was a mistake for us," Rick said. "If his people confirm their inauthenticity, they will know someone is on to them. Then who knows what will happen. Goulet could be a dead man."

A collective gasp carried through the room.

"Can we intercept the diamonds before they are examined?" Rocky said.

A moment of silence followed.

Sandy Yoe said, "That might be possible."

"Really? How?" Buck said.

"You may have noticed, but I was a minute or two late for this meeting. I had just finished confirming that we had been able to target and track the drone that snatched the diamonds the vice president had thrown into the air."

"Why wasn't this brought to my attention?" Buck asked Sandy.

"We weren't sure we had the correct drone. After the snatch, eighteen different bird drones formed a flock, and they flew in a southwest direction."

"What? A flock of drones?" Hamilcar asked, incredulous. "This keeps getting more insane!"

Sandy said, "Then some of the drones broke off and others continued on. It required some time for us to integrate our tracking and satellite surveillance to finally locate our bird, the one that grabbed the diamonds."

Wide-eyed, Rocky asked, "Well, where is it?"

"It landed in the Great Falls area."

"Is it still there? Can we get to the diamonds?"

Sandy thought for a moment. "Maybe. Our drone surveillance and satellite imagery have the bird drone sitting on top of an out building at a remote farm."

"Then let's go get it!" Dr. Parson's said.

"How?" Director Hamilcar asked.

"Send our net throwing drones down there and bag it!"

"Excuse me," Lynn Elle said, holding up her hand.

All turned toward her.

"We have those assets at the ready." Lynn said.

"How far away are they from the target?"

"A couple of miles, but the drone's batteries are running low. If it's going to happen, it'll have to happen soon."

Rocky said, "Director Hamilcar, Buck, Trish, your thoughts."

"I say, do whatever we need to do to get them back," Trish said with authority.

"I agree with her," Buck said.

"Director?" Rocky asked.

The director sat for a few moments. "I think we are in this far too deep not to take action. We are definitely going to need some presidential pardons when this is all over. Go for it."

"Okay, let's do it now," Rocky said. "We'll break for an hour and return here once everyone has done what they need to do."

The meeting reconvened in the East Wing conference room, with the president in attendance.

"Goulet is hosting a late dinner at his residence," Dr. Parson's said, "for the leadership of the House and Senate Democrats and Republicans this evening. He is politicking for votes."

"Do you think it will make any difference," Rocky asked. "as to the outcome of the vote?"

"Only if," Trish Smart said entering the room, "we don't have a super-majority in our favor. In that case we will not have a mandate."

"Hello, Trish, glad you're here," Nick said.

"Pardon my tardiness, sir. Was on a call with the party leadership. You look good, Mr. President, after your long day."

In a jocular tone, he said, "Well, I've just had a nice long nap while you were all conspiring in here earlier."

The mood lightened.

"At least we will be the fly on the wall at the veep's party," Rocky said. "We will hear and see everything being said. The placing of the surveillance equipment was well timed."

"Maybe that won't be necessary," Rick commented.

"What do you mean? We need to know what Goulet is planning," Nick said.

"We'll know that, regardless," Rick replied. "I suggest we have Gage Goulet arrested for narcotic trafficking just after everyone arrives."

Stunned silence permeated the room.

"That part of the investigation is legal and can be used in court," Rocky said, not convinced what he said was true. "Good thinking, son."

"Thank you, Dad,"

"Yes, Rick, that idea might have some legs," Nick said.

"Thank you, Dad. One can only imagine the collective reaction on the faces of all those in attendance when the FBI arrives to arrest their host's son. Just think how dramatic it would be if they are all seated at the table!"

"By the way, how do we know the kid will be home?" Dr. Parsons asked.

"His father has restricted him to the residence," Rick said, "until the vote has been taken. The Secret Service has been posted at all the entrances and the tunnel has been sealed."

"I suppose you learned this from the surveillance in the residence?" Nick asked.

Rick smiled and shrugged his shoulders.

"Got it," Nick said.

"We got the diamonds!" Lynn said, entering Rick's office, later that afternoon. "We have their intact drone too. The drone's tracking device is disabled, and it is on its way via corporate jet to Chamber's Enterprises for a complete systems analysis. Hopefully, we will learn even more about this group and how it operates."

Dr. Parsons asked, "Do we think that they have any idea we have their drone?"

"Not likely," Rick said. "There was no traffic in the area when we snatched it and according to satellite imagery, none for hours prior to it landing there. My guess is, when they can't locate it, they'll conclude, or at least hope, it disappeared due to some sort of malfunction."

"I sure hope so," Trish said. "But they will certainly be on an even higher state of alert now that the diamonds are missing."

"Those folks are going to be very unhappy," Lynn said. "It scares me to think what they might be up to."

"Can you imagine how Goulet will react when he finds out the diamonds are missing?" Rick remarked.

"Who knows if they'll ever tell him." Rocky said. "Where do we go from here? We know the guy is guilty. We have the evidence. Evidence we can't use in court. From what we can tell, the president will be reinstated, with or without a mandate. What do we do with Goulet, then?"

"I think," Rick said, "we need to press harder to find out who the culprits are that helped or managed Goulet. We need to know who the hell these bastards are."

Everyone nodded.

"I agree, Rick," Rocky said. "Let's do exactly that, find out who these people are before the trail totally disappears."

Rick said, "Lynn, where are we on all that? What's the latest?"

"We think we have a half dozen multinational companies that are in some way shape or fashion connected to Goulet. He has been involved on some level with them for years. First in the House, then Senate. These are companies that have repeatedly benefited from his voting record. We are looking into more companies and entities. The list we came up with earlier is just the tip of the iceberg."

"When do you think you will have made a compilation of all the conspirators?" Dr. Parsons asked.

The president said, "Days, weeks, months. Hard to tell. These guys have dug in deep and concealed their activities. It's definitely an international conspiracy. Lots of layers and not so friendly host countries to deal with."

Trish folded her hands on the table and took a moment to individually look each attendee in the eye. "It is safe to assume that Congress will vote our way. Once that happens, the White House will become a very busy place again. All the presidential work will be moved back to the White House from the Executive Building. We will not have the luxury of meeting like this."

"It's time," the president said, "to move the investigation out of the White House."

Dr. Parson's said, "Mr. President, I hope you are not suggesting we turn it over to the government."

"Absolutely not," Nick said. "Rick, Buck, your thoughts?"

"I think it is rather obvious. We will have to move the entire operation to Chambers Enterprises, Boston." Rick said.

Rocky nodded. "The further away from DC, the better."

Trish said, "In my capacity as chief of staff, I will have to remove myself from further investigation discussions. The only interaction I will have will be with those in the Federal Government." She paused. "It does not appear they have anything substantial to offer at this time. Director Hamilcar will also have to abstain from any further discussions, as will you, Dr. Parsons."

The mood in the room darkened.

Nick stood. "Trish, please take care of this. The rest of you, do what you were doing, and let me know if you need me for anything. I need to get more rest. Tomorrow is a big day. And thank you, all of you."

"Should we advise you when the arrest has been made, Mr. President?" Dr. Parson's asked.

"No, I don't think so. Only if there are complications. Tomorrow morning will be fine. Thank you."

While they were gathering their things, and preparing to leave, Rocky held up his hand. "I know I am speaking for myself and on behalf of the president when I tell you how much we appreciate all that you have done, every one of you. The hours you've kept over weeks has been grueling. You have been successful. We know who many of the conspirators are, their reason for wanting Goulet to be president, greed."

The president nodded in agreement.

"This is a win," Rocky said. "We unequivocally confirmed Goulet is part of a conspiracy that attempted to murder the president. We are also moving closer to identifying the other conspirators." He paused, placed his hands in his pockets and looked down at the floor. "Yes, it is a crime for which Goulet may go unpunished."

Rocky took a moment to let his last statement sink in, then said, looking at everyone in the room, "Importantly, Nick is alive and assuming the duties of the office to which he was elected, a victory not only for us, but the American people."

If Rocky's victory speech had any effect on anyone, it wasn't evident.

The room emptied leaving Rocky and Rick alone.

"You really don't believe that crock, do you Dad?"

"I have no choice. I am married to the president of the United States. I will have to spend all my energy supporting him. It will be very difficult as he continues to recover and *get back in the saddle*, so to speak. I hate the idea of Goulet and those bastards going scot-free, he and his band of conspirators. But my hands are tied."

"Mine aren't, and Vice President Goulet will not go unpunished.

CHAPTER 19

Headlines on social media and papers read:

VICE PRESIDENT'S SON BUSTED FOR DRUG DEALING
GAGE GOULET SON OF VICE PRESIDENT ARRESTED!

VEEPS RESIDENCE INVADED
FBI ARREST VP'S SON

BAIL DENIED FOR VICE PRESIDENT'S SON'S ARREST
ON DRUG CHARGES

LEADERSHIP MEETING AT VP'S RESIDENCE
RAIDED BY FBI

VICE PRESIDENT'S SON JAILED FOR DEALING DRUGS

Rocky slurped his coffee, exhausted. "I didn't get much sleep last night, fielding the calls for Nick," Rocky said to Gene. "Yeah, that's quite a mess!"

"Most of the complaining came from members bitching about being caught up in a drug raid. It's kind of funny really. Ol' Goulet will never live this down. Talk about people getting the cold shoulder, this guy is persona non grata extraordinaire!"

They both had a laugh as they imagined the chaos at last night's dinner. They were well into their breakfast when Nick walked into the room. "What are you two laughing about?"

"It appears the dinner party at the veep's resident was crashed, a real 'showstopper'!" Gene said laughing at his own pun.

"Yeah, I've been checking the feeds on my phone this morning. Sounds like quite a party." Nick grinned. "Sorry I missed it."

"Nick, you'll never guess what the Senate Leader did. She insisted that all protocols be followed when the FBI showed up. Most of the members were headed out the door when the FBI refused to let them pass. Senator Tatsu supported the FBI's insistence everyone be searched. Each member had to give up their cell phone until they were allowed to leave, not one by one, but as a group!"

Gene said, "For Christ's sake, are you telling me the entire Congressional Leadership of the most powerful country in the world was held hostage by one of the least reputable agencies in the country?"

"I wouldn't want to be representing the FBI in the next budget meeting," Nick said.

"Also," Rocky said, "when searching each member, they found weed on three of them and Viagra on two others. Fortunately for the potheads, weed is legal in DC."

"Not on federal property," Gene said.

"They gave them a pass," Rocky said.

"Can you imagine those poor bastards in the cloak room putting up with the razzing over the Viagra. Oh my God!" Gene said.

The men broke up laughing.

"Give me the names! That might be useful to us," Gene said to Rocky.

"Get 'em yourself," Rocky said.

"Hm, how do you know all these details anyway?" Gene asked.

"You don't want to know," Rocky said.

"Oh, one of those, again."

"Well, you're the one that insisted you be kept out of all this. Just following your rules." Rocky grinned.

"What about the boy? What happened to him?" Nick asked. "I feel kinda bad, him being pulled into all of this. Might not have happened if his father wasn't vice president."

"Like hell," Gene said. "That cowboy has been getting away with shit for years. He wasn't sent away during the election for good behavior." He looked at Rocky. "Out with it, what happened to the kid other than he was booked and denied bail."

"That denied bail thing came as a huge surprise. I couldn't believe it when I saw it on the feeds," Nick said. "I guess that's what happens to repeat offenders, and especially when lots of paraphernalia and cash are involved. Oh, and yeah, and getting put before a judge whose daughter died a year ago from a fentanyl overdose."

"That'll do it," Gene said.

"I agree," Nick said. "I was thinking it is a shame I have to go to the Hill today. I think the deal is done. We got it."

"You know that won't fly, don't you, buddy?" Gene said to Nick. "You need to go to the Hill and seal the deal."

"Yeah, I just had to say it though. It'll wear me out again but will certainly help get that mandate we need. Besides, my administration is beginning to look like a train wreck with my being laid up and last night's fiasco with the VP."

"Yep, Mr. P," Gene said. "When you get up there today, please do not bring up Goulet or his son. If someone brings it up, just say that your thoughts and prayers are with the family and that you will do anything within your power to be there for them."

"Like Goulet was for you, Nick," Rocky said in a sarcastic tone.

A pregnant pause followed.

"I didn't need to say that. Sorry. Go on Gene."

"All anyone will want to talk about will be the bust. Sit quietly and listen. Tell them you left a message for the vice president and look forward to speaking with him and offering your support."

"Everyone takes the call when the president calls," Rocky said.

"Yeah, you're right," Gene said. "You didn't make a call. Just say you sent a message telling the vice president you would be happy to take his call whenever it was good for him."

"Rocky, will you get that message to the vice president's office for me?" Nick asked.

"Sure, Nick. Consider it done."

"Time to saddle up, Mr. P. Let's trot on up to the Hill and wow them!"

CHAPTER 20

"We need to finish our conversation," Rick said.

"I agree, that's why we're having it here in this bar and not the White House," Buck said.

"And I'm sorry the way I spoke to you, Buck. I didn't mean it. I'm just so upset with losing you."

"You're not losing me, Rick."

"Don't kid yourself. Brooke, my guess is, has you now," Rick said observing his mug, leaving a ring of condensation on the table, rotating his beer round and round as he spoke. "Buck, have you rethought, or thought any more about what we discussed? What you're giving up between you and me?"

"Of course, I have, Rick. How could I not? Even in the midst of all that chaos at the White House."

"Well, what have you decided? Have you reconsidered?"

"Nothing really. I feel the same as I did a couple of nights ago, sitting in this very spot. I want to see you and get to know Brooke better."

"Goddamnit! That just won't work. You know Brooke won't go for it. Neither will I. Have you talked to her about it? Been honest with her?"

"Mostly, I told her that people change and that she and I might be able to make it work."

"Basically, you are going to ditch me if it works with her." Rick's face reddened.

"I didn't say that! I said I didn't want to let her go without seeing if things could work out. This is the twenty-first century. Things are different now. Who knows what kind of relationship we could end up in?"

"You must be out of your mind, Buck. There is no way that Brooke or I would do something like that. Who do you think you are? For that matter, who do you think we are? You can't have it both ways!"

"What the fuck are you talking about? Christ! Get real!"

Rick laughed an uncomfortable laugh. "You know what I'm talking about. Besides, you're not even on first base with her. And think about it, you and I have been fucking each other for over a year."

Buck shook his head and exhaled. "You're right. I'm not on first base, yet. But I'm at bat. I don't plan on just making it to first base, I plan on hitting a home run!"

"Cute, metaphor, bitch. Well, you've struck out with Brooke so far. I doubt she'll be back in the game any time soon. Until then, what am I, your pinch hitter?"

"We'll see. You gonna hold it against me?"

"What, trying to hit a homer, homo?"

"Yeah."

Rick leaned forward, placed his elbows on the table and rested his chin on steepled fingers. "If you hit that ball over the fence, I'll come back and even the score!"

Buck leaned forward and growled, "Is that a threat?"

"It's a promise!"

∞

"I am not sure I totally agree with you, Trish," Rick said. "Not sure how you can walk away from this mess. Goulet gets off scot-free and that's that." The two walked side by side down Pennsylvania Avenue.

"Did you know, Rick, this is the first time I have gone for a walk, or been outside the White House or my condo since the morning of the inauguration? It seems like I've been in some sort of captivity or even a time warp of sorts for weeks."

"You have."

They walked in silence for a couple of blocks and took a right on Ninth Street and headed towards the Mall.

Stepping up onto the grass, Trish said, "I understand how you feel. And no doubt you understand the position I am in. I need a clean slate to protect your father and serve him to my utmost ability. I cannot do that thinking about the scumbag of a vice president, that traitor."

"If anything is to be done to bring justice to all of this, it appears that it has fallen on my shoulders," Rick said.

"Your shoulders are big enough, you have the intellectual, financial, and corporate resources to do anything you choose."

Rick stopped in place and stared at Trish.

She turned and faced Rick. "With all my soul I hate to have to take this position. The venom I feel for that prick of a vice president knows no bounds. I could have vomited in that meeting when I had to pull back. I feel cheated that I no longer have an opportunity to avenge what has been done. But Rick, I know you will avenge us all. I will do whatever I can to facilitate anything you do. Remember, Goulet works for my boss. I won't go to meetings. I won't have phone conversations or email exchanges. Forget text. If you have anything I need to know or do, it will be face-to-face."

Rick stood speechless.

"It is time for you to pack up your investigative team and head back to Boston. You have plenty of opportunities to return when you need to, after all, your father is president of the United States."

"That sounds like orders."

"This is an order, from me. Get revenge. Destroy the bastards that tried to murder your father."

∞

Rick entered the East Wing and taking note of an army of men and women packing up their equipment. "Wow, it's moving quick around here. Looks like most of it is done. Hey Lynn, I've been looking for Brooke, have you seen her?"

"She was here about a half hour ago getting her things. She said she was headed back to her law practice and would probably be swamped for weeks."

"Anything about me?"

"No," Lynn said, her head cocked. "Should there be?"

"Nope, just wanted to say goodbye. You and Sandy taking the corporate jet back with Buck and me?"

"Sandy and I are, but Buck is hanging back for a couple of days. Said he had some personal business to take care of."

"Personal business, wonder what that could be?" Rick looked around the room. "Hey Lynn, I've got a question or two for you."

"Shoot, what ya got?"

"Not here, too many ears. But I was wondering, do you think you and Sandy might be interested in working on a special project with me? It'll demand total secrecy and discretion."

"Sure, I'm in. Why not? I mean just on what I know about what you might want, and I know zero." She grinned. "My guess is Sandy would be too. Just ask her."

"Okay, we can talk about it later on the flight to Boston."

Sandy walked in the room. "Just spoke to Buck while he and Brooke were laughing it up and heading out to get something to eat. He said he's going to meet us back at corporate in a couple of days. Looks like he's got Miss Brooke on the mind. Ooh la la!"

Under his breath, Rick said, "We'll see who laughs last."

"Huh, did you say something, Rick? I didn't hear you," Sandy said.

"Naw, I just remembered, I forgot to send an email. Gotta get on it." He walked out of the room and hollered back from the hall, "See you two at the Reagan corporate jet terminal!"

Walking down the hall he said, "Revenge! Revenge! Revenge!"

CHAPTER 21

President Nicholas Chambers–Jefferies did not head directly to the residence when he returned from Capitol Hill that afternoon. Instead, Gene in tow and having texted Rocky to meet him, he found Trish and Rocky sitting in the Cabinet Room.

"Welcome back, Mr. President," Trish said.

"Hi ya, Nick," Rocky said and walked over and gave him a hug.

"Hey, Gene," Trish said.

"Hi, Gene, thanks for squiring my man around the Hill," Rocky said.

"You're very welcome," Gene said. He patted the president on the shoulder. "This man is a workhorse. I could hardly keep up with him today. At one point I thought he was going to ditch the walker!"

Rick entered the Cabinet Room, his face drained and morose.

Nick took note. "Hey, Rick, why so downcast? We're almost there!"

Rick forced a grin. "That's awesome, Dad. Sorry, just a busy day packing up and everything. Headed to Boston shortly."

"I bet you're not going to miss leaving this circus behind," Rocky said.

Rick smiled broadly. "You got it Dad. I'll miss you guys, but gotta get back in the driver's seat at corporate. You stockholders would appreciate that, right?"

Nick nodded and motioned Rick toward him. "Come here, give me a hug before you leave."

Rick and Nick embraced, and Nick said, "I love you, son. Always will. Thank you for everything." Nick pulled back and kissed Rick's forehead.

"I love you too, Dad. Make sure and listen to your docs." He swallowed hard, turned, embraced Rocky. "Love you, Dad. I'll call you in a couple of days."

Rocky bear-hugged his son. "You know I love you too, and always will. Make me proud!"

Rocky patted Rick's back and they shook hands.

"Bye, Gene, see ya, Trish," Rick said, waved his hand, and walked out the door.

Nick cleared his throat. "That was tough. Something's bothering him. I've never really seen him so sad."

"Yeah," Rocky said. "It's more than sad. It's something bigger. I can think of a few things." He sighed.

"Let's change the subject," Nick said. "Rocky and I'll follow up with Rick later."

"Gene," Nick said, "would you like to share your thoughts on how things went today and what you anticipate happening tomorrow?"

"Well, Señor Presidente, today was almost like a celebration. Everyone we ran into was dumfounded with what had happened at the veep's residence last evening and damn glad that decision has cleared the way for most everyone to vote for you. The vote, a mandate, is in the bag!"

"Congratulations, Mr. President," Trish said, while she, Rocky, and Gene applauded.

"Well, other than the last few days spent waltzing around the Hill with my trusty walker, I've done nothing to bring this about. It's thanks to you and the team."

"What's on the schedule for tomorrow?" Gene asked. "Plan on politicking?"

Nick turned to Trish. "Trish?"

"There is nothing on the schedule, other than making a statement to the nation from the Oval Office following the vote. We have some remarks prepared for your review. They've been sent up to the residence."

"Thank you. I think I would like to meet with you, Trish," Nick said. He then looked at Rocky and Gene. "You two gentlemen as well and Director Hamilcar. Please schedule that for mid-morning tomorrow. Also, arrange a meeting with the vice president for the following morning."

"Yes, sir," Trish said.

"Good afternoon, everyone, and thank you." Nick said, standing.

Gene and Trish stood. "Good afternoon, sir."

Rocky, having also gotten to his feet, placed his hand in Nick's. "Let's go, it's been a long couple of days."

∞

Brooke and Buck met at Annie's Paramount Steak House on Dupont Circle for a quiet dinner away from the circus.

"I am so glad you selected a booth. It's a bit more private than the front room," Brooke said.

"Glad you approve." Buck smiled. "Cocktail?"

"Please, I'll have a Gibson."

"I don't remember, but what is the difference between a Gibson and a Gin Martini?" Buck asked.

"I don't think anything, really. I love the martini onions and a splash of dry vermouth. These days most bartenders think a martini is just a lot of gin or vodka. Boring. Ordering a Gibson ensures I will get what I want without a fuss."

"You're right," Buck agreed, smiling. "You never know what you'll get when you order a martini these days. I'll have the same."

Small talk ensued as the Gibsons arrived followed by fried calamari.

"I thought you would be on the corporate jet with the others heading back to Boston about now."

Buck's face took on a reddish hue. "Well, that was the plan until, rather, uh, well, you accepted my invitation."

Brooke cocked her head, "I hadn't planned on accepting any invitation from you, or even speaking to you. For at least a little while anyway."

"I'm really happy you changed your mind. So, why did you change your mind?"

"Pretty basic, really. I like you a lot, and I didn't want you to leave without our ending up on good terms, friends."

Buck looked down and toyed with his martini glass while she continued to speak.

"It's not your fault things are the way they are. I can't blame anyone for that. It's just the way it is. Besides, I sure don't want to poison things between you and my brother. After all, you've had a thing going on, you live in the same city, and you work for him."

Buck looked back up at Brooke and smiled gently. "Thank you. Thank you for understanding and your generosity in offering your friendship. It means a lot to me." He raised his glass. "Cheers! Here's to our friendship, may it blossom!"

"I'll toast to our friendship." She raised her glass.

They ordered dinner.

"Hadn't seen you around the East Wing the last couple of days," Buck said.

"I've been at the law offices. Things have really gotten behind. After our last conversation, well, I just needed to get away. Besides, I'd done just about all I could do. The rest of you had things well in hand. It just seemed that it was the best thing for me to blend into the woodwork and move on. Oh, and I moved back to the townhouse. Can't live in the White House. Need my own space."

Nick successfully hid his surprise learning Brooke had decided to move out of the White House. "That sounds like a good idea. I wouldn't want to live there. It will be interesting to see how difficult it will be to get back to normal. Gotta be rather mundane after all this drama," Buck groaned.

"Here's to normal!" Brooke said raising her glass.

"To normal!" Buck clinked his against hers and they both downed what remained in their glasses.

JR STRAYVE JR   276

"Shall we have another?" Brooke said smiling, her green eyes twinkling in the low light.

"We shall." Buck laughed.

Dinner arrived and Brooke asked for two more Gibsons.

Well into their meal, Buck said, "I spoke to Rick about us."

Brooke placed her fork on her plate and her hands in her lap and waited for Buck to continue.

"I told him you and I were an item. A small white lie, I know. But one can hope, can't I?"

"Well, aren't you incorrigible? You know we're not an item. And we weren't an item then. Just a kiss, which was all it was. You shouldn't have told him we are together. He's been a bit of a prig the last few days. Not himself. I'm concerned. Figured it was about you. Anyway, as you probably know, he saw us. What a fucked up situation."

"Well, maybe it was just wishful thinking on my part, us being an item. To be fair, it still is."

Brooke glared at him.

"I know! I know! Not to worry," Buck said, sipping his cocktail. "Just friends."

"I'm not worried about you, Buck, I'm worried about me falling for you and regretting it the rest of my life. I don't want to have the kind of marriage my parents had. I want a traditional marriage, a normal family."

"What do you mean your parents?"

Brooke shook her head, picked up her fork and stabbed at the food on her plate. "Never mind, forget what I said. I shouldn't have said that. See what you and three Gibsons do to me?"

Buck smiled and watched her assault her food. "I told him you are very important to me and that you are my priority."

She continued eating, focused on the disappearing food and nursing her cocktail.

"He didn't take it very well. Not well at all. He's not given up, but things are not what they were." He paused. "Just wanted you to know."

Five minutes passed, both consuming their meal and well into their cocktails.

Brooke held up her glass, gaining their waiter's attention. "Two more of these please."

"Are you sure, Brooke?"

"Couldn't be surer."

When the drinks arrived, Brooke asked the waiter to clear the table.

After the waiter had taken their plates, Buck said, "You know, I really hadn't finished."

"Sorry," Brooke said. "I'm a strong-willed independent woman. I am in charge of my life and will remain so. If you want to sleep with me and have a relationship, you better get used to it. And it will be on my terms. My brother and any other guy are off limits!"

A quizzical look crossed his face.

She tossed her napkin on the table. "Don't look at me like that! Pay the bill and let's go fuck!"

"It looks like it's just going to be us moving forward from here," Rick said to Lynn and Sandy over the sound of the

Gulfstream's G800's engines. The sleek plane lifted up into the night sky, jetting them toward Boston.

"Not sure what you mean, Rick," Sandy said. "Move forward where?"

Rick looked over at Lynn and then back to Sandy. "I suppose you two haven't had time to discuss my proposition."

"Rick, know that we are open-minded," Sandy said. "And you haven't provided specifics to either of us, yet." She leaned forward and continued, "Just give it up. We've been working closely for weeks, not to worry, we're pretty cool, and discreet."

"Would either of you like something to drink, an adult beverage, or something to eat?" Rick asked, almost pleading. "We've got a full pantry on board and a three-hour flight."

Both women nodded.

"Let's have champagne. Why not, it's not often we get to travel like this!" Lynn said.

"Champagne it is!" Rick said cheerily and beckoned the steward.

The steward arrived; a towel draped over one arm. "Yes, sir?"

"The ladies and I will share a bottle of Veuve Clicquot La Grande Dame Rose. Also, in about an hour please serve the lobster dinners I ordered." He turned to Lynn and Sandy. "Lobster? Okay by you?"

They both said, "Yes, thank you."

Speaking to the steward, "And we will have the Roederer Cristal with dinner."

"Yes, sir. I will return in a moment with the Veuve Clicquot, sir."

Rick settled back in his leather chair, releasing a sigh of satisfaction. "Well, now that the first order of business has been taken care of, let's get to it." He paused. "What I am proposing is of a very delicate matter. It is something that cannot be discussed outside this very small circle of three."

The steward placed an ice bucket containing an opened bottle of champagne alongside the table. He poured a small amount of champagne into one of the crystal flutes and handed it to Rick. Rick sipped, savored, then nodded his head in approval. The steward filled the ladies' flutes and topped off Rick's and placed the bottle in the bucket and covered it with a rose-colored napkin.

As the steward walked away, Rick said, "Please do not disturb us until dinner."

He turned to face Rick. "Yes, sir." And he returned to the rear of the cabin.

"Cheers! To our new adventure!" Rick said, hoisting his glass.

The ladies lifted their glasses, and Lynn said, "Cheers to whatever it might be."

Sandy laughed. "Cheers!"

The party sipped the crisp bubbly, and all settled back into their oversized leather seats.

"Here we go. What I am proposing is we continue full throttle with the investigation."

Lynn and Sandy exchanged incredulous glances.

"Our activities must remain just between us. I know I am repeating myself, but I cannot stress how important it is that our efforts be kept from everyone. Our project involves getting to the bottom of who tried to kill the president. Our primary objective is to identify and name every conspirator and provide that information to the government. The techniques we have been using and will no doubt continue to use are, in most cases, those with which the government is not legally allowed to implement. But, most importantly, I do not have confidence in the investigation being successful should the government organizations tasked with doing this sort of thing attempt to find the perpetrators. The president and I have no doubt and are convinced there are those embedded in several agencies whose agenda does not complement finding the criminals who tried to kill my father. It does not mean they are necessarily in league with the conspirators, but nonetheless have demonstrated no interest in finding the perpetrators. With of course, one exception, the Director of the Secret Service. That being said, it is better we move on, navigating our own course to find the perpetrators and bring them to justice."

Empty flutes in hand, Lynn and Sandy stared at Rick.

Rick, noticing their stares, and then empty glasses, said, "I beg your pardon." He took hold of the champagne bottle, refilled all three glasses and returned the bottle to the bucket.

Lynn said in a flat tone, "Thank you."

"Yes, thank you," Sandy said with similar emotion.

"You are very welcome. Now, our successes to date are in large part the result of the work both of you have done. Your ability to manipulate surveillance assets and provide the analysis needed to achieve the results we have obtained is truly quite remarkable. This project needs more of the same."

Sandy nodded. "When you speak to our objectives, what specifically are you asking us to do and what qualifies as having achieved your goals? Do you want names, addresses, phone numbers, email addresses? What exactly do you want?"

"I want everything. I want to know every detail possible about who they are, who they work for, and everything about their personal and professional lives. Their strengths and their Achilles' heels."

"That is a tall order, Rick," Sandy said.

"Indeed, it is," Rick replied.

"Rick, I am sure you must have taken into consideration how difficult it could be to keep the project confidential in our current shared space working environment," Lynn said.

"I have. You will not be working on the corporate campus, but at another site, a safehouse of sorts, located not far from Logan airport. Having a close proximity to the airport will prove convenient, as I anticipate considerable travel for both of you."

Lynn and Sandy stared, mouths agape.

"As to the location, you will be working alongside four other team members tasked according to our needs to unearth and validate our research."

"Security types, ex-military guys?" Sandy asked.

"Ex-military guys and gals," Rick said. "If they cannot handle the workload, there are more assets available to augment our requirements."

"This is beginning to sound very over the top. Does Chambers Enterprises have experience in this sort of thing? A history?" Sandy asked.

"Interesting question. I'm impressed. The company was founded by my great, great, great, great, grandfather sometime in the mid-1700s. Don't remember the exact year. The company has grown quietly for centuries. Expert management and extensive knowledge are the prerequisites of a successful business. We are fortunate in that Chambers Enterprises has had the best of both for five, six generations."

The women sat in shell-shocked silence.

Lynn brought her gaze back to Rick. "That's quite a corporate background. I guess you must know what you're doing. But this is certainly something the company, you, and us have never done before."

Rick said, "You will have a lot of flexibility and autonomy. Of course, I will be in regular contact and will spend moderate amounts of time working with you. Your salaries will be doubled."

"Okay! Sounds good to me," Sandy said.

"No argument here, but I hope you know what you're doing," Lynn said.

"But one more thing," Sandy said. "Buck Gerard. Why isn't he involved in this? After all, we work directly for him."

"Not any more. You work directly for me."

"Oh—" Sandy said.

"Yes, you work for me. I have other plans for Buck. I just need to clear them with a few people first."

The stewards came alongside the table and began the dinner service.

"My I offer you a cup of New England Clam Chowder?"

CHAPTER 22

Twenty-seven days following the assassination attempt that shocked the nation and the world, the vote returning to power was held late morning in the House of Representatives. The president received one hundred percent of the Republican votes and seventy-five percent of the Democrats. The Senate followed suit an hour later, all one hundred Senators voting in the president's favor.

It was time for President Nicholas Chambers-Jeffries to grab the reins of power and reassure the world he was mentally and physically fit and could fulfill his role as the most powerful man in the free world.

The White House staff, assembled along with members of Congress and executive branch personnel applauded as the president entered the gilded East Room and stepped on to the dais.

President Nicholas Chambers-Jeffries stood confidently in front of Gilbert Stuart's Lansdowne portrait of George Washington waiting for the applause to subside.

The president raised both his hands in the air. "Look at me! No wheelchair, no walker!"

Cheers, laughter and applause erupted.

"Thank you everyone for your support these past weeks."

He turned and faced the painting behind him and then back to his audience. "It is interesting. Interesting that I am standing here in front of the painting saved by Dolly Madison from a burning White House when the British attacked in 1814. Like that painting, I was saved from certain death. Perhaps physical death and if not that, political demise.

"Today, the rescued painting and a rescued president stand before you, both in their rightful place. The American people fought off an invasion in 1815. You, my friends held fast against an attempted assassination of your president. Once again, the American people have prevailed!"

The room burst into applause lasting several minutes. No attempt was made to quiet the crowd as all knew it was vital that the fear and pain be released, and the victory celebrated.

"All of us are experiencing great frustration and perhaps discomfort not having the who, why, and how of the attempt on your president's life. It is of grave concern for all of us. But we will not be deterred from living our lives. We will not allow those evil souls to stain and discolor our daily lives. They will be discovered, and the truth, one day, will be revealed. I have the fullest confidence in the Justice Department, the FBI, and the host of other government agencies investigating this heinous crime. Let the rest of us move on with our lives."

Applause rang out.

"Standing here today, I commit to you, the American people, that I will remain faithful to you and the Constitution of the United States, the world's longest surviving written government charter!"

Applause erupted again.

"You are all well aware of my staunch belief in the rights of all individuals and their right to pursue their own lives on their own terms."

More applause.

"While, as of yet, I have no proof as to who and why someone tried to assassinate me, it is my opinion, a widely held opinion, that it was a direct attack on the people of this country. An attack on their right to elect the man or woman they feel would best serve them as president. What they couldn't kill at the ballot box, they chose to murder in broad daylight, in plain sight of the entire world! They have failed!"

Applause and cheers rocked the room. So raucous, so rage-like, the chandeliers were seen to sway, and many found it necessary to protect their ears from the deafening sound.

Minutes later the cacophony died down allowing the president to continue, "They failed! They failed! They failed! You, the people, prevailed!"

More applause.

"As you must surely know, I and my administration have a great deal for which to be thankful. And a lot of work to catch up on! The people's work!"

The president looked toward Vice President Chris Goulet sitting in the first row. "Vice President Goulet, let me take this opportunity to thank you for standing in my stead while I was incapacitated."

Muttering could be heard interspersed throughout the assembly.

The president started clapping, "Please give it up for your vice president. No one can imagine how difficult it must have been to be called to serve the country under such trying circumstances. Please!"

Tepid applause lasted less than five seconds.

"But, before I go," the president said, "let me acknowledge the love and compassion of the American people during my time in need, and that also of my family."

The president motioned to those standing off to his left. Rocky and Brooke walked over to the president and joined him on the platform.

"My husband, Rocky, and our daughter, Brooke, and our son, Rick, who returned to Boston last evening, thank you. Thank you for always being there for me through thick and thin. You are all amazing and I love you dearly. God bless you, my family, the American people and God bless America!"

The president embraced them both. The family stepped off the platform and exited the East Room to thunderous applause.

CHAPTER 23

Life in the White House and on Capitol Hill returned to normal. Vice President Goulet faded into the background.

In the Oval Office, the president addressed those he had asked to join him—his husband, his chief of staff, and his congressional advisor. "Rocky, Trish, Gene. We need to jump-start this administration. The first thing I want to do is to put this assassination attempt and the vice president's involvement in it behind us. I know it sounds naïve, maybe dangerous, not to pursue Goulet's involvement, but I don't think focusing on the past is in the country's best interest at this time. There are, in my opinion, much higher priorities. Including getting our nominees' confirmations out of the way. The administration will never be able to move forward until we get the Cabinet nominees in place.

"Then there are the judicial appointments. Very important for our long-term plan strengthening diversity and equality. We have a very short window to bank on Congress's good feelings following the attempted assassination to get everything accomplished."

Trish said, "We've withdrawn the list the vice president sent to the Hill during your hospitalization and forwarded the original list of nominees to the Hill, sir."

"Excellent. As you all know, I have signed the executive orders we drew up and held during my hospitalization. Later today, I will make the announcement of their signing to the nation from the Press Briefing Room. That will allow me to get in and out and not have to spend too much time on my feet."

"Do we anticipate any push back from the reporters on any of the orders?" Rocky asked.

"Not sure they can push back," Gene said. "No one's seen them yet. As far as we know the contents has not leaked from Justice—"

"Surprise!" Rocky said.

The president gave a brief smile to his spouse. "Right, Gene. I will briefly describe each executive order and after the press conference is over the press secretary will release copies of the orders online."

"What are your thoughts on taking questions from the White House Press Corps, Mr. President?" Trish asked.

"Let me offer my opinion on that, Mr. President, If you don't mind, sir." Gene said.

"Gene, did you just say Mr. President?" Rocky quipped, smiling and scratching his chin.

"Roll with it Rocky," Gene said.

"What are your thoughts, Gene?" the president asked.

"I believe you will certainly get a lot of softball questions, mostly referring to your health, etc. However, there is always that possibility you will get a hardball thrown at you. Not that you can't handle it, but if you are to move quickly forward with your agenda you must control the narrative."

"Are you suggesting I make opening remarks, sign the documents, and leave without fielding questions?"

"Precisely. I would address the questions that would likely come up regarding your health. Then quickly move on. Jump into each executive order, one by one. Outline each respective order and how it relates to your campaign promises, sign it, and then on to the next one."

The president thought for a moment. "Anything else?"

"Yes, Mr. President," Trish said, "I think it is good idea for you to stress how important it is for the nation that Congress ratify your appointments as quickly as possible."

"That makes sense to me. When I've done that, I'll simply thank everyone for their support and make some sort of excuse that I need to get back to work and attend to the nation's business."

"Throw them a bone, Mr. President," Gene said. "Something like, you will hold a press conference later in the week—"

"Good, I'll do that."

Brooke paced outside the Oval Office waiting for the meeting to end.

The appointment secretary said. "Ma'am, the president will see you now."

"Thank you." She stood, walked toward the open office door, braced herself, slapped on a happy face and briskly entered.

"Hello, Dad! How're you feeling today? Good meeting?"

The president was still sitting on the sofa, soaking in the heat from the crackling fireplace. "Hi, Brooke." He patted the cushion next to him. "Come over here and sit next to me."

She plopped down close to him and gave him a peck on the cheek. "Okay! Oh, that fire feels so good."

"So nice to see you! You look wonderful." He took one of her hands in his. "I am feeling better every day. I tire easily, but the staff is very attentive and careful not to put too much on me. Dr. Samson hovers over me. I think he'd move into the Oval if I'd let him."

"Gosh, even though it's the White House and all, this feels so normal, so intimate and like the old day's taking a moment to get caught up. I hope the bubble doesn't burst. I am so happy you are recovering and looking better. I love you so much and feel terrible about the way I handled some things."

"Honey, please don't concern yourself. I think you are doing really well, considering you learned that your twin is a half-brother and, well, you know, the part about your mother, Rocky, and me. All that is enough to send anyone into a tailspin."

Brooke looked down at her lap, sat for a moment. "Yes, it was emotionally devastating piled on top of the fact that you lay in a hospital bed recuperating from someone trying to kill you."

"Will you forgive me and Rocky for not sharing the truth with you and Rick long ago?"

She took her free hand and placed it atop his, looked into his eyes. "I forgave you weeks ago. Actually, I don't know when I forgave you both. It's just at some point it seemed unimportant, almost like it never happened. But every now and then I feel a pang when it comes to mind. I suppose the pain will disappear with time."

"Thank you, darling Brooke. Our closeness means so much to me. I need you, and our family, more than ever."

"I think we all do, you, Rick, Dad, and me."

"About Rick, have you had an opportunity to speak to him about this? I mean with all that has kept the four of us occupied, we haven't really spent much time on protecting the most important thing in our lives, each other."

"We spoke briefly, but no real resolution type therapy talk. Too busy with all that's happened. I suppose we will at some point." She paused. "There's something different about him though."

"Such as?"

"Such as he appears to be distant. Skulking. Caught up in his own world. Kinda like Rocky, I mean, when Dad was running Chambers Enterprises. Before he moved over to chairman of the board and made Rick CEO. But in a different kind of way. Except, Rocky never skulked. Rick seems hard, surprisingly insensitive, like he doesn't care about anyone very much. Rocky and you always have been loving and caring no matter what garbage or pressure you were dealing with. Rick is hurting."

"I know it's none of my business, and we don't have to talk about it if you don't want to, but does it have anything to do with Buck?"

A flush crept across her face.

"Sorry, Brooke, I didn't mean to—"

"Not to worry, Dad. I'm sure it has something to do with that. You know, huh?"

"Yeah,"

Brooke exhaled. "It's so weird, like you and Mom and Dad all over again. I don't know how I can live with that. I don't want to live like that. How did you do it?"

The president rolled his lips. "I think I was so in love with Rocky and cared very deeply for your mother. To me, it was like having the best of both worlds. I was allowed to continue to love and be with the love of my life and at the same time have a family. You kids mean everything to me. Being part of the family expanded and enhanced my life."

"How did Mom deal with it?"

"Your mother was something special. I'll never forget when they shared with me, your mother and Rocky, about that rainy day in Brussels. She and Rocky were sharing a glass of wine just before she and I were to head to Paris for a weekend. This was only a couple of months prior to our wedding. First of all, Rocky had no idea she knew about him and me. That was a shockeroo when she let him know she knew. I remember hearing he knocked his wine glass off the table." He gave a quick laugh. "That is a story unto itself."

Wide eyed and smiling ear to ear, Brooke said, "I know about that! Well sort of. Mom told me a story about one time Rocky and her were drinking wine and she caught his wine glass careening off a table." Brooke snorted. "I thought she was exaggerating, guess not."

"Yep, it's true. Now you know why Rocky knocked over the glass. He recounted the story more than once. He said it was a big surprise to learn that she loved me so much that she planned to marry me and was committed to growing my political career. So much so, that she said she would be supportive of the relationship between Rocky and myself, as long as she could marry me."

Brooke inhaled, and said, "This is weird, but that reminds me of the 1930's famous song writer, Cole Porter, and his wife Linda. Somewhat of the same kind of thing, akin to what the three of you must have had. She knew he was gay before they married. She supported his sexual orientation and affairs and his career. Incredible. Lives filled with mountainous love and support, unconditional." She sat for a moment, then reached over and took both her father's hands in hers. "Thinking about this makes my head hurt, and my head spin,"

She then released his hands and sat back. I am trying to put my head around this. "Okay, but why did Mom have to do that, I mean agree to support the relationship between you two? It is so hard to fathom. Love? Really? It seems so surreal."

"She didn't have to do that. Perhaps, because I had told her that I was in love with Rocky and couldn't marry her."

"Holy crap!"

"Exactly."

"I really wish I had known all this before now. And, by the way, no details on how you three hooked up. TMI."

"No problem here. By the way, it was only once."

"Hm. Meant to be, I guess." Brooke sighed.

CHAPTER 24

A series of text messages the months following Nick's recovery and return to power led to Rocky and Jack meeting again at the Arlington townhouse. Rocky had just finished bringing Jack up to date on what had transpired since they had last seen one another.

"I am so glad we, the family, have got some normalcy back in our lives," Rocky said. "Once things calmed down, I slept for at least twelve hours the first night, and have slept longer than normal ever since. Nick got a little worried and suggested I get some lab work. That's not gonna happen. I've had enough of doctors and all that with what Nick went through. I'm just catching up on my sleep. That's all it is."

"Well, I missed you. That was a special time we had, reigniting our relationship," Jack said. "It was therapeutic, for me, on so many levels. How about you?"

"You know, I look back at it and I can't believe it happened, but I can, actually. I suppose I should feel guilty or something like that. But I don't. And yep, you're right. It was therapeutic. I really needed what our time together gave me."

Jack looked into Rocky's eyes, and asked, "So, what now?"

Rocky stood and began to walk around the townhouse library.

Jack, a look of loss crossing his face, watched Rocky pace the room.

Rocky, turned, smiled, and went back to his place next to Jack. "I've been thinking about that. But first, my daughter Brooke lives here now. She's gone for a few days. But back to your question, it would be nice to have a friend with benefits. Nick is so busy he has no time for himself or me. It's like when I was running Chambers Enterprises and he was in the Senate. But at least then, when we could find time for each other, we had some privacy. Not now. In the last three months since he got back in the saddle, I bet we haven't had any real alone time. Always an interruption. Sex? Forget it. He's honestly too tired and or preoccupied. I know he would if he wasn't just totally exhausted. His body is still on the mend, his emotions, his psyche, all mending. Our conversations aren't what they used to be. Everything has changed. I'm not complaining. It is what it is. Things will get better."

"Oh man, that sounds tough. Particularly since you guys were so close before the campaign and the assassination attempt."

"Yep, it is. But I shouldn't complain. At least he's alive and thriving."

"But you're not thriving. Not happy?"

"No. I'm not thriving and not really happy. More lonely than anything." Rocky sat back against the couch and looked up at the ceiling. "What does a guy do as First Spouse of the United States? I'm not into all that stuff my predecessors have occupied themselves with. Hell, we've hired someone to handle the social falderal."

"That blows the stereotype of a gay guy right out of the water." Jack laughed.

"I just show up when asked. I know how Prince Phillip must have felt when he was alive and stuck in nowheresville. I'm fucking bored out of my mind. I have to find something to occupy my time."

"Can you go back to Chambers Enterprises?"

"Everything must be in a blind trust as long as Nick is the president. The good news is, as you know, my son is the CEO. The bad news is the CEO is my son. He appears to be doing a great job and running the company well. No way for me to participate in running the company on any level as long as Nick is president. As it stands, I have nothing to do. Nothing I am interested in, anyway."

"That makes sense to me," Jack said. "Hopefully you can find something you can enjoy doing and feel good about."

They sat silent for a few moments.

Jack reached over and placed his hand on Rocky's thigh. "And what about us?"

"That's really why we are here, isn't it?" Rocky asked.

"I suppose so. It's certainly why I'm here. I would really like to continue seeing you."

"That would be really nice, but—"

Jack interrupted, "But you're afraid we'd get caught and that would cause Nick international embarrassment and possibly undue all his work, especially the LGBTQ stuff."

"Exactly, it would destroy him. Not that you and I had something on the side. It'd decimate his life's work."

Jack said, "Men can be so strange. Sex for one man is so different than for another man, and yet not always. Straight guys can spout fidelity and monogamy and then fool around on the side, not giving a shit about the hypocrisy. Now, if a gay guy does the same thing, people will say that is why homosexuality is evil. Yet, and at the same time, the straights are doing it too. Some studies have shown seventy percent or more of the heteros are doing or have done the same thing. not just men. Huge numbers of women too."

"You're right, Jack. But that sounds a lot winey. This isn't like Europe. It's the US. In Europe they don't give a shit who sleeps with whom. In America, if I, as first spouse, or a first lady got caught fooling around, the husband, the president, would be run out of the White House. But other than Kennedy, Johnson, and Clinton there isn't much attention given to presidents cheating. And remember, they got caught cheating in a straight relationship. Also, think about it, there is no documented history of first ladies cheating on their husbands."

Jack raised one eyebrow. "What about Eleanor Roosevelt and Lorena Hickok? Hell, they had adjoining bedrooms in the White House?"

Rocky laughed. "Hey that was over eighty years ago. And ladies have always been allowed to have a best friend. Jeez, furthermore, the press wasn't allowed to take pictures of President Roosevelt in his wheelchair. They sure weren't going to take pictures of Eleanor and Lorena getting it on. Things have changed.

"You know we would be discovered. You know that, right? Do you want that for Nick and me?"

Jack dropped his shoulders and looked to the side and, in a monotone, said, "No, I don't. I wouldn't wish consequences that would fall out from that on anyone."

"Lincoln and Van Buren were supposed to have been gay. It's documented," Jack said.

Rocky put his hand on the side of Jack's face. He pulled him in and placed his lips on Jack's. "One last fling, and we're done, right?"

Jack drew back. A smile emerged from a frown. His eyes regained some of the luster they had lost. He nodded. "One last fling."

CHAPTER 25

"The vice president has not given up his burners," Sandy said, facing Rick seated at a first class linen draped table for two on the Amtrak Acela. The train sped along at 150 miles per hour, the countryside and small towns whipping by as they raced towards New York City.

"Okay," Rick said, "Let's use pronouns, just in case we're overheard."

Sandy looked around the dining car. Four tables were occupied, and none within twenty feet of where they were seated.

She nodded. "We have everything recorded, but rather than risk them falling into the wrong hands, they have been placed on servers not connected to the net or Chambers Industries' corporate web."

"No transcripts on paper?" Rick asked.

"No. In fact no notes anywhere. What I am about to share with you is from my memory."

"That's the way I like it. Go ahead fill me in as soon as the attendants serve our lunch." He looked around the dining car. "God, it never changes, no matter how often I do it, I love going first class."

Sandy smiled. "I sure could get used to it." She raised her wine glass and toasted, "To going first class!"

Rick returned the toast.

The train seemed to fly effortlessly through the New England countryside at top speed. A reassuring constant humming cast a surreal air about the superliner's cars.

"It's odd not hearing the clickity-clack of the wheels on the track. Are we just going too fast to hear it?" Sandy chased down Atlantic Salmon with her wine.

"No, oddly, there are very few seams in the tracks. They are almost totally smooth. At least the sections that Acela uses. Pretty much clickity clack is disappearing for all rail travel nationwide, just like on Acela."

"Fascinating. I heard at some point, in the near future, the Acela train will be allowed to go 160, maybe 180 miles per hour.

Rick said, "As far as speed, the Eurostar connecting London and Paris through the Chunnel can go 186 miles an hour and has been doing it for years. Premier Class, their first class, is well worth it."

"Ah, so you've traveled on Eurostar?" Sandy asked.

"Yes, a wonderful experience and I recommend it."

Sandy turned her attention to the rolling countryside flying by. "Everything goes by so fast. It is somewhat visually uncomfortable."

"You'll get used to it. I used to think the same thing," He said, and changed the topic. "In these recordings, what have you heard of interest? Is he still conniving?"

She said, "He is definitely in contact with some or maybe all of the people he was communicating with right after the assassination attempt. Not as often, maybe once each week. Most of the conversation is one-sided, his side. He provides those listening on the other end with the specifics of what the administration is doing. It's a little unnerving to listen to all the very sensitive information being given to who knows who."

"Once again, he is a traitor," Rick said.

"Listen to this, not only does he tell them what is happening and being discussed but provides attribution on all parties, including the president."

Rick drummed his fingers on the table. "This means that they know the inner workings and who thinks what. Very dangerous. This is treasonous."

Sandy said, "We have no indication or idea of what or if they are planning to do anything at the moment. Goulet has not referred to any sort of operation being put in place." She paused and leaned forward. "But get this, Lynn and I believe they are trying to arrange some sort of meeting, like face-to-face between all of them."

"You mean, between Goulet and the conspirators?"

"We think so," Sandy said nodding.

"That doesn't sound very smart. He's too high profile. So, too, are several of the conspirators we've identified as being involved. Must be desperate or something." Rick leaned back in his seat and rubbed his chin. "Keep me up to date on this, real time. And get me that list of suspected conspirators."

"Will do."

"Whatever happened to the diamonds he sent to them that never arrived? Anything on that?" Rick asked.

JR STRAYVE JR   304

"Yes, well not really. He asks about them. He talks like he is being stonewalled. He makes noises about not providing any further information. They appear to have calmed him down by putting money in an offshore account."

"What? Why didn't you tell me this earlier. How much?"

"It just happened this morning before we left Boston. Five million." She cocked her head. "Saving best for last, I suppose."

Rick stared out the window, ruminating, not saying a word.

Entering Pennsylvania Station in New York City, Rick said, "None of this can ever be revealed to anyone."

She nodded.

"Only you, Lynn, and I can know the contents of his conversations. That is the only way we can move forward with a plan to eliminate that son-of-a-bitch with little or no collateral damage. This man is putting the lives of every American at risk and many other people in the world as well."

He reached down and removed an envelope from his valise. "When you get off the train, take this to Hudson Yards. Go to the Vessel, the honeycomb-like 16 story structure. You can't miss it. Climb to the top, do not take the elevator, you want to avoid pickpockets."

"Hm, now, Rick, I understand why you made that funny request to wear comfortable shoes. So grateful you did!"

Rick chuckled. "You're welcome. When you arrive at the top wait until you are contacted by a young athletic Asian male wearing a long sleeve French cuffed yellow shirt. The cufflinks will be mismatched. He will ask you if your name is Naomi. You will say no, but I have a cat with that name. You will ask him if he has a cat, and if he replies he does, but it doesn't have a name, as he doesn't like cats, he is your man. Give him the envelope."

"That's it? Why all the secrecy and James Bond stuff?"

"Yes, that's it. And you do not want to know. It's better this way."

She shrugged her shoulders and took the number 10 envelope from him.

"Sandy, I cannot stress how important it is for you to do exactly as I say. After the hand-off, leave immediately. Spend a couple of hours shopping and use the Acela return ticket to get back to Boston. If anyone asks about where you were, tell them it was a shopping trip. Wear some of the things you buy on your shopping spree for the first few days following your return to Boston. I will cover the costs. Have fun!"

The train came to a halt alongside the dark platforms under Penn Station.

"See you in Bean Town," Sandy said and disembarked.

∞

Rick caught an Uber to Teterboro Airport and boarded a corporate jet to Reagan National Airport.

An hour following his arrival in D.C., early evening, he was seated at the dining room table in the residence with Brooke, Rocky, and the president.

"So glad everyone is here, one big happy family," Rick said. "Like the old days."

"Not really like the old days," Nick said, glumly. "But close enough."

Rick and Brooke exchanged glances that spoke, *WTF*.

"Rick, you've been up in Boston running your empire about four months now," Rocky said, "and from what I can tell, doing a superb job. Proud of you, son."

Rick gave a week smile. "Thank you." He turned to Brooke. "What have you been up to, sis?"

The family engaged in superficial conversation throughout the meal. A low level tension permeated their conversation. Rocky thought, *will things ever get back to the loving free-flowing fun conversations we had before? Before they found out. I love these kids, but things just aren't the same. They're growing up and have been through some pretty dramatic shit. Not fair.*

Nick said, "What's on your mind, Rocky? You appear a little distracted."

Rocky's cheeks inflated as he exhaled. "It's the elephant in the room."

As if on cue, everyone placed their silverware on their plates and folded their hands in their laps.

"Oh, that," Nick said.

Rick rolled up his napkin and tossed it on his plate. "I'm okay with it."

Brooke folded her arms. "Okay with what, Rick?"

Rocky was about to interject when Nick held up one finger shushing him.

Rocky tightened his jaw and looked down at his half eaten dinner.

Rick said, "I am okay with, with both of them keeping us in the dark as to who our real fathers are. If any of us was affected by their purposeful omission, it's me. I wouldn't change it. We were a happy family unit then. And we are a happy family unit now. Everything is cool. I like having my real dad as my dad."

Rocky looked up, eyes glistening, and swallowed.

"So, your dad, Brooke, is my stepdad," Rick said. "Lots of people have stepdads. We both have stepfathers."

Brooke said, "It's the duplicity of it that irked me the most. I'm not okay with it. I am, however, over it. I've moved on."

Rick said, "I don't think you, me, or any of us are over it totally. I don't know if we ever will be. Look at us now, this isn't the fun family group we had."

"Maybe with time," Nick said. "Time will deaden the pain."

"You just never forget," Brooke said. "It's like some sort of trust or something has been violated. It hurts too much."

Rick pushed his plate to the side, leaned forward, folding his arms and placed them on the table and said, "Brooke, would you agree that there is no point in telling anyone else about this?"

"Well, I would only tell one person. That is, if I were to get married, my husband would have to know."

Flexing his fingers repeatedly, Rick said, "Anyone I know?"

Brooke narrowed her eyes, glaring at Rick.

Nick and Rocky sat contemplating the dining room table.

Moments later, Nick sat back and placed his napkin on his plate.

"Your father and I," Rocky said, looking up, "apologize again for not sharing with you before now. It was our intent to protect you and the family. When your mother died, and then with the campaign frenzy, we just figured you both were overloaded. We really did want to tell you, but life got in the way."

Nick said, "What's done is done. We're sorry. There is nothing more we can do. There was no malice or untoward intent on our parts. Action taken, or rather not taken, was done with love."

Nick stood. "I have a meeting with the vice president in a few minutes. I doubt I will see you before you turn in. Please plan on breakfasting together in the morning. Love you all."

Rick stood. "Dad, may I have a moment?"

"Sure, walk with me."

The two men left the room and headed toward the residence elevator.

Rocky turned to Brooke. "So, how's it going with Buck? You two seem to being seeing a lot of each other."

"How do you know that, Dad?"

He drew his breath in through his teeth making a hissing sound. "Well, now that you are living back at the Alexandria townhouse, your protection has been inquiring about arrangements they need to make at the house to secure it. Buck's name came up as spending a lot of time there and how his being there would impact their planning."

"Ugh," Brooke said. "Well, he's been coming back and forth between DC and Boston on the weekends."

"Rick and your father are talking about bringing him on at the White House."

"The White House? Why? He's not political. Actually, hates politics. He prefers numbers to people. Feels he can trust them."

"C'mon, Brooke. You know that's not entirely true. He's very personable and a great team player."

"Well, maybe. That just sounds good. Being cynical, helps me maintain this contrarian persona I've developed since Dad got shot."

"I can understand that. I thought you finding a relationship like the one that is developing with Buck would be good for you. Get you back to your old happy, hard-working, compassionate young woman self."

"I'm not unhappy, just a little disillusioned. Life has really taken on an *adult* dimension. It's been hard on both Rick and me. I think that is one of the reasons he is so distant and depressing to be around."

"My guess is it may be somewhat related to essentially losing a father and a lover on top of everything else associated with the assassination attempt."

"You don't mince words much, do you, Dad?"

"I think there were two elephants in the room. We just took a little longer getting to the second one, you, Rick, and Buck."

"That's for sure."

Rocky said, "Keep your hopes up and your eyes wide open. When it comes to love and sex, one never can know what lays down the road."

"Sounds like you are speaking from experience."

"Perhaps I am."

Brooke stood up. "Up for a game of chess?"

"Hell, yeah! I'll meet you in the East sitting room. There's a set on the bookshelf."

"Don't dilly-dally, Dad."

"Maybe just long enough to fill two tumblers with some smokey Scotch."

∞

After leaving the residence and taking the elevator to the main floor, Rick suggested they have their conversation somewhere private. "The West Wing will still have some people working late. What about going to the Green Room?"

"Sure, let's go," Nick said placing his arm around Rick's shoulder.

They entered the dimly lit parlor. Taking note of a fire blazing in the fireplace, Nick said, "You've had this planned all along, haven't you? Very nice. I like it. Good place to have a one-on-one conversation."

"Thanks, Dad. One thing for sure, you've always appreciated the little things."

"Indeed, I have. So, what's on your mind, son?"

"Several things," Rick said motioning to the chairs. "Dad, all that I am going to share with you I have shared with no one. Only two members of my staff are aware of what I am going to tell you."

"Okay." Nick nodded.

"First of all, I would like to address my idea about Buck being assigned to the White House for the foreseeable future."

The president said, "I like the idea. He is exactly what we need for us to bring the IT assets up to date around here. My hope is he will bring a new comprehensive perspective that will get our people into the 21st century."

"If anybody can do it, he can," Rick said.

"I have a question though. You and Buck. It's no secret within the family you two are or were an item. It is abundantly clear his interest in Brooke has not gone over well."

Rick's eyes tightened as he ground his teeth.

"I can see I hit the nail on the head, son. I am so sorry you are going through this. Is there anything I can do?"

Rick glared into the fire, an edge in his voice. "Just keep him away from me. As far away as possible."

Nick sat up. "So, there is more to this, sending him to the White House. Isn't there?"

Rick turned from the fire wearing a hard look. "Do that. Keep him away from me. That is all you can do. I'll take care of the rest."

"What rest? What are you talking about?"

"I don't want to talk about it anymore. That's not why I'm here anyway."

"Rick, you know you can come to me any time you want to talk. One last thing, please consider your sister. Keep a dialogue going with her. You two barely exchanged words at dinner. That is not healthy for anyone. It's hard on her as well."

Rick let loose an icy laugh his father had never before heard, "Right! This is hard for her! Horseshit! She's got what she wants, and I lost what I had. Time to change the subject."

The president's face went blank.

In a cadenced monotone, he said, "Nice segue, Rick. What is it that you want to speak to me about? It couldn't have been about your sister and Buck."

Rick sat back. "Goulet is still using the burners to communicate. He is in touch with whoever he was working with. He has taken payment, we think, because of the diamonds, not sure. But a lot of money. Five million dollars was put in an offshore account for him. And on top of that, he is telling his people everything, I mean everything that is happening in the White House and who is doing what and their opinions on policy?"

"Treason. That bastard should be hauled out of his office and executed," the president said.

"I need to know something, Dad. You mentioned how you were not going to let on to Goulet that you knew what he was up to. Did you hold to that? Do you think he suspects you know something?"

"I did exactly as I said I would. He knows nothing of what we have ascertained. I called him into my private office and said I understood that he only had the country's interest at heart when I was shot, and that his actions were understandable and that I might have done the same thing if I had been in his position."

"Nice crock of shit, Dad."

"Thank you. I even went further; I have included him in all our policy meetings and always solicit his input. It's amusing to watch him get more and more puffed up as I give him more responsibilities. Perhaps your people have heard some of this on his calls."

"Uh, huh, we have." Rick crossed his arms and stared back at the fire. "Has Goulet made any special requests, like along the lines of travel, especially international economic summits, that sort of thing?"

"Funny you should ask. He dropped a few hints about wanting to have the US represented at a high-level economic forum hosted by some of the largest corporations in the world."

"But that doesn't sound like an event politicians would attend. Interesting. Did he say what corporations were hosting? And who was invited?"

"No, he did not. But I bet you can get that information."

"No doubt I can. If he's got it, it's floating around out there in the open."

"I believe he said something about Macao," Nick said. "

"Macao?"

"Yep."

"Okay, thanks. I'll look into it."

"Rick, are you keeping tabs on the veep's residence?

"Oh yeah. He's into some weird shit. You know he checks on the diamonds regularly? He's also doubled his son's detail. Poor kid can't take a crap without someone being on top of him. The house arrest bracelet has definitely limited his ability to deal drugs. I understand he is, for the time being, popular at school. Here is the vice president's son, former drug dealer, wearing an ankle bracelet, and has his own personal protection team.

"So, Dad. This is how I see it. I'll keep tabs on Goulet and let you know if anything is up. As far as that trip goes, I think we ought to look into it more. What if it's his way of getting in touch with his comrades face-to-face?"

"I can see that, Rick. But why would he do that? It's dangerous for him and them."

"I think they're spooked. Feels like they need to get back their control, maybe make another move. Maybe setting up a powwow sort of thing. Make sure everyone is loyal. I'll have to think about it. Put some feelers out. Please, Dad, do not share any of this information with anybody. Not even my dad."

"Not to worry. The last thing I want to do is get him all riled up again. It's taken months for all of us to calm down. This stays just between us."

"Thanks, Dad."

"Rick, I really appreciate what you are doing. You have enough on your shoulders running Chamber's Enterprises. You didn't need this too."

"Not a problem. I have good people working for me. And back to Buck, let's get that worked out. I want to keep him out of Boston."

"Okay, son. I'll take care of it.

As he left the building, Rick called Boston. "Lynn, I need you to do some research, some deep digging. We need to know everything we can find out about a corporate conference being held in Macao in a couple of months. I want to know who is hosting and who is attending. And where it is being held. Probably some high-end resort hotel. Dig deep on all attendees. Nothing is off limits. When I get back to Boston, I'll share more with you and what I need." Rick terminated the conversation and returned the burner to his pocket.

CHAPTER 26

"Mr. President, I think we need to revisit the assassination attempt investigation," Gene said, sitting with the president in the Oval Office.

"What, more jitters, lack of progress on behalf of the FBI or anyone else?"

"Speculation. People want a resolution. Having this hanging over the nation's head makes people uneasy, nervous. There are signs the public doesn't think you or the administration have a handle on things. There is an undercurrent being promoted by your detractors that you are a nice guy, but not tough enough to run the country."

"Naturally, that plays into a weak sissy-type gay guy, right?" The president quipped.

"I'm afraid so, Mr. President. It is what it is, and we have to deal with it, or it may deal with us. To make things worse, there is some far left-wing and right-wing crap being tossed about speculating on some sort of cover-up conspiracy."

"That's rich," the president said. "Imagine that. The right and left working together on something."

"Regardless, sir, we have to address the issue of vacillating political support and an agitated public."

"I suppose what they want me to do is go kick some ass," the president said. He thought for a moment. "Well, I am. I spoke with the speaker of the House and the Senate leader this morning. I've asked them to establish a joint bi-partisan commission to look into the assassination attempt. Maybe that will light a fire under our investigative agencies to produce some answers."

"Glad to hear that, Mr. President. But let's get some mileage on that to help quell some of this rampant speculation."

"Okay, what do you suggest?"

"Have both parties' leadership come down here to the Oval and announce the formation of the commission. They'll be happy to do it. Good press, and makes them look like they're doing something, leadership, that sort of thing. The photo op with them standing behind you seated at your desk gives you the look of a leader as well."

The president clenched his teeth. "Like I'm not a leader, now?"

"Come on, you know what I mean." Gene said.

"I suppose I do. I get it. I don't like it. And I resent all this hullabaloo about something I cannot control. But you're right. Take care of it. Make the arrangements."

"Will do, sir."

The president said, "Let's move on. Next item. We need to talk about the progress we are making on the nominees sent up to the Hill. It's been over four months now. What can we do to get the last three Cabinet members confirmed?"

∞

"Try as I might, Trish," the president said, "I can't seem to get far enough away from the investigation that isn't going very well. Lack of progress only serves to distract my administration and give the Dems fuel to cast doubt on me and my ability to run the country." He paused. "I don't know why I'm telling you this, you are as much aware of it as am I."

"I understand, sir."

"Trish, there is something I need to share with you. I can't provide all the details, because I promised I would only share what was absolutely necessary."

"Does this have anything to do with your meeting behind closed doors with your National Security Advisor, sir?"

"Yes, it does. It is amazing. Ever since I replaced my predecessor's National Security Advisor with Dr. Parsons, things seem to be happening, moving forward, relative to the investigation. I was tempted to tell Gene about it when he was here earlier, because it has an indirect impact on his and my conversation. But I couldn't. Only because he doesn't have the security clearance."

"That's a shame. Of all people, he has proven to be a wise and prophetic advisor. Kinda like having one hand tied behind your back by not giving him all the info he needs."

"Totally. Let me share a little from my meeting. It appears that there is a modicum of progress being made regarding the investigation. NSA, as you know is constantly monitoring all international calls."

"And a lot of domestic calls too." Trish sighed.

"No doubt. Everything is recorded. Because the analytics get overwhelmed by volume, often times the analytics are rerun. The rerun eliminates a lot of the chaff-like chatter. Clutter is mini-mized and the traffic reanalyzed."

"When over 5 billion or more people worldwide own phones, that's bound to be a pretty chatter-clutter filled universe," Trish said.

"Hadn't thought about that number of people owning phones. Wow. Anyway, NSA, no doubt, through prodding from Dr. Parsons, came across phone conversations that caught their interest. A string of ongoing conversations. These conversations are, fortunately for us, a legal wire-tapping operation, international in scope." The president paused and sat back. "Unfortunately, they involve the vice president."

Trish blinked, her jaw slackened, she exhaled. "Not surprised, but so very disappointed to hear this again, our fears perhaps confirmed by another entity." She folded her hands in her lap. "So sorry, Mr. President."

"Me too, I had always deep down hoped it wasn't true. I know that was naïve thinking. I just want it to go away. Go away so we can get on with our lives and running the country."

"Do they have anything?"

"Very difficult. As you know we are only able to record and hear one side of the conversation. I am still not sure how this happens, but our people can only hear one side. The other end is garbled sometimes and then quiet sometimes. The VP is sharing with someone or some people and relaying intimate details about the goings-on here inside the White House."

"What is he thinking? Have to gain? That's reason enough to impeach him, sir."

"It is. But getting rid of him will not facilitate, but will certainly infringe upon, our discovering who his cohorts are. We need to know who they are."

Trish said, "How would you like to proceed, sir?"

"The first thing we need to do is mitigate the damage he is doing. Knowing what we know about his leaking White House activities, we can handle the situation by limiting his access to sensitive information."

"That will be tricky, as he will surely suspect something is up when doors are closed to him," Trish said.

"We'll keep the doors open, but we will keep him away from the building, the White House."

"Sir?"

"I am going to ask him to take on a nationwide tour assessing the nation's education systems from prekindergarten to post graduate school. He will visit every state over the next three months prior to his trip to Macao."

"Macao? You approved that trip?"

"I will. I'll tell him just before I let him know about what he'll be doing for the next three months. He won't like it. It may cause him to tip his hand by doing something stupid in the meantime. We need to give NSA time to do their homework and we can't have him snooping around here. Sending him on a three-month field trip will solve both problems."

"Excellent, Mr. President. I will get to work alongside his chief of staff, Merrill Spaulding, putting together his fact-finding tour as soon as you meet with him. What happens after Macao?"

"That will depend on where the investigation has taken us by then. We have the answers, but no admissible proof. Quite the quandary."

"One more thing, sir. Have you thought about creating some sort of unofficial liaison between Dr. Parsons and your son? Rick has a great deal of data that could be useful to her teams."

"I broached that with Rick. He is very reluctant, even adamant that no relationship be traceable between the government and Chamber's Enterprises. In his opinion, and Rocky's, and White House counsel, connection with the two would open Pandora's Box to the government initiating future inquiries into the corporation. Potentially exposing corporate intellectual property to competitors."

"I understand. Just a thought."

"Now, that doesn't mean that any private conversation I have with Rocky or Rick, well you know what I mean—"

Trish smiled.

"Now, what else is on our agenda, Chief?" the president asked.

Rick returned to Boston and went directly from Logan to meet with Lynn and Sandy.

"Find anything yet?" Rick asked.

Sandy nodded, pushing a sheet of paper across the table toward Rick. "This is the list of companies we suspect are in league with the vice president."

He picked up the paper and studied it. "Hm, these are many of the same companies uncovered by Dr. Parson's. And more. Good work!"

"They are all listed there," Lynn said. "Interesting coincidence."

"I don't believe in coincidences, and neither should you," Rick said, "That is if you want to continue to work with me on this project."

Both Sandy and Lynn sat speechless and shared an OMG look.

"What else do you have?" Rick asked.

Lynn said, pensive. "I don't want any job bad enough to be spoken to like that."

Rick leaned back from the table. "I beg your pardon. I have no idea where that came from. I apologize."

Lynn and Sandy both looked down at paperwork laid out in front of them.

Sandy picked up another sheet of paper and handed it to him. "This is a list of the corporate executives we believe will be attending representing the corporations in attendance. What is most significant is the CEOs of all the entities on Dr. Parson's original list will be there. And some of the CEOs from the list we have recently compiled."

"For lack of a better word," Rick said, "that cannot be a coincidence."

Lynn said stiffly, "No, not likely."

"This is excellent work, ladies. And again, I apologize for my earlier remarks."

Lynn and Sandy sat as Rick continued to review the list.

"Hm," Rick said, "Infinite Systems is one of the largest military equipment suppliers in the world. Interesting, a Swiss company. Hm." He pointed at the list. "These two Canadian companies complement each other. One satellites and the other the latest entry into launching reusable rockets."

Lynn said, "I was particularly interested in the Russian conglomerate, the precious minerals firm. They control seventy percent of the earth's minerals used in high tech armament command and control. A bit disconcerting, don't you think?"

"I do. Very disconcerting. And this one, the Chinese shipping firm. I believe it is government owned. But listed on the New York Exchange. Masquerading as independent."

"Rick," Sandy said, "Every one of these firms has ties to the worldwide military industrial complex. All of them do a significant amount of work for either the United States military or defense suppliers, contractors, and importantly, research companies."

"Yes, I see that. This is the answer to the question. Why and who has a vested interest in eliminating my father and placing Goulet in the White House. My father has a history of voting to limit military spending and is somewhat of an isolationist. No war, no outrageous profits for these companies. Goulet on the other hand, has proven to be a lapdog for the Defense Department and the military industrial complex. Now we know."

"Rick, don't you think we should share the information with the president?" Lynn asked. "He should know this. NSA, the CIA, and FBI should know this."

"I think this is too much to share. Let them figure it out for themselves if they can. We'll keep it under wraps until we know more."

"But why? The vice president is a danger to the country," Sandy said. "Every call he makes endangers national security."

"I have my reasons. In the meantime, I think the next step is to continue delving deep into the professional and personal aspects of these people's lives. Also, let's do a further analysis of what these companies have in common. What are their mutual interests, and why would it be beneficial for them to assassinate the president? How and what would they gain? That will, of course, mean you look into my father's history as it would relate to these entities' domestic and international economic interests."

"But we pretty much have figured out what they have in common and have to gain," Lynn said.

Rick scowled, tilted back and looked upward. "Ladies, let me make myself clear. I am in charge here. Just do as I say. I have my reasons. Until we have documented proof of their interests and motivation, I cannot pass it on to the president. Understand?"

"Okay, we're on it," Sandy said.

"One more thing," Lynn said, "the vice president has communicated again with whoever he is speaking with on the burner. He has reserved the Imperial Suite at the host hotel. I've looked into it. It is beyond luxurious. Ten thousand square feet, a two-story suite on the top of the sixty-story hotel."

"Really!" Rick said. "I've driven by that hotel. It's an over-the-top resort. Doesn't that suite have a cantilevered meeting room that extends high above an artificial lake? A glass floor. You can see the lake below and the underwater light show from that vantage point. It is supposed to be extraordinary."

"That's the one. It costs thirty-five thousand dollars per night."

"Fuck! That is a chunk of change." Rick whistled.

"And it looks like the taxpayers will be footing the bill for his four-night stay," Sandy said.

"I heard," Lynn said, "the Ritz-Carlton in Tokyo has the most expensive suite in the world. This one has it beat."

"I wonder," Rick said, "why Goulet would want such a grand and expensive suite, other than ego. He's planning something."

"Like a private meeting. One that will impress the participants," Lynn said.

"How large is the cantilevered part of the suite?" Rick asked.

Sandy turned and began a search on her laptop. A moment later she said, "It says here the multi-purpose glass floored room can accommodate parties for up to fifty people and conference room configurations handling up to twenty-five."

"We may be on to something here, Lynn," Rick said. "Your idea that he might be planning to meet privately with his cohorts and impress them at the same time may have legs."

"My guess," Lynn said, "is he needs to do this to regain stature and the credibility he lost following the unsuccessful assassination and the way he blundered through the aftermath."

"This is a ruthless group," Sandy said. "If he wasn't vice president, my guess is they would have taken him out by now. Just to protect them from any other blunders he would inevitably commit. Like, maybe this meeting."

Rick crossed his arms, looked down at the list. "You may be more right than you could ever have imagined."

Sandy and Lynn exchanged quizzical looks.

"I will be making a trip to Macao."

CHAPTER 27

"Brooke, I have some good news."

"I think I know what it is," she said, rolling over in bed, looking into Buck's eyes.

"I've taken the day off. We have the entire day together."

"It's Tuesday, I have to go into work." She kissed him. "Nice try, why didn't you give me a head's up. I could have scheduled it off."

He took her into his arms and rolled on top of her, peered into her eyes. "I think you're going to call in sick."

Their naked bodies pressed together.

"Oh, maybe so," she said, "I feel a penetrating headache coming on."

An hour later they lay under the sheet, half awake, watching the ceiling fan's blades turn slowly overhead.

"I think it's interesting you have the fan on during the winter," Buck said.

"It's my environmental consciousness," she mused.

"Like you don't want to perspire during hot sex?" Buck laughed and poked her.

She giggled. "Not really, silly. But maybe. Also, circulating the furnace's heated air keeps the temperature consistent throughout the room and uses less energy. Especially if you reverse the rotation of the blades dependent on the season."

"On the season? Are you kidding me? You're making this up."

"No, I'm not. Dad, the president, told me that one direction pushes air down and the other draws it up."

Turning toward Brooke and propping himself up on his elbow, he said, "Which is which?"

"What?" She said sitting up. "Which what?"

"The direction. Which direction pushes and which one draws upward?"

She sighed, "I don't know."

"You don't change it seasonally?"

Grinning, focused on the fan, she said, "Heck no, I can't be bothered with that!"

"You silly goose!" Buck said, tickling her.

"Ah! Stop it! You know I hate that!" Brooke said, playfully punching his chest.

"Okay, I'll stop." He placed a kiss on her lips.

"That's better. You know I like that." she said. "But isn't there something else you are supposed to share with me? Tell me something. Remember?"

"Maybe."

"Out with it, then!"

"Okay," he said.

"Okay, what? What else?"

"I said, *yes*."

"You're making me work too hard for this. Hurry up, tell me."

"We have all day, remember, you're supposed to call in sick," he said. "I have some more good news."

"Buck! Tell me!"

"All right, all right. I accepted the president and Dr. Parson's request that I serve as a consultant to the White House, NSA IT, and ASI."

"I am soooo glad to hear that, yeah! Smart move. I love you! Thank you!"

"You are welcome. Where's my thank-you kiss?"

"Come and get it!" she said pulling him close. "Let me show you, my appreciation."

Thirty minutes later, showering and toweling each other off, Brooke asked, "Is my brother going to give you some sort of sabbatical or leave of absence from Chamber's Enterprises? You won't want to stay at the White House forever. You'll bring them up to speed, get bored and want to move on."

"For sure. My coming to the White House was Rick's idea. He's keeping me on payroll, too."

"Rick's idea?" she said. "I thought it was my dad's idea."

"Nope, the president said it was Rick's idea."

"Huh, interesting. He's up to something."

"How can you say that? He is doing the government a favor. Besides, he'll be doing without my expertise at the company."

"I know my brother. Remember, he's my twin and your spurned lover."

∞

The president and Rocky had taken the weekend and returned to their secluded Charlottesville country home.

"You know, this is getting old fashioned," Nick said. "Sitting around reading the papers. Most people just look at their phones and haven't read a paper in years."

"True, sweetie. If you weren't president, we probably wouldn't have easy access. Like bringing them in from DC every morning with the rest of the White House stuff they send you."

"Enjoy it while you can, babe," Nick said, turning a page. "I see Goulet's getting some negative press."

"Yeah, Nick," Rocky said. "Have you been keeping up with the pushback we've been getting on the vice president's interactions with educators?"

"A little. I really haven't focused on it. The worse he does, the better I feel. But that's not helpful."

Rocky said, "Yep, it doesn't help in the long run. Midterms will be here before you know it."

"I have been mulling it around a bit. He is not an asset," Nick said looking at the paper.

"Nick, he is still not totally supportive of your initiatives, especially the education ones. You ran on a progressive education platform. This guy is not pushing your agenda. He's really pissing some people off. They're confused. You campaigned on inclusive progressive change, and he's pooh pooing it."

"I know," Nick said, closing his newspaper and placing it on the table. "He's headed to Macao for the economic conference in a couple of weeks. When he gets back, I will have a *Come to Jesus* meeting with him."

"And say what?"

"Join the team, play ball, by my rules, or resign."

"How do you think he will react to that? And what can you do to make him resign if he's reticent?"

"Those are good questions."

∞

Later that afternoon Rocky paused the football game on TV and turned to Nick. "Well, did Brooke decide whether or not she and Buck are going to have a White House wedding?"

"Christ, Rocky, I was really hoping not to have to think about that yet. I'm still dumfounded they're moving so fast. It's six months into their relationship and they're getting married. Too fast. I'm worried about them not giving the relationship more time."

"Yep, they're living together at the townhouse," Rocky said. "I'd hoped that would have been enough to keep them content for a while. Get to know each other better."

"Another thing that bothers me is, and please don't think me overthinking this," Nick said.

"Overthinking what, Nick?"

"What if this is somewhat of a rebound? You know Buck and Rick's thing being over with. Also, what if Brooke is moving too fast to protect her interests, if you will, vis à vis Rick and Buck and wanting to secure her hold on Buck?"

"Rick is the one likely to have a rebound. Buck just moved on. Oh my God. She's smarter than that, right?"

"I hope so. I know, who better than me and you can understand their positions. Being with Sheila and loving you at the same time made me crazy. I really thought I was going to lose it.

Then telling her I couldn't marry her because I was in love with you and her accepting our relationship was totally unexpected."

"Hey, think about where we've been," Rocky said. "I certainly had all kinds of weird thoughts when you and Sheila were seeing each other. Especially when you and I were also together. It's a hell of an emotional roller-coaster being on either side of the equation. But it worked, didn't it?"

"For us. But we are not the same. Their situation is different," Nick said.

"It is," Rocky agreed.

CHAPTER 28

The door to the Oval opened, and the president, turning to Dr. Parsons, said, "I asked the chief to join us at the end of your briefing. I hope you don't mind."

"Certainly not, sir."

"Good morning, Doctor," Trish said taking a seat.

"Hello, nice to see you, Chief," Dr. Parsons said.

"Doctor, when we last met, on Friday," the president said, "I asked you to come up with a way to create a little tension between the vice president and his conspirators. Have you come up with anything?

"Well, I have something you might be interested in. But if you don't mind, Mr. President, why now? What is the purpose? I thought you wanted to move on, forget about his involvement in the assassination attempt."

"Doctor, I feel it's best I keep my own counsel on this one. But we need something to keep Goulet off-balance. Three and a half years remain before we can get rid of him. He is a thorn in my side. His behavior indicates he will continue to undermine the administration. His poll numbers are in the tank and there is no foreseeable future for him politically."

The women nodded in agreement.

"He is part of my administration. His actions reflect directly on the administration and my ability to run the country and deliver on the promises I made. His actions, like it or not, work in the Dems' favor. He is, for all intents and purposes, perhaps inadvertently, their tool. He is misguided and living in some sort of alternative universe. I suspect he is trying to remain in the good graces of those he has been working with to get rid of me. Maybe they'll try again."

"All too true," Dr. Parsons said. "Well then, as far as my idea, I thought perhaps we could have the CIA orchestrate some sort of disinformation that would culminate in a misunderstanding between two of Goulet's conspirators."

"What kind of disagreement?"

"We will release information that the Chinese government has made surreptitious arrangements to purchase a predetermined amount of oil for a premium through some OPEC members."

"Why would they pay a premium when they can save a lot of money hedging oil prices and buying on the open market?" the president asked.

"Consistency. This guarantees uninterrupted oil for their burgeoning industry. Also, all the oil is transported on Chinese oil tankers. China is growing their shipping lines to secure its trade routes, the modern Silk Road."

"That makes sense. Go on."

"This arrangement would produce higher revenue for certain OPEC members and keep oil prices paid by other countries elevated. A key point is, this would be portrayed as being done surreptitiously and the real price paid by the Chinese is not revealed. OPEC collectively sets the price of oil which all members are to adhere too. Should the other members find out, well, all hell could break out."

"And this relates to Goulet's cohorts, how?"

"How about we say the deal was brokered and administered by two corporations, one Canadian and another Indian. Both of these companies should be part of the cabal working with Goulet."

"I don't see how this could be disruptive to the cabal. They would be making a lot of money."

Trish leaned forward. "This is where the fiction gets interesting. If all goes according to plan, several of the other members of the cabal will want to protect their bottom line. They'll be pissed. They'll be at each other's throats."

"But that is just business, competition," the president said.

"Nothing is purely competition in globalized trade, sir. Those negatively impacted will feel cheated, used."

The president sat; his hands clasped behind his head. "This is interesting. We don't appear to have anything to lose. And the dissention provides Goulet an opportunity to try and elevate his standing with these folks by getting them together to resolve their issues in Macao." He paused, sat up, and folded his arms. "Let's do it. Find a way to leak the information to the disaffected OPEC countries and to the Canadian and US oil industry."

"Yes, Mr. President," Dr. Parsons said.

"I understand Rick is next on my agenda."

"Yes, sir," Trish said, "I'll let the appointment secretary know you are ready to see him on my way out."

"Thank you, Trish, and thank you, Doctor."

The women left the Oval.

Rick walked into the Oval Office moments later. "Hi, Dad!"

Father and son embraced.

"Hello, son. Please sit," the president said gesturing to a chair. "How was your trip?"

"Uneventful. Flew in this morning from Boston."

"I heard you were overseas on Chambers Enterprise's business."

"Yes, I was. Returned a couple of days ago. Good trip, thanks for asking."

"Are you in DC for a couple of days or in and out, son?"

"I'm here today and gone tomorrow. Thought I'd camp out here, if that's okay."

"Please do, you know you are always welcome. Plenty of room. We'll have dinner tonight with Rocky and Brooke. That is, if Brooke is available. She's so tied up with her work and everything."

"Everything, meaning Buck?"

The president ignored the comment.

"So, what's up?" The president asked.

"Like I said before, I think you should send Buck to Macao."

"We've had this discussion before," the president said.

"He could be very helpful keeping an eye on the vice president."

"I agree. I have asked him, and he has accepted and agreed to go."

"Oh," Rick said. "Okay, that was weird. I didn't know you had taken care of it, or I wouldn't have brought it up."

The president chuckled.

Rick said, "I know you don't want to hear this, but my sources tell Goulet has stepped up his communications with his people."

"Yes, I am aware. NSA. And you have a good point. Yeah, we need to keep an eye on him. He certainly didn't do me or my administration any favors on his nationwide jaunt minimizing my education initiatives.

"Back to Buck, Dad. We agree he will be part of the White House Communications Team, right?"

"Right."

"Communications," Rick said. "By that, I mean, he would be in a good position to tap into Goulet's conversations."

"Okay. And?".

"As a member of the communications team, he will have access to all the spaces where the vice president finds himself."

The president said, "Got it. Okay, I'll make that happen. Good thinking, son."

Rick stood. "Great. Good seeing you. Gotta go?"

"Remember when we discussed months ago making those bastards pay?"

"Hey Dad, aren't all conversations in the Oval videoed and recorded?"

"Not this one."

"Okay, got it. I have something in the works. But I think it is best you have no knowledge of it. Plausible deniability."

The president nodded. "Okay, but why are you rushing out? I have time to chat and catch up on anything else you might want to discuss."

"Tons to do. See you tonight. We can catch up then.

CHAPTER 29

Buck and Rick ran into one another in the White House mess.

"Hey Rick, care to join me for a bite?" Buck asked, sticking out his hand.

"This is a bit awkward," Rick said. "Not really." He shoved his hands in his pant pockets.

"C'mon, don't do that." Buck placed an arm around Rick's shoulders. "My office is just around the corner, let's chat."

"Fine," Rick said and followed Buck from the mess to his office. Rick wrinkled his nose. "This is where you work?" He gazed around the windowless room and took in the elaborate workstation festooned with six monitors and a keyboard.

"Yeah, it's not much, but it is what it is."

They both took a seat at a worktable. Rick sat back in his chair and crossed his legs. "I suppose I should congratulate you and Brooke on your engagement."

"That would be nice. But I understand if you don't."

"I don't approve. And I won't."

"I totally get where you are coming from, Rick. And I'm sorry for you."

Rick slammed his fist on the table. "Don't feel sorry for me. I'm not the asshole who left our relationship! You should feel sorry for fucking things up between you and me!"

Buck leaned forward and placed his hands on the table. "Rick, I'm sorry. But we were just seeing each other. There was no commitment."

"I was committed!"

"That was your choice. I might have handled things different from the get-go, if I had known how serious you were. But just the same, I would still have ended up moving on."

"You sure as hell have moved on. Looks like you are running away from being gay."

"Wrong. I love Brooke, pure and simple."

"I thought you loved me."

"Rick, it just wasn't that way for me. I can't help that."

Rick glared at Buck.

Buck sighed. "I hope you can find a way to reconcile yourself to Brooke and me being together. You and I will be family, brothers-in-law."

Rick shot to his feet. "Fuck you!" He stormed out of the room slamming the door behind him.

∞

Five days later Dr. Parsons sat alone with the president in the Oval giving him his daily security briefing. "The Canadians have contacted us with some interesting information. They have indicated that they have intercepted some chatter that may compromise the vice president."

The president sat up straight. "No shit! What specifically, did they say?"

"It appears the leak has accomplished what was intended. The Australians and the Brits are also hinting at the same thing. Once people's attention was drawn to the Chinese arrangement, all stops have been pulled out and just about every sophisticated intelligence agency in the world is on this like a fly on you know what."

"This will prove interesting. With Goulet leaving later today for Macao, things could come to a head quickly. My hope is that they reveal their hand while they, the cabal, are in Macao," the president said.

She said, "I know Buck Gerard is there assisting the communications team. Even if we have them on tape admitting guilt, what good is it?"

"Leverage. We'll keep the information. Present it to Goulet. He'll have to resign and go away. We'll be rid of him."

Parson's said, "And you'll have leverage on every one of the corporations involved, international leverage so to speak."

"Exactly," the president said.

Three days later, the economic conference adjourned. Vice President Goulet invited his twenty-four accomplices in the assassination attempt to dinner in the Tiānshàng Resort's Imperial Suite. All accepted his invitation, including the recently slandered Chinese and OPEC members.

"Mr. Vice President," Buck said, "I believe that everything is in place and ready for you and your guests."

"Thank you, Buck. I appreciate your team sweeping the room. The last thing we need is to have our conversations overheard. These are very private and important individuals."

"Yes, sir."

"Is the repository box for the guest's phones ready to go?"

"Yes, sir. As the guests enter the room, they will be asked to place their phones in the RF shielded box. They will be assured that they can retrieve them when they depart."

Goulet said, "I hope this doesn't meet with too much pushback. I know it's not unusual to remove phones from secure meetings. But this is different. That leak, the story, the one about OPEC rigging oil prices has really made a lot of people jumpy. We want our guests to be comfortable and can't be too careful." The vice president rubbed his hands together. "We'll return them as they leave. When we . . ." He paused. "By the way, it wasn't my idea to secure the phones. I had forgotten all about that. It was a good catch. Whose idea was it?"

"I believe a security consultant forwarded it to our people."

"Do you know who?"

"No, sir. Makes sense, though."

"Hm, yes, it does."

The guests arrived and without much comment surrendered their phones. They passed through the metal detector and entered the large, cantilevered room. The guests, initially taken aback by the twelve-inch-thick glass floor, not confident of their footing, drew back, hesitating before stepping into the room.

Moments later, growing more accustomed to the dizzying light show dancing sixty feet below they moved tentatively forward. Laughing and talking, pointing out the amazing kaleidoscope of multi-colored lights that whirled beneath the water's surface. The myriad of undulating vivid colors swept across their faces, creating a carnivalesque ambience.

Festive popular Asian music radiated from speakers embedded in the twenty-five-foot-high ceiling. Themed chandeliers with fantastical figures and symbols depicting the dynasties of China caught the light and added to the dizzying lightshow.

"Look at this thing," one of the guests said, accepting a champagne flute offered on a tray by a life-sized robot. "She, I mean, it looks so real, like one of those Chinese Dragon Dancers."

Fascinated by the mechanical servers, the guests chatted among themselves questioning the province of the robots. Several reached out and fingered the fine embroidered silk covering their lifelike frames.

"Their faces," a German CEO said, "They look ... are so, so beautiful, enchanting." He sighed, reaching up toward one of the robot's faces. "Ah, only if they were real." The robot gave a slight bow and scurried off.

A female Australian corporate executive said, "I would love to have one of these machines in my home. I wouldn't have to lift a finger, and I could get rid of all the staff. I could remain at work, tending to my conglomerate."

Goulet approached one of the guests, a Muscovite, admiring one of the robots, and said, "Yes, we thought it wise to utilize robots instead of humans during our dinner meeting. Much better for security and privacy."

"Novel idea," he said. "I commend you, Mr. Vice President. That and this spectacular venue. It has always been a goal of mine to stay at the Tiānshàng. I am looking forward to whatever else you might have in store for us. Hopefully, our plans for the world will be put back on track when all is said and done." He nodded curtly, turned, and made his way across the room, avoiding the Chinese shipping executive and the OPEC member who stood together, off to the side, ignored by the other executives.

Cocktails flowed and the guests took refuge in traditional etiquette prohibiting serious discussions prior to dinner. The stunning venue and fascinating humanoids dressed in multicolored opaque silk robes filled the relaxed conversation.

The thud-like sound of a large gong being struck reverberated throughout the room. Guests brought their conversations to an end and moved to the large dining table.

The vibrant dancing colors rising through the floor morphed to slow, relaxed, undulating waves in muted shades of gold as the music calmed to Chinese Zen melodies.

"It is as if the sun is rising over a sea of gold; a sign of good fortune," a United Kingdom bank executive said.

Guests marveled at the oval table made of malachite. It was streaked with spidery veins of gold and silver set off by flickering light from the miniature tourmaline lanterns extending the length of the table.

The chandeliers' light faded, and the diners turned their heads as the double doors leading into the room opened wide. Twenty-four robots dressed in shimmering mother-of-pearl dragon robes and elaborate headdresses floated in, carrying ornate covered soup bowls on red Chinese hand painted wooden trays. The dinner service had begun.

∞

While the guests chatted and dined, Buck and his team set about downloading the digital content from the appropriated phones, in accordance with the plan devised by Rick. Several engineers worked together on the more difficult phones, implementing a myriad of different techniques in their efforts to access the data.

An hour into the process, all but four of the phones had been copied and returned to the box. Each phone was placed into the same red velvet slot from which it had been removed. The engineers continued to work on gaining access to the data on the remaining phones.

Growing impatient, Buck said to the engineers, "We need to decide whether or not we will be able to break into those phones. If we can't, we can't. No taking chances getting caught and having our plan discovered."

The engineers nodded and increased their work tempo.

∞

Halfway around the world, unbeknownst to Buck, Goulet, or the dinner guests, Rick, Lynn, and Sandy were listening in, monitoring the real-time recordings being collected by the robots. They recorded every conversation in the room.

As they ate and drank the men and women attendees openly discussed how their plans for Goulet to become president and serve their corporate interests had failed.

One of the women said, "There is little that we can do at this point to fix the situation. It is obvious that there are those present we cannot depend on to work with us as a team. This reality leaves us all vulnerable to compromise."

"I'm curious about these robots," the OPEC member said, changing the subject to divert the attention from himself.

The Chinese shipping executive said, "Yes, they are quite realistic. Where were they manufactured? They look familiar, perhaps they were at the Hong Kong robotics expo last year."

Suddenly, the Muscovite stood. He grabbed the closest robot and ripped off its headdress. And inspected the crown of its plastic head.

Goulet stood and exploded in a rage. "What the hell are you doing?"

The eyes of the guest manhandling the robot bulged. He stepped back and pointed at the exposed corporate logo. "Look here! I knew it! Chambers Enterprises developed these!"

Rick, listening in, eight thousand miles away, smiled, and congratulated himself.

All conversation ceased. A hush descended over the room.

The meditative music filled the void.

The Russian said, "I saw these things when visiting their manufacturing plant in Shanghai six months ago!"

The Vice President, still standing, asked, "Are you certain? This must be a mistake. I had no idea!"

"Yes, goddamn it!" the man said. "I am more than certain!"

The London banker stood, raised his fist. "You son-of-a-bitch, Goulet!"

Goulet, his face ashen, looked around the room. "We're fucked! They've been listening to everything we say!"

He grabbed the handset from the house phone on the table next to him. "The meeting is over, Gerard! Get those phones in here, now!"

Buck flew into the room, box in hand, and began distributing the phones to their owners.

Three rapid explosions shook the room. The floor shuttered as the concrete and steel trusses supporting the cantilevered room heaved.

Chandeliers swayed, several popped and shorted out.

The golden hue of the floor disappeared. Once again, the kaleidoscope-like dancing lights entered the room from the lake below.

Horror crossed the guests' faces, magnified by the cruel demonic pulsating light that seemed to laugh at their fear.

The floor rolled.

Goulet stood frozen as people scrambled away from the heavy malachite table. He watched in horror as the table split down the middle, crashing to the floor. People were pinned, legs severed under the weight of the falling stone.

Panicked screeching filled the room.

The room heaved, walls cracking.

Vomiting ensued.

The room tilted, the floor to ceiling windows shattered. Shards ricocheted and embedded in furnishings, guests, and robots, slicing through skin tissue and decapitating those in their paths.

The glass floor separated, as if a sink hole had appeared, claiming the malachite table as an offering bound for Hades.

The room imploded.

Buck ran for the only entrance, the double doors. He yanked on the handles. They wouldn't budge, sealed by the explosion from below which had compromised the door's frame. He pounded and called for help.

Screams were blanketed by the sound of groaning beams being torn from the side of the hotel.

An Indian IT executive, a Taiwanese chip maker, and a German arms dealer jumped out broken windows, arms pinwheeling as they fell to their deaths.

Goulet watched the table fall in pieces and disappear into the fogging mist below.

Remaining guests stumbled and fell, grabbing anything they thought might save them, grasping for heavy objects and clinging to one another attempting to flee the glass chasm swallowing furnishings and people and robots. One by one people lost their grip or were sliced in two as the glass, plaster, steel beams and walls crumpled around them.

Diminishing screams punctured the bedlam as fewer and fewer remained, sacrificed by the disintegrating room.

Goulet climbed on top of a large side table and clung to a wall sconce as the glass floor funneled the final furnishings and guests.

Losing his grip, he toppled from the table. Flailing and shrieking, he joined the people and debris cascading down through the night to certain annihilation and death.

Buck dangled midair holding onto the door handles, the floor having disappeared from beneath him. He watched the remaining room's structure break apart, piece by piece. His aching hands grew numb. His legs dangled. Perspiration soaked every inch of his body.

Resigned to his fate, he said, "I'm done . . . Brooke."

One of the handles separated from the door. The other hand, unable to hold his weight, let go.

He fell, replicating da Vinci's Vitruvian Man and joining the trail of debris raining from the sky piling into the lake's depths.

A series of meteoric splashes sent gigantic surges of water, one after the other, across the resort's grounds.

People sipping cocktails at tables on the water's edge, witnessed pieces of the Tiānshàng's famed cantilevered room, its occupants, and furnishings crash onto the unsuspecting boaters.

The onslaught of tsunami-like waves, caused by the falling debris, spun people, furniture, vehicles, and anything not bolted down into the surrounding lobbies, hotel rooms, meeting facilities, and ultimately neighboring streets. Once benign objects, transformed into missiles of every size and shape by the relentless stampeding waves, destroyed everything in their path.

Local residents, observing the massacre from higher vantage points, videoed the carnage. The spectacle lasted only ninety seconds from the first explosion to the final collapse.

Cable news and social media filled the airwaves with firsthand accounts and videos of the catastrophic collapse of the world-famous cantilevered room.

Reports that the vice president of the United States and many international corporate executives had been lost along with over five hundred hotel guests and staff quickly spanned the globe.

Within hours reports circulated suggesting the collapse had not been an accident, but perhaps a terrorist attack, igniting worldwide fear.

∞

The president, Trish, Dr. Parsons, Director Hamilcar, and the director of the CIA met in the Oval Office to watch the coverage and videos of the unfolding catastrophe.

"Mr. President," Trish said, "members of the vice president's communications team have confirmed Buck Gerard was in the room when it collapsed."

The president covered his eyes for a brief moment and sadly shook his head.

Dr. Parson's said, "It appears that all the corporate guests, Buck, and the vice president were lost, sir. It would have been impossible for anyone in that room to have survived."

"It was no accident," the director of the CIA said. "Our analysts believe precisely placed explosives caused the room to separate from the building and fall."

"Why was the vice president with these people? Who were they? Was Goulet the target or was someone else the target?" the president asked.

No one answered him.

"What a shit-show! Has the FBI expedited its team to the site?"

"Yes," Trish said.

The president turned to address Director Hamilcar. "Did you lose any agents, Director?"

"Apparently not, sir. The vice president had cleared the room of everyone but the attendees and himself for the duration of the dinner. As a matter of interest, robots had been used to serve the cocktails and meal."

The director's use of the word robots caught everyone's attention.

"Robots?" the president asked.

"Robots, sir," Hamilcar said.

"This sounds like some sort of preplanned, well laid out scheme," the CIA director said. "It all sounds so implausible. Any idea who provided the robots?"

"It's too early in the investigation to know," Dr. Parsons said. "As of this moment, everything and everyone is at the bottom of a lake and spread throughout the resort and neighboring area. Many bodies will have been torn apart."

"God knows when we will be able to recover the bodies or even if they will find them," Hamilcar said.

"Why was Buck the only one of our people in the room?" The president asked.

"It is too early to know why," Dr. Parsons said.

The president sat for a minute, exhaled, and said, "Okay everyone, please keep me informed of any developments. We need to stay on top of this." He paused, scanned the room and, looking at Trish Smart, said, "Anything else?"

"Mr. President, we have begun the process of preparing a list of potential nominees for you to consider replacing the vice president. Once his body is located, we will officially begin the process of looking for a nominee to submit to the Senate.

The president nodded.

Trish stood. "Excuse me, sir. The Cabinet has assembled and are waiting for you."

The president did not respond.

She continued, "Once you have finished your meeting with the Cabinet, the White House staff and press corps are gathering in the East Room where you will simultaneously address the room and the nation."

"I don't understand why Buck Gerard was in the room when it collapsed," the president wondered aloud.

That weekend Nick, Rocky, Rick, and Brooke gathered at their Charlottesville home. The family sat at the kitchen table. All four clutched coffee cups. Brooke stared out the window. Rick contemplated his hands while Rocky and Nick looked at Brooke.

Rick took a bite from a biscotti.

"Honey," Rocky said to Brooke, "We are so sorry about Buck. What can we do?"

Brooke shook her head side-to-side, still staring out the window.

"It just doesn't make sense," she said. "I just don't get why he had to go in the first place."

"He was just doing his job," Rick said.

"Doing his job?" Brooke asked. "His job was to be improving White House IT and ASI, not babysitting the vice president."

She looked at her father. "Dad, why did he go on that trip? When he said he was going, it didn't make a lot of sense to me. Now, it makes no sense at all."

"We had an opportunity," Rick said, "to utilize some new technology that Chambers Enterprises developed to extract data from the attendee's phones. Data we felt could help us figure out who tried to assassinate Dad and why. Buck was familiar with the technology."

Rocky said, "I agree with Brooke. Anyone on the communications team could have utilized that technology. Whose idea was it to send him in the first place?"

Nick shifted in his chair and took a sip from his cup and set it down.

"What's the point?" Rick said as he settled back and crossed his arms. "What's done is done. We lost someone important to Chamber's Enterprises, you Brooke, and me. It's a loss we'll have to deal with. And that's it."

"Kinda cold, don't you think?" Rocky said.

Brooke turned her attention to Rick. She glared. "You were part of this, weren't you?"

"C'mon, Brooke, don't be silly," Rick said.

"Brooke," Nick said, reaching over and placing his hand on her forearm. "Rick came to me and thought it would be a good idea for Buck to go on the trip to not only help with the tech but to keep a close eye on Goulet. We have been concerned with his having an agenda that would compromise what we are trying to do to serve the nation. We had lost all confidence in him."

Brooke stood and pointed at Rick. "You, you!" Her nostrils flared, "You SOB, you couldn't deal with the fact that Buck and I were going to get married!"

Rick opened his mouth, paused, then said, "That's ridiculous!"

"Please, Brooke," Nick said. "Rick was doing the job I asked him to do."

Fists balled, she said, "I'm right! I know I'm right!"

"You're just overreacting. You're emotional," Rick said in flat tone.

"Emotional? You bet I'm emotional!" She took a deep breath. "Why did you go to Macao anyway? Buck said you stopped there on your overseas trip a couple of months ago."

"Macao?" the president asked. "You didn't mention Macao. I asked you specifically about your trip after you got back. Remember? In the Oval. You brushed me off. I remember that."

"What the hell is going on here?" Rocky asked pushing away from the table. "You and I also discussed your trip in detail. You left out the part about Macao."

Rick said, "You all are making a big deal out of nothing."

"No, we're not, Rick! You had it all planned. You've been planning it since Buck and I got together. If you couldn't have him, no one was going to have him. You went to Macao. You planned whatever it was you were going to do and when it was done, you made sure he'd be there!"

Rick shot up out of his chair, unsettling the table, toppling his and Nick's coffee cups onto the tray of biscotti.

He stepped back, pointing his finger at the family. "You think you are so fucking high and mighty! Who do you think has been protecting this family?" He pointed his finger back at himself. "Me, goddamn it! Me! The rest of you walked away when the real work had to be done. Protect your precious reputations. But not me! No, me! I am the one that carried on while the rest of you went about your lives!"

His face flushed; he curled his lip. "And you, Brooke! You stole Buck from me!" He teetered, then regained his balance. "Fuck all of you!"

He turned, storming out of the kitchen.

Brooke sprang to her feet, her hands clenched by her side, and screamed,

"YOU KILLED HIM!"

ACKNOWLEDGEMENTS

In addition to my great appreciation for Tamara Merrill's unending support, content editing, and cover art. I would like to thank members of the SD Writers group, Tamara, Craig McCleod, and Elle Ravenswood, and Tom Courtney. They helped me craft the story and provided mountains of encouragement.

Thank you, Sandra Yeaman, my line editor. Her expertise allowed me to move confidently forward publishing POTUS DOWN.

Finally, to my family and friends, thank you for your unconditional love and belief in me and my work. Cheers!

ABOUT THE AUTHOR

J.R. Strayve, Jr. was born to a nomadic military family, attending nine schools before entering college. Following service in the United States Marine Corps, he raised a family. It is here that he discovered his talent for "spinning tales," regaling his young children with spontaneous bedtime stories.

His bestselling book, and best seller, *First Spouse of the United States*, received critical acclaim for its insightful look at modern day politics and diversity.

The dystopian, alternative, historical series, *Braxton's Century*, *volumes 1,2, & 3*, written by Strayve, unravel an exotic and adventurous tale. This passion filled epic takes place in the late 18th and early 19th century.

While Strayve is best known for his fiction, he has also collaborated on an explosive exposé of the Veterans Administration. *Broken Promises* is an in-depth account of one man's turbulent crusade to right the wrongs of compromised mental health care for veterans.

Strayve's work is featured in *Another Marine Reporting, Sir!*, a collection of true sea stories written by USMC veterans. He has also written numerous short stories and novellas.

He resides in San Diego, CA, where he is active in his community and participates in educating and mentoring other writers.

OTHER BOOKS BY JR STRAYVE JR

BRAXTON'S CENTURY Vol 1

"A riveting escapist fantasy I couldn't put down." Red, white, and orange light fiendishly dances within Aurelio Palace's soaring glass dome. The midnight sky of England's rolling countryside has been set aglow. It is 1870.

The palace has been set on fire by the ten year old Prince Braxton, third son of the fictional Prince and Princess of Wales.

Intense heat soaring up into the glittering dome, loosens the lead securing the glass panes to the massive onion shaped dome's latticework.

The panes shift then plummet down to the rotunda's glittering marble floor, exploding in all directions, a million knife-like shards sure to dissect all within their murderous path.

This is the first of many bizarre but calculated turns of events Braxton sets in motion during this 19th century alternative historical epic.

Readers that enjoy exotic travel, magical settings, beautiful women, handsome men, brilliant dialogue, action, adventures, twists and turns, and fluid sexuality are sure to be seduced by Braxton as he comes of age.

Buckle up and dive into this saga, journeying alongside Braxton tearing through life on his own terms, crafting history's greatest hundred years.

Amazon:
https://www.amazon.com/J-R-Strayve-Jr/e/B08SHQ78CD 238

BRAXTON'S CENTURY Vol 2

When Prince Braxton departs Vienna in the 1880s, following a night of debauchery dressed in gold as the ancient God of War, Mars, he leaves behind a tangle of threats, promises, and compromised nobles, his trading empire intact. Or is it?

Braxton's larger-than-life wheeling and dealings take him from Russia to Japan, Hong Kong, and India. But his obsessions are sucking every ounce of Braxton's being from within.

Continue your journey through history's most dynamic century as Prince Braxton tears through life on his own terms. When life forces him to decide his path, what and who, will he choose?

This second volume of three scorches a trail spanning from 1880 to 1884. The entire saga features a century of world wars and engineering marvels that one might recognize with requited and unrequited love, romances that defy social mores, death, revolutions, and espionage that casts this tale into one that could have been had Prince Braxton been real.

Available on Amazon: https://www.amazon.com/dp/B08YNH7KWX

FIRST SPOUSE OF THE UNITED STATES

First Spouse of the United States: Star Athlete & War Hero Battles Societal Boundaries and Washington Elite parallels today's political and social unrest.

They thought he had it all. But what he had was secrets in his closet.

Lt. Ricardo "Rocky" Chambers has always been the epitome of what women want and who men want to be. Handsome. Star athlete. Fighter pilot.

Heroism and prowess do not clear a path for happily-ever-after, as a dark secret could derail all this family man, captain of industry, and gay civil rights advocate has worked for.

And secrets aren't meant to stay hidden.

And the mysterious Sheila fit into both of the men's lives?

With adversaries lying in wait, the secret is exposed in the national media. Can Rocky and his husband overcome the fallout on the quest for the White House?

In a coming-of-age story that parallels today's political and social unrest, there are no taboo subjects.

Available on Amazon: https://amzn.com/B07PNS1FD6

THE LIEUTENANT & THE VINTER - A Novella

German SS Lt. Georg von Reichenau, recently recovering from wounds sustained in battle has been assigned to French Burgundy. Andre Beaulieu, a gold medal winning Olympian down-hill racer is working to maintain his family's vineyard during the WWII German occupation. The Lieutenant remembers

Andre. Andre has no recollection of how they met, for he lives with a different memory of a woman he cannot forget or find. Adult Content.

Available on Amazon: https://amzn.com/B08F9N7GW7 240

VAINGLORIOUS - A Short Story

Prequel to the Braxton Century Series Set in the fabulously glittering court of the early 1830s, Russian Grand Duchess navigates the treacherous gauntlet thwarting the powerful men attempting to control her.

She has no choice but to obey the czar, her father's every command or she, too, would become "forever indisposed," as had her mother. If you think Henry VIII was tyrannical ... read this novella. The czar's court is as villainous as is he. Ekaterina violently opposes the marriage and ultimately surrenders to her father, the czar's, politically motivated marriage betrothal. Her future husband, Prince Gregor, handsome and sexually attractive, is not her prince charming. His wedding gift to her is blatant womanizing and ceaseless conniving to steal power and prestige, planting the seeds for the contempt and disdain further fueling her hatred for him.

Through the years, even the czar comes to share Ekaterina's hatred for Prince Gregor. The saying, "misery makes for strange bedfellows," draws the czar and Ekaterina together in a devious plan of imperial proportions to rid themselves of Gregor. A plan that would succeed beyond their wildest nightmare.

Author JR Strayve, Jr is a master storyteller, adept at weaving fact and fiction together in a seamless, jaw-dropping tale of

Ekaterina's determination to rule her own life amidst Russian political intrigue and savagery. Join Ekaterina in her story, A prequel to Braxton's Century Volume I. Readers are further mesmerized by the young Grand Duchess Ekaterina, fully understanding why she is later so closely drawn to Prince Braxton, becoming his confidante and benefactor.

Available: https://books2read.com/u/3n7k15 241

JR STRAYVE JR is available for speaking engagements
at book clubs & professional groups.

Please forward inquiries to: info@jrstrayvejr.com

If you would like to keep abreast of the author's upcoming
projects; subscribe to his newsletter.

CPSIA information can be obtained
at www.ICGtesting.com
Printed in the USA
LVHW031119050423
743446LV00001B/44

9 781737 124351